OPEN ME CAREFULLY

Open Me

Edited by ELLEN LOUISE HART *and* MARTHA NELL SMITH

Carefully

EMILY DICKINSON'S INTIMATE LETTERS TO SUSAN HUNTINGTON DICKINSON

PARIS PRESS *Ashfield, Massachusetts 1998*

Library of Congress Cataloging-in-Publication Data
Dickinson, Emily, 1830-1886.
Open me carefully : Emily Dickinson's intimate letters to Susan Huntington Dickinson / edited by Martha Nell Smith & Ellen Louise Hart. -- 1st ed.
p. cm.
Includes bibliographical references and index.
ISBN-0-9638183-7-6 (alk. paper). --
ISBN 0-9638183-6-8 (pbk. : alk. paper)
1. Dickinson, Emily, 1830-1886--Correspondence. 2. Women poets, American--19th century--Correspondence. 3. Dickinson, Susan Huntington, 1830-1913--Correspondence. I. Smith, Martha Nell, 1953- . II. Hart, Ellen Louise. III. Title.
PS1541.Z5A45 1998
811'.4--dc21
[B] 98-31033
CIP

First Edition.

0987654321

Printed in the United States of America

Open Me Carefully is dedicated to the memory of Martha Dickinson Bianchi, Mary Hampson, and to the love of Susan and Emily Dickinson.

CONTENTS

PUBLISHER'S NOTE

PARIS PRESS hopes that this collection of Emily Dickinson's "letters" to Susan Huntington Dickinson helps to enhance and perhaps change your understanding of Emily Dickinson's life as well as her work. Dickinson lived like many of the great writers throughout history: Ensconced in literature, philosophical and spiritual concerns, the natural world, current events, and family, Emily Dickinson managed to integrate solitude into the demands of nineteenth-century responsibility in order to think and to write. She felt deeply and lived her desire, vision, humor, and pain onto the page. Her work was inspired by all the components of daily life, including the deeply intimate and passionate relationship with her friend, neighbor, and sister-in-law, Susan Huntington Dickinson. For thirty-six years, Susan Huntington Dickinson was a primary source of solace, intellectual challenge, and love for Emily Dickinson. It is with great pride that Paris Press offers you a pivotal collection of writings from our most beloved American poet to her most beloved and inspirational companion.

This selection of Emily Dickinson's letters, letter-poems, and poems to Susan Huntington Dickinson is presented as precisely as possible. We have followed the dating, line breaks, spacing, capitalization, spelling, and punctuation of documents as they were compiled and presented to us by Ellen Louise Hart and Martha Nell Smith, authors of the Introduction, Section Openers, Bridge Notes, and End Notes. We offer our deepest gratitude to these ground-breaking scholars.

Paris Press extends heartfelt thanks to the many individuals and organizations that made the publication of *Open Me Carefully* possible. We are grateful for the guidance and advice of Cathy N. Davidson, Daniel Lombardo, Patricia McCambridge, Ken Wissoker, Eleanor Lazarus, and David Wilensky. For generous financial support we thank Laura Slap Shelton, the Council of Literary Magazines and Presses, the Sonia Raissiz Giop Charitable Trust, the Lydia B. Stokes Foundation, the Massachusetts Cultural Council, the Massachusetts Foundation for the Humanities, and the Xeric Foundation; we are grateful to an anonymous contribution made in memory of EG. Many thanks to Ivan Holmes and Judythe Sieck for their elegant designs, to Jeff Potter for the fine composition of the book, and to Susan Kan and Maryellen Ryan for their hard work and loyalty. Thanks also to Elspeth and Nick Macdonald for use of their quiet retreat during the editing of this book.

—Jan Freeman

INTRODUCTION

In June 1852, Emily Dickinson sent a letter to her friend Susan Huntington Gilbert, who was away from home teaching mathematics at Robert Archer's school for girls in Baltimore, Maryland. The letter was carried and delivered to Susan by Emily's father, Edward Dickinson, on his way to Baltimore to serve as a delegate to the national Whig convention. "Why cant I be a Delegate to the great Whig Convention?" asks Dickinson in the letter's postscript. "Dont I know all about Daniel Webster, and the Tariff, and the Law? Then, Susie, I could see you, during a pause in the session." Placed for Susan to see when she first unfolded the letter is Emily's tender instruction, "open me carefully – "

Over the next four decades, Emily Dickinson would write to Susan more frequently than to any of her other ninety-nine known correspondents, including editor Thomas Wentworth Higginson. The voluminous correspondence with Susan constitutes one of two major bodies of work that Dickinson bequeathed to the world — the other being the more than eight hundred poems that she collected in her handbound manuscript books, or fascicles.

Open Me Carefully presents a selection of this extensive body of correspondence, inviting a dramatic new understanding of Emily Dickinson's life, creative process, and poetry. These intimate letters tell the story of a passionate and sustained attachment between Dickinson and the beloved friend who was her central source of inspiration, love, and intellectual and poetic discourse.

Dickinson's poems, letters, and letter-poems to Susan give us a rare glimpse into the poet's process of writing and revising. They also indicate that Susan, herself a published writer of poems, reviews, essays, and stories, was Emily's primary reader, the recipient of both drafts and finished poems. Yet, in spite of the sheer volume of correspondence between Susan and Emily, and despite compelling evidence of an ongoing literary dialogue between the two women, the relationship between Emily and Susan has been neglected, distorted, and obscured. Whereas pages and pages of academic speculation have been devoted to a mere three letter-drafts that Dickinson wrote to a mysterious real or fictional character identified only as "Master," the correspondence between Dickinson and Susan has received disproportionately little attention.

Audience and Muse, Confidante, Collaborator, and Critic

Emily Dickinson died in 1886, and her poems were not introduced to the reading public until 1890, when editors Thomas Higginson and Mabel Loomis Todd released the first edition of *Poems by Emily Dickinson.* In the hundred years since that first publication, the story of Emily Dickinson and Susan Huntington Dickinson has only gradually emerged in the annals of Dickinson scholarship. In fact, most readers of Dickinson are unaware of the intense and long-lived relationship that was at the very core of the poet's emotional and creative life.

Susan Huntington Gilbert and Emily Elizabeth Dickinson were born within days of each other in December 1830. They may have known each other from girlhood; they certainly knew each other from adolescence; and they had begun to correspond by the age of twenty. Their relationship spanned nearly four decades, and for three of those decades, the women were next-door neighbors. Together, Susan and Emily lived through the vicissitudes of a life closely shared: Susan's courtship, engagement, and eventual marriage to Emily's brother, Austin; Susan and Austin's setting up home next door to the Dickinson Homestead; the births of Susan and Austin's three children, and the tragic death of their youngest son, Gib; anonymous individual publication of at least ten of Dickinson's poems; and the deaths of parents and many friends.

Open Me Carefully includes, for the most part, only Emily Dickinson's side of this correspondence. Nearly all of Susan's letters to Emily were destroyed at the time of the poet's death. This would have been the result of a routine "house cleaning," reflecting the common practice in the nineteenth century to either destroy or return to the senders all letters received by the deceased. That even a handful of Susan's letters to Emily have been preserved, when letters from all other correspondents were irretrievably disposed of, is itself a testament to the vital nature of this correspondence.

A Story Left Untold

The correspondence reproduced in *Open Me Carefully* debunks much of the common Dickinson lore served up for decades by high-school literature textbooks, television sitcoms, song lyrics, and literary biographies. According to these tenacious popular legends, Dickinson was an inaccessible, ethereal hermit, too rare for this earthly plane, and probably undone by unrequited love for any or all of several male suitors whose identities have been the stuff of speculation for countless readers.

But why has this important correspondence — which lasted until Dickinson's death in 1886 and preoccupied Susan until her own death in 1913 — been relatively ignored, if not suppressed? Emily Dickinson's writings to Susan were certainly not unknown; they have long been recognized as passionately literary, and many scholars have bickered and argued over the nature of Dickinson's obvious devotion to her sister-in-law.

Two cultural factors may have contributed to the discounting of this pivotal relationship. The first is the stereotypical nineteenth-century vision of the "Poetess" as a tortured, delicate woman dressed in virginal white, pining away in seclusion, removed from the vibrant nit, grit, and passion of normal life. It is this stereotype, encouraged by Dickinson's early editors — particularly Mabel Loomis Todd — that has preserved the popular image of Emily Dickinson as the recluse spinster belle of Amherst.

The second factor is the view of intimate female friendships in the nineteenth century. According to this view, women of Dickinson's time often indulged in highly romantic relationships with each other, but these relationships were merely affectionate and patently not sexual. Such same-sex attractions, so the popular wisdom goes, had the character of an adolescent crush rather than a mature erotic love. As this correspondence shows, however, Emily and Susan's relationship surpasses in depth, passion, and continuity the stereotype of the "intimate exchange" between women friends of the period. The ardor of Dickinson's late teens and early twenties matured and deepened over the decades, and the romantic and erotic expressions from Emily to Susan continued until Dickinson's death in May 1886.

The Makings of a Myth

Though details of Emily and Susan's relationship were known to their contemporaries, much of the information about the two women has been passed along through sometimes questionable testimony. The strongest testimonies, and the ones that have been most pivotal in determining the presentation of the relationship until now, have been provided by two controversial sources. The first is Martha Dickinson Bianchi, Susan's daughter and Emily's niece. Bianchi, who compiled *The Single Hound* (1914) and dedicated it "as a memorial to the love of these 'Dear, dead Women,'" then continued to carry out her mother's plan by presenting extracts from letters in *The Life and Letters of Emily Dickinson* (1924) and *Emily Dickinson Face to Face* (1932). For various unfair and unfounded reasons, many scholars have characterized Bianchi as an always unreliable source. However, we believe otherwise, and we have cited her comments and observations about Susan and Emily throughout this book.

The second source is Mabel Loomis Todd, editor (along with Thomas Higginson) of the first three volumes of Emily's poems. In her desire to hide Susan's central role in Dickinson's writing process,

Loomis Todd went to great lengths to suppress any trace of Susan as Emily's primary audience. Much of the reason for this is obvious: the young Mabel Loomis Todd, born the year Susan and Austin wed, had become Austin's mistress; she was the "other woman" to Susan's "wife forgotten."[1] The affair continued until Austin's death in 1895 and was quite public, an inexpressibly painful situation for Susan. Loomis Todd made no mention of Susan when she produced the *Letters of Emily Dickinson* in 1894. There is even evidence in Emily's letters to Austin that someone, probably Loomis Todd, sought to expunge affectionate references to Susan.

When the Dickinson fascicles were turned over to Mabel Loomis Todd, Susan's crucial position as primary audience for Emily's poetry became an inconvenient and irrelevant piece of information that did not jibe with the popular image of a nineteenth-century poetess. To editors of the time, the most marketable image of Dickinson the poet was that of the eccentric, reclusive, asexual woman in white. This mysterious figure necessarily wrote all alone, harboring some "secret sorrow" that no one else could understand or be privy to. There was simply no place in the official Dickinson biography for the revelation of an immediate confidante and audience for her poetry — particularly not one who lived next door. Loomis Todd was therefore willing to play up this "solitary spinster" characterization of Emily Dickinson in her editorial productions, and thus the role of Susan went entirely unmentioned in the earliest publications of Dickinson's works. Loomis Todd even refused Higginson's recommendation that Susan's obituary of Emily (which emphasized that although she kept her own company she was "not disappointed with the world"[2]) serve as the introduction to the 1890 *Poems*. Instead, Loomis Todd used a three-paragraph introduction by Higginson that proclaimed that Emily was "a recluse by temperament and habit,"[3] and hence the mythology of Emily Dickinson, the "recluse of Amherst," was cast.

Susan's Book of Emily's Writings

Between Dickinson's death in 1886 and the first printed volume of her poems four years later, Susan began to work on an inclusive volume of Emily's writings. Seven months after Dickinson's death, Susan submitted to an editor of *The Century* "a poem of Miss Emily Dickinson's on the 'Wind' thinking you might like to print it."[4] That letter's reference to "a novice's attempt at type-writing" shows that Susan was already at work transcribing Emily's poetry. Susan was determined to depict Dickinson in her complexity, making a collection that was "rather more full, and varied"[5] than the conventional presentation in *Poems by Emily Dickinson* (1890). Rather than separating the poems from their original contexts and dividing them into the predictable subjects that audiences of the time expected ("Life, Love, Time & Eternity, and Nature"), Susan wanted to showcase the entire range of Emily's writings: letters, humorous writings, illustrations — in short, everything left out of the Loomis Todd and Higginson edition.

Forty fascicles, or manuscript books, and scores of poems on loose sheets had been found after Dickinson's death, and Emily's sister Lavinia (Vinnie) wanted poems from that trove to be incorporated into a printed volume. Vinnie turned to Susan to accomplish the task. Susan struggled with the problem of making a book from those fascicles, reading through the astonishing production of her friend and marking individual lyrics with initials (D, F, L, N, P, S, W) and "X's" in order to categorize them. In doing this, Susan was not only deferring to Vinnie's wishes but also bowing to Higginson's market judgment that the kind of "more full and varied" volume she had first imagined was "un-presentable."[6] Susan tried to make her book of Emily's writings conform to Vinnie's and Higginson's vision, but she could not accomplish the task because it went against her better judgment, informed by decades of her creative work with Emily. Distracted and grieved both by the loss of Emily and her husband's flagrant affair with Mabel Loomis Todd, Susan moved slowly. Vinnie, growing impatient, demanded that the fascicle poems be returned so that another editor, one who could get the job done more quickly, could work on the project.

Though Susan continued to work on designs for her book of Emily's writings until her death in 1913, she returned the fascicle poems to Vinnie, knowing that they would be given to Loomis Todd and edited into an acceptable printed volume that would not amply reflect Emily's genius or her goals as a writer.

Solitary, But Not Removed

Understanding of Dickinson's life and her utterly original and daring poetry has been obscured by a combination of deliberate suppression, easy stereotyping, and convenient but misleading categorization. In *Open Me Carefully,* we see that Emily was not the fragile, childlike, virginal "bride who would never be" writing precious messages about flowers, birds, and cemeteries from the safety and seclusion of her bedroom perch in Amherst, Massachusetts. Dickinson was devoted to her craft, and she was dedicated to integrating poetry into every aspect of her day-to-day life. She was engaged in philosophical and spiritual issues as well as all the complexities of family life and human relationships. She knew love, rejection, forgiveness, jealousy, despair, and electric passion, and she lived for years knowing the intense joy and frustration of having a beloved simultaneously nearby, yet not fully within reach.

While it is true that Dickinson went to extraordinary measures to preserve her privacy, the facts of her solitude have been taken out of context. Like many artists, she needed a great deal of time alone for reading, contemplation, and writing — a requirement that has rarely been questioned when enjoyed by male writers. However, in the case of Dickinson, the need for solitude and contemplation has been interpreted as a pathological reclusiveness and an indication of intense vulnerability and wounding, not as a consciously chosen way of life.

The Subject Matter of Daily Life

Dickinson's most intense and constant relationship moved from "Emilie" to "Emily" and "E." and from "Susie" to "Sue" and "Susan." Focus on any other single correspondent cannot possibly offer the diverse array of insights rendered by scrutiny of these writings to Susan, for no other addressee was as intimate with Emily for as long a period of time, and no other was privy to such a range of her work. The comfort and informality of the correspondence (reflected in the content and in the types of paper used for the missives, as well as by the "rough draft" style of handwriting), reveal the "dailiness" of the intimacy between these two women. Emily did not rely on special occasions such as birthdays, holidays, or deaths to inspire the need for contact; the most ordinary and extraordinary events alike could prompt a poem or letter to Susan. Every aspect of their lives is deemed worthy subject matter in their correspondence, from shared meals and just-read books to personal unveilings about desire and loneliness; from mundane family matters to political situations reported in the newspaper, which both read every day.

Literary and biblical references abound in the correspondence, and many of Emily's favorite writers, such as George Eliot, Elizabeth Barrett Browning, and Shakespeare, are mentioned and quoted. Frequently, characters and situations in novels and plays are referred to in a manner that suggests a "masking" function, implying that Susan and Emily related their secrets through the personalities of literary and biblical characters with whom they were both familiar.

Within the documents, Emily frequently refers to family members, and a Chronology following this Introduction presents the people, places, and important events that the correspondence refers to directly or indirectly. For the most part, Emily writes to Susan from the Homestead in Amherst, Massachusetts, and Susan receives the letters during visits with family members and friends from Manchester, New Hampshire to Grand Haven, Michigan — but most often the letters travel directly next door, to the Evergreens.

Infused with eroticism, the poetry exchanged between Emily and Susan was part of the texture of their daily life. They simultaneously lived and screened their passion. However much the love between Emily and Susan has been overlooked or diminished by commentators, one thing is clear: the letters and poems are standing proof of a devoted correspondence that has had a profound impact on the history of American literature. Though popular Dickinson lore has veered far from the romantic and intellectual essence of this primary relationship, the work can now, more than a hundred years later, finally speak for itself.

A NOTE ON THE TEXT

In preparing *Open Me Carefully*, there were two main challenges before us. The first was to make a book that, although arising from academic research, would be appealing and informative to the general reader, as well as to Dickinson scholars. The second challenge was how to make a cohesive book that would most effectively relate the human story behind this most generative of literary and emotional unions. Thus, a great deal of thought and effort went into such overarching issues as which principles should serve as a guide to selection of materials to be included; how the chosen writings should then be contextualized; and how the documents should be organized.

A Comfortable, Everyday Correspondence

Even as attention to Dickinson's manuscripts has increased in the past decade, the assumption has been that any knowledge discovered through analyses of the original documents is of primary interest only to specialists. Yet the textual body of the correspondence — Dickinson's manuscripts and all their material facts — forms a powerful witness to Susan's involvement in Emily's writing practices, and is therefore of importance to anyone interested in the life and poetry of Emily Dickinson.

Emily wrote to Susan on different types of paper (graph, scrap, and formal embossed paper of all sizes), while with other correspondents she almost always used more formal, gilt-trimmed stationery, in effect dressing her texts like a gift edition of poetry or a deluxe edition of biblical scripture. Sending writings in one's casual script (as Emily does to Susan), in the handwriting more similar to one's private notes for developing expression, is an act that speaks of trust, familiarity, routine. Using less formal stationery for those writings — scraps of paper lacking gilt edges or elegant embossments — likewise signals the intimacy of comfortable everyday exchange, a correspondence not bound by special occasions, but an everyday writing habit that takes as its subject any element of life, from the monumental death of a loved one to the negligible nuisance of indigestion.

Poems Newly Associated With Susan

Emily's expressions to and about Susan — uttered in pencil and ink, on elegant stationery and on small torn squares of paper — were powerful enough to drive Susan herself to destroy those "too personal and adulatory ever to be printed."[7] Other individuals, most likely Mabel Loomis Todd, erased Susan's name and affectionate references to her; identifying some of these erasures for the first time has enabled us to identify poems not previously known to have been sent to Susan.

Twenty poems and one letter not previously associated with Susan are reproduced in this collection. These include the late 1850s letter to "Susie" discovered in 1992 and the new copy of "The feet of people walking home" addressed to "Darling" (both housed at Amherst College), a new version of "The Overtakelessness / of Those" addressed to "Dollie" (at Princeton), and a new version of "Two – were immortal – / twice – " (at the Morgan Library in New York City). We include manuscripts that editor Thomas W. Johnson did not link to Susan, though material evidence (Susan's markings, paste marks, pinholes, and/or folds) shows that according to his editorial principles, they should have been. We also include drafts of poems. Although Johnson asserted that Dickinson "never sent rough or semifinal drafts to her friends,"[8] we have found drafts we believe were sent to Susan.

For letters and poems that are not actually addressed to Susan, we have a variety of evidence to support our claim that the documents belong in this correspondence, including physical characteristics, paper types, signs of handling, notes written on the manuscripts, transmission and publication history, and work by previous editors.

The Importance of Manuscript Study

Over the past decade, technological advances in textual reproduction — such as photographic representations of the manuscripts and the creation of electronic archives providing digital images of Dickinson's writing — have worked hand in hand with critical advances such as feminist analyses to reveal more clearly Susan's immense importance as a participatory reader of Dickinson's works. *Open Me Carefully* makes use of facsimile reproduction. By studying Emily's writings to Susan in manuscript, readers can examine Dickinson's development from girlhood to advanced middle age, and the parallel maturation in her creative practices. We have made our selections with an eye toward presenting a wide range of textual forms, and in arranging these documents we have emphasized chronology.

All of Dickinson's letters and poems are handwritten, and certain manuscript features — calligraphic orthography, punctuation, capitalization, and line breaks — help to convey meaning. After the late 1850s, Dickinson's letters and poems came to look alike, both with short lines, and rarely any indentation or spacing to separate lines of poetry and lines of prose in a letter. Therefore, in Sections Two, Three, and Four we present Dickinson's line lengths, while previous editors have joined her lines of poetry according to schemes of rhyme and meter and disregarded the lineation of her prose. For consistency, we provide transcriptions, showing line breaks, for Susan's letters of the 1860s. Dickinson does not indent paragraphs in her letters but indicates their start and finish in other ways. In Section One we leave lines of space between passages to represent paragraphing.

Dickinson used the page itself, and the placement of words in relation to embossments, attachments, and margins to convey meaning, and in ways that typography cannot sufficiently transmit. We describe such poetic designs in the End Notes. Other aspects of Dickinson's handwriting which influence our editing and interpretation cannot be fully translated into type.

In reproducing her unusual capitalization, editors' decisions will vary since Dickinson's lower and upper case letters are difficult to distinguish. She generally has four or more sizes of an individual letter in a single piece of work. We call it as we see it, acknowledging that some of the fun of working with this writer's manuscript art, translating it into print, is the pleasure of interpretation and debate. Punctuation is another matter of translation. Dickinson's famous "dashes" are often angled, pointing up or down, curviform or curving with a dot to look like a bird's eye, but for simplicity we show all these "pointings" as short, standard en-dashes, with the exception of one mark that angles up and frequently appears in the later writing. This we translate as an apostrophe, a near approximation, in order to give readers a feel for its pronounced angular difference from other dashes. The calligraphic orthography (unusually shaped "S's," extravagantly crossed "T's," etc.) is described in the corresponding Notes at the back of the book. In our translation of a draft poem, a word that appears in brackets is a word Dickinson crossed out.

Not surprisingly, as Susan's poems echo Emily's in choice of subject, so the physical characteristics of her compositions often reflect Emily's. Any one of these compositional habits may be fairly common, and any one is not enough to argue for significant similarities. But the fact that many of their habits of abbreviation and punctuation mirror one another's is suggestive: like Emily's, Susan's shorthand to reorder words is to place numbers above them to indicate their position in a series (for example, "2" above the word or phrase to be placed second); Susan's quotation marks "sashay" like Emily's, and her dashes are sometimes directed decidedly up or down. Taken all together, and with the fact that in the 1870s and 1880s, Susan begins to space her alphabetic letters as Emily does, such similarities suggest at the very least Susan's intimate familiarity with, and appreciation of, Emily's work.

Descriptions of material elements of the documents, their subsequent handling and publication, are all primary parts of the story of Susan and Emily's writing exchange and are provided in the Notes.

Editions by Thomas H. Johnson and Theodora Ward, and by Ralph W. Franklin incorporate, amend, and sometimes radically revise work of earlier Dickinson editors (Thomas Wentworth Higginson, Mabel Loomis Todd, Millicent Todd Bingham, Martha Dickinson Bianchi, and Alfred Leete Hampson). Our editorial, critical, and biographical presentation also builds on the work of others, most specifically *The Letters of Emily Dickinson* edited by Johnson and Ward. We revise and correct errors in Johnson and Ward's painstaking transcriptions, and impart more information than they about the material elements of the documents, while benefiting from their research and commentary. We also benefit from the research and commentary of literary historian Jay Leyda. *Open Me Carefully* is engaged in a critical conversation with other editorial endeavors, past and present, including those of Ralph W. Franklin, Marta Werner, Edith Wylder, Susan Howe, Sharon Cameron, Jerome McGann, and Jeanne Holland, and we welcome ongoing discussion and debate about ways of reading and representing Dickinson's manuscripts.

The Question of Genre

Some editors have used genre distinctions as the dominant way of organizing Dickinson's writings, and so the Dickinson corpus has often been divided into separate volumes of poems and letters. *Open Me Carefully* breaks with this method of presentation by integrating various genres in which Dickinson wrote: poems, letters, and the genre identified by Susan as the "letter-poem."[9]

The letter-poem, a category that includes signed poems and letters with poems or with lines of poetry, will be seen here as a distinct and important Dickinson genre. Johnson arranged lines in letters to separate poems and make them look the way we might expect poems to look. We do not do this here. Neither do we divide the correspondence into "Poems to Susan" and "Letters to Susan." Instead, we follow Dickinson's commingling techniques, mindful that conventional notions of genre can limit our understanding of Dickinson's writing practices. Elizabeth Barrett Browning, one of Dickinson's literary heroes, called *Aurora Leigh*, one of Dickinson's favorite works, her "Novel in Verse." We see Dickinson's blending of poetry with prose, making poems of letters and letters of poems, as a deliberate artistic strategy.

The Accuracy of Dating

It is impossible to date and order most of the Dickinson manuscripts with precision, particularly the correspondence of the middle and late periods. Rather than using Johnson's dates, we have attempted to situate each document based on Emily's handwriting, the paper used, and particular references within each missive. These methods of dating result in a grouping of the documents into four categories: 1850 to mid-1850s; mid-1850s to mid-1860s; mid-1860s to mid-1870s; mid-1870s to Dickinson's death on May 15, 1886. With the exception of some early letters, which can be more specifically assigned a month, year, and sometimes even a day, the dating of most individual manuscripts is approximate. Our dating calls into question the supposed gap in the writings from Emily to Susan during 1856 and 1857 — a time during which the Dickinson family returned to the Homestead and Austin married and set up home with Susan next door at the Evergreens. Susan's marriage to Austin was no doubt bittersweet for Emily; while it ensured that her dear friend would be close to the family, married life occupied much of Susan's time. But it is obvious that this transition in their lives never put an end to their correspondence. Because we believe that some documents of the mid-1850s may have been destroyed, we do not concur with Johnson and Ward that Emily did not write to Susan during these years; in fact, we regard the gap in previous editions of letters as an editorial construction.

Marks by Other Hands and Other Telling Details

Marks on the manucripts made by Susan, by her daughter Martha Dickinson Bianchi, and by her children include editing notes, commentary, and signs of household use. Susan marked many poems and letters with an "X" indicating a selection process; she recorded dates and events associated with the writing for editorial purposes, as did Martha Dickinson Bianchi, and she made notes to herself to read various poems to friends. Penciled lines drawn through or beside passages of early letters, also likely to be Susan's editorial markings, resemble lines penciled in books in the Dickinson households, probably made by Susan as she read. On the versos of these manuscripts are word games, shopping lists, mathematical calculations, children's drawings, bearing witness to the fact that these documents had their place in family life. Physical aspects of the manuscripts tell the story of how these letters and poems were delivered, handled, and preserved.

Folds. Rather than placing a letter or a poem in a sealed envelope to be delivered to Susan, most often Dickinson folded the manuscript into thirds or quarters, wrote Susan's name on the verso, and then handed the letter to Susan face-to-face or, alternatively, had a family member (one of the children) or someone who worked in the households carry the letter next door to Susan's house. Of all Dickinson's correspondence to others, only writings to Susan are on very small pieces of paper (11.2 x 12.5cm.) and when folded, small enough to fit into the pocket of her dress.

The fact that many manuscripts have multiple folds suggests that they were unfolded and refolded in the process of being read and reread by Susan. Some letters were certainly shared with Susan's friends and family members. Since manuscripts in library collections are not stored folded, we can be reasonably sure that a manuscript with worn folds and more than one configuration of folds was handled during Susan's lifetime and that the wear is not the result of handling by scholars. (In contrast, the wear to a sheet's central fold created by paper manufacturers to produce two leaves, four pages, is likely to have resulted from scholarly and editorial handling.)

When a manuscript is not addressed, the fact that it has been folded does not necessarily mean that it was ever sent to a reader. Evidence suggests that Dickinson folded paper before writing on it to avoid writing directly over folds. Thus, in determining which manuscripts were actually sent to Susan, we do not consider the presence of folds alone to be sufficient evidence; there must also be other markings or signs of handling, use, and preservation unique to this correspondence.

The multiple folds and worn folds are consistent with Martha Dickinson Bianchi's statement that Susan read and reread these letters, letter-poems, and poems late in her life as she made preparations with her daughter for an edition of Emily's writings to be published after her death. Folded manuscripts were often pasted into scrapbooks, so the process of unfolding, reading, and refolding would be repeated. The care Susan took in keeping these manuscripts attests to the value she placed on them. When Susan reread the letters and poems pasted down in this way, she would have been recreating the experience of unfolding, opening, and reading them for the first time.

Paste marks. Many manuscripts to Susan were once pasted onto sheets of paper, as indicated by residue remaining on the verso when sheets were removed. Occasionally, pasty fingerprints appear on the manuscripts. In the 1890s, Susan and Martha may have been compiling an edition, or their work may have been done closer to Susan's death in 1913 and the publication of *The Single Hound* in 1914. Some paste marks show traces of blue-ruled sheets, the tablet paper on which Susan and Martha pasted manuscripts and on which Martha recorded information received from her mother about a document. Some manuscripts appear to have been pasted onto sheets of stationery by Susan, perhaps to be placed among loose sheets kept in a scrapbook or notebook.

Pinholes. Many of the manuscripts to Susan show that they once were pinned to some other surface. Pinholes may indicate a variety of uses and handling. Susan pinned manuscripts in scrapbooks. A slip of paper with Susan's name could have been pinned to a poem or letter when it was sent. A folded manuscript may have been pinned inside Dickinson's clothing until she had the opportunity to deliver it to the Evergreens. Or, a sheet may have been pinned to a piece of cloth on a tray or to one covering a gift of bread, candy, or fruit. In addition, before the invention of paper clips, manuscripts were pinned together. The pinholes with traces of rust may mean manuscripts were pinned for a long period of time, stored and preserved.

These salient material facts all argue for embodying Dickinson's most important correspondence, her writings to Susan, in a book all its own. By presenting this most passionate and diverse of all of Dickinson's correspondences, *Open Me Carefully* relates Emily and Susan's devotion to one another and to the craft of poetry. Through all the decades of poems, letters, and letter-poems from Emily to Susan, we are constantly reminded that for these two remarkable women "Poetry" and "Love . . . coeval come."

CHRONOLOGY

December 10, 1830	Birth of Emily Elizabeth Dickinson, daughter of Emily Norcross and Edward Dickinson, sister of Austin Dickinson (b. 1828), in Amherst, Massachusetts.
December 19, 1830	Birth of Susan Huntington Gilbert Dickinson, daughter of Harriet Arms and Thomas Gilbert, the youngest of six children, in Deerfield, Massachusetts.
1832	The Gilbert family moves from Deerfield to Amherst, where Thomas Gilbert becomes proprietor of the Mansion House, an inn and stagecoach stop.
February 28, 1833	Birth of Lavinia (Vinnie) Norcross Dickinson, Emily's sister.
March 1833	Samuel Fowler Dickinson, Emily's grandfather, sells half of the Homestead to General David Mack and moves to Ohio.
late spring 1833	Emily lives with her aunt Lavinia Norcross in Monson, while her mother recuperates from childbirth.
September 7, 1835	Emily begins four years at the district Primary School.
February 13, 1837	Harriet Arms Gilbert, Susan's mother, dies of consumption.
1837	Susan Gilbert and her sister Martha (b. 1829) move to Geneva, New York, to live with their aunt Sophia Arms Van Vranken.

late 1830s–1840s	Susan attends Utica Female Seminary.
January 1838	Edward Dickinson assumes his first term in the Massachusetts General Court.
April 1840	Edward and Emily Norcross Dickinson and their three children move from the Homestead on Main Street to "the Mansion" on South Pleasant Street.
September 1840	Emily and Lavinia Dickinson begin education at Amherst Academy.
December 23, 1841	General Thomas Gilbert, Susan's father, dies.
June 22, 1842	Susan's eldest sister Harriet (b. 1820) and William Cutler are married in Ashfield, Massachusetts, and move to Amherst.
early 1840s–early 1850s	Susan and Martha Gilbert live in Amherst with Harriet and William Cutler as well as in Geneva, New York.
September 1847–August 1848	Emily attends South Hadley Female Seminary (Mount Holyoke College).
fall 1847	Susan attends Amherst Academy for one term.
1850	Emily sends first known letter to Susan.
February 1850	Amherst College *Indicator* prints Emily's "Magnum bonum" Valentine Eve letter.
September 1851–early July 1852	Susan teaches mathematics at Robert Archer's school in Baltimore, Maryland.
February 20, 1852	Emily's first printed poem, "A Valentine," appears in the *Springfield Daily Republican*.
December 17, 1852	Edward Dickinson is elected to Congress, Representative of Tenth Massachusetts District.
March 23, 1853	Susan Gilbert and Austin Dickinson are engaged at the Revere Hotel in Boston.

mid-November 1855	The Dickinson family moves back into the renovated Homestead.
July 1, 1856	Susan and Austin are married in the home of Susan's aunt Sophia Arms Van Vranken in Geneva, New York, then move to the Evergreens, next door to the Homestead.
late 1850s	Emily sends poems regularly to Susan; Emily begins to make her "fascicles" or manuscript books.
1858–1866	Emily publishes eight poems in the *Springfield Republican, Drum Beat, Round Table, Brooklyn Daily Union, Boston Post.*
June 19, 1861	Birth of Edward (Ned) Dickinson, Susan and Austin's eldest child.
April 1862	Thomas Wentworth Higginson's "Letter to a Young Contributor" appears as the lead article in the *Atlantic Monthly.*
April 15, 1862	Emily writes to Higginson and sends four poems.
April–November 1864; April–October 1865	Emily receives medical care from a Boston ophthalmologist and lives with cousins Fanny and Louise Norcross in Cambridgeport, Massachusetts.
November 29, 1866	Birth of Martha (Mattie) Gilbert Dickinson, Susan and Austin's second child.
spring 1872	Emily and Susan are seen attending church together.
November 5, 1873	Edward Dickinson re-elected to the Massachusetts General Court.
June 16, 1874	Edward Dickinson dies.
June 15, 1875	Emily Norcross Dickinson, Emily's mother, suffers stroke.
August 1, 1875	Birth of Thomas Gilbert (Gib) Dickinson, Susan and Austin's youngest child.

February 8, 1882	Susan introduces Mabel Loomis Todd to Emily's poetry.
November 14, 1882	Emily Norcross Dickinson, Emily's mother, dies.
October 5, 1883	Gib Dickinson, Susan and Austin's youngest child, dies of typhoid fever; Susan and Emily go into seclusion.
May 15, 1886	Emily Elizabeth Dickinson dies from Bright's disease. Susan prepares Emily's body for burial and writes the obituary that appears in the *Springfield Republican.*
December 31, 1886	Susan submits "A Poem of Miss Emily Dickinson's on the 'Wind'" to *The Century.*
November 1890	*Poems by Emily Dickinson,* edited by Mabel Loomis Todd and Thomas Wentworth Higginson, published by Roberts Brothers.
August 16, 1895	Austin Dickinson dies.
May 3, 1898	Ned Dickinson dies of angina.
August 31, 1899	Lavinia Dickinson dies.
May 12, 1913	Susan Huntington Dickinson dies.
1914	*The Single Hound: Poems of a Lifetime,* edited by Martha Dickinson Bianchi, published by Little, Brown and Company.

SECTION ONE

Why Susie!

Early Writings, 1850 to mid-1850s

DURING THE EARLY AND MID-1850s, Emily's correspondence to Susan is effusive and filled with puns and references to the act of writing. The first letter that is preserved from Emily to Susan is dated 1850. While it is not certain how Emily and Susan met, it is likely that they were friends by 1847 or 1848. In an 1850 letter to Susan, Emily's brother Austin remarks on the previous Thanksgiving and expresses his happiness when Emily and their sister Lavinia (Vinnie) asked Susan's "family into the circle which had for two or three years been gradually forming."[1] The letters from Emily to Susan and drafts of letters from Austin indicate that Susan is the object of passionate attachment for both brother and sister.

The boundaries of the correspondence from Emily to Susan are defined by what Susan saves rather than by what Emily writes, and it is likely that Emily sends letters to Susan that have not survived. Perhaps Susan begins to keep letters from Emily following the 1850 death of her sister Mary, in childbirth. Or Susan may save Emily's letters when she begins to keep letters from Austin.

In the early years of the correspondence, between 1851 and 1852, Susan moves to Baltimore to teach at Robert Archer's school for girls. Her decision to go away is sudden, and she writes to her brother Dwight, declaring that she has left her "good friends in Amherst actually staring with astonishment."[2] Susan is independent, outspoken, deeply engaged with spiritual concerns, and like Emily, she is committed to pursuing intellectual growth without benefit of continuing education.

Emily's and Susan's impatience and resentment of household duties are nearly identical. In a letter to her friend Samuel Bartlett, Susan says: "I've fairly commenced the Spring siege of sewing, and such quantities of garments and furbelows, to be made, lie stretching away before my crooked needles, I am quite in despair, and continually wondering and fretting, that we are not clothed like the lilies, without any spinning and toiling — I find no time to read or think, and but little to walk — but just go revolving round a spool of 'Coat's cotton' as if it were the grand centre of mental and moral life — "[3]

While Emily sends Susan passionate and playful letters, Austin formally courts Susan, and Emily secretly delivers his letters to her "Darling Sue." In 1853, humor suffuses an edge of envy for Austin's heightened status in the family as an ambitious and "learned" person; having graduated from Amherst College, he now attends Harvard Law School. Although Emily "loves the opportunity to serve those who are mine," she writes to Susan in markedly shaky handwriting, identifying with Miss Julia Mills in *David Copperfield,* whom Dickens describes as "interested in others' loves, herself withdrawn."

The intellectual intimacy between Emily and Susan begins in the early years of their relationship. In her letters to Susan, Emily frequently refers to the novels she is reading and uses various characters as metaphors or codes to relate her feelings about herself and Susan, and comment about friends, relatives, and literary and political luminaries and events.

In early 1853, Susan travels to Manchester, New Hampshire, to visit Mary and Samuel Bartlett, her sister Mary's in-laws. On the return rail trip from Manchester on Wednesday, March 23, Susan arrives in Boston for a tryst with Austin at the Revere Hotel, and the couple becomes engaged. When Susan returns to Amherst, she shares the news with Emily who then writes to Austin: "Oh my dear 'Oliver,' how chipper you must be since any of us have seen you?" and "I hope you have been made happy."[4] In this letter, she blames Austin because Susan seems distracted and absent, and Emily devises punishment: "You deserve, let me see; you deserve hot irons, and Chinese Tartary . . ." She then reminds him how often she is seeing Susan while he is away at law school and closes with: "Dear Austin, I am keen, but you are a good deal keener, I am something of a fox, but you are more of a hound! I guess we are very good friends tho', and I guess we both love [S]us[ie] just as well as we can."[5] As the brackets indicate, Emily's references to "Susie" have been altered or erased. In another letter written several weeks later beginning, "Do you want to hear from me, Austin?" affectionate references to Susan are erased as well, though kindly references to Lavinia remain untouched. Emily asks Austin, "How long it is since you've been in this state of complacence towards God and our fellow men?" She then follows with, "I think it must be sudden."[6] Facetiously she recommends religious texts to guide Austin in meditating on self-discipline and submission of his will. She hopes that he has "enjoyed" "sanctuary privileges."

In April 1854, Austin, Lavinia, and their mother visit Washington, D.C., where Edward Dickinson is serving as a member of Congress. They arrive on April 7, and stay for several weeks. At this time, Susan lives with Emily, in the company of John Graves, a cousin from nearby Sunderland, who is attending Amherst College. In mid-April, Susan writes to Mary Bartlett saying, "I am keeping house with Emily, while the family are in Washington — We frighten each other to death nearly every night — with that exception, we have very independent times."[7]

Three months later, Susan becomes seriously ill with "nervous fever." Describing Susan's condition to a friend, Emily writes that "every hour possible I have taken away to her." Susan recovers in August and travels to Geneva and Aurora, New York, where she stays with family for nearly three months. Austin, now graduated from Harvard Law School and admitted to the bar, prepares to seek his fortune in the West.

From Aurora, New York, Susan travels to Grand Haven, Michigan, where she stays with her brother Dwight through the early winter. In a letter mapping out her travel plans Susan tells her brother, "I have always felt so like a child the idea of really being married seems absurd enough and if the event ever occurs I think I shall experience a feeling of odd surprise — "[8]

When Susan accuses Austin of interfering with her correspondence with Emily, Austin writes: "As to your deprivation of 'Spiritual converse' with my sister — I Know Nothing — I was aware that you had been in correspondence for some time, but had never had an intimation that the correspondence was at an end — . . . So you will not suspect me of having interfered with your epistolary intercourse with her."[9]

In the letters that follow, Emily and Susan are in their early twenties. Though Emily's feelings of love, desire, and longing for Susan have often been dismissed as a "school-girl crush," the letters resonate with intelligence, humor, and intimacy that cannot be reduced to adolescent flurry.

1

Thursday noon.

Were it not for the weather Susie – my little, unwelcome face would come peering in today – I should steal a kiss from the sister – the darling Rover returned – Thank the wintry wind my dear one – that spares such daring intrusion! Dear Susie – happy Susie – I rejoice in all your Joy – sustained by that dear sister you will never again be lonely. Dont forget all the little friends who have tried so hard to be sisters, when indeed you were alone!

You do not hear the wind blow on this inclement day, when the world is shrugging it's shoulders – your little "Columbarium is lined with warmth and softness," there is no "silence" there – so you differ from bonnie "Alice." I miss one angel face in the little world of sisters – dear Mary – sainted Mary – Remember lonely one – tho, she comes not to us, we shall return to her! My love to both your sisters – and I want so much to see Matty.

Very aff yours, Emily

autumn/winter 1850
In this letter Emily refers to Susan's sister Mary, who died on July 14, 1850. In December, Susan's sister Martha ("Matty") came from Michigan, and the Gilbert family was temporarily reconstituted in the Amherst home of their eldest sister Harriet. The allusion to "Alice" is to Alice Archer of Longfellow's

Kavanagh (1849) whose room is "that columbarium lined with warmth, and softness, and silence." Throughout the correspondence, and long before Susan is actually her sister-in-law, Emily addresses Susan as "Sister."

2

Thursday evening

I wept a tear here, Susie – on purpose for *you* – because this "sweet silver moon" smiles in on me and Vinnie, and then it goes so far before it gets to you – and then you never told me if there *was* any moon in Baltimore – and how do *I* know Susie – that you see her sweet face at all? She looks like a fairy tonight, sailing around the sky in a little silver gondola with stars for gondoliers. I asked her to let me ride a little while ago – and told her I would *get out* when she got as far as Baltimore, but she only smiled to herself and went sailing on.

I think she was quite ungenerous – but I have learned the lesson and shant ever ask her again. To day it rained at home – sometimes it rained so hard that I fancied you could hear it's patter – patter, patter, as it fell upon the leaves – and the fancy pleased me so, that I sat and listened to it – and watched it earnestly. *Did* you hear it Susie – or was it *only* fancy? Bye and bye the sun came out – just in time to bid us goodnight, and as I told you sometime, the moon is shining now.

It is such an evening Susie, as you and I would walk and have such pleasant musings, if you were only here – perhaps we would have a "Reverie" after the form of "Ik Marvel," indeed I do not know why it would'nt be just as charming as of that lonely Bachelor, smoking his cigar – and it would be far more profitable as "Marvel" *only* marvelled, and you and I would *try* to make a little destiny to have for our own. Do you know that charming man is dreaming again, and will wake pretty soon – so the papers say, with another Reverie – more beautiful than the first?

Dont you hope he will live as long as you and I do – and keep on having dreams and writing them to us – what a charming old man he'll be, and how I envy his grandchildren, little "Bella" and "Paul"! We will be willing to die Susie – when such as he have gone, for there will be none left to interpret these lives of our's.

Longfellow's "golden Legend" has come to town I hear – and may be seen in state on Mr. Adams' bookshelves. It always makes me think of "Pegasus in the pound –" when I find a gracious author sitting side by side with "Murray" and "Wells" and "Walker" in that renowned store – and like him I half expect to hear they have "flown" some morning and in their native ether revel all the day – but for our sakes dear Susie, who please ourselves with the fancy that we are the only poets – and every one else is prose, let us hope they will yet be willing to share our humble world and feed upon such aliment as we consent to do!

You thank me for the Rice cake – you tell me Susie, you have just been tasting it – and how happy I am to send you anything you love – how hungry you must grow before it is noon there – and then you must be faint from teaching those stupid scholars. I fancy you very often descending to the schoolroom with a plump Binomial Theorem struggling in your hand which you must dissect and exhibit to your incomprehending ones – I hope you whip them Susie – for my sake – whip them hard whenever they dont behave just as you want to have them! I know they are very dull – sometimes – from what Mattie says – but I presume you encourage them and forgive all their mistakes. It will teach you patience Susie – you may be sure of that. And Mattie tells me too of your evening carousals – and the funny frights you give in personating the Master – just like you Susie – like you for all the world – how Mr Payson would laugh if I could only tell him, and then those great dark eyes – how they would glance and sparkle! Susie – have all the fun wh' you possibly can – and laugh as often and sing, for tears are plentier than smiles in this little world of our's – only dont be so happy as to let Mattie and me grow dimmer and dimmer and finally fade away, and merrier maids than we smile in our vacant places!

Susie, did you think that I would never write you when you were gone away – what made you? I am sure you know my promise far too well for that – and had I never said so – I should be constrained to write – for what shall separate us from any whom we love – not "hight nor depth["] . . .

October 9, 1851
Susan is now teaching in Baltimore and Emily writes to her frequently. Ik Marvel's (Donald G. Mitchell) *Reveries of a Bachelor* (1850) was a bestseller and enjoyed by Emily, Susan, and Austin, as was Longfellow's *Golden Legend* (1851). Both books celebrate romantic passion and emotional attachment. Lindley Murray, William Harvey Wells, and John Walker were lexicographers and grammarians. In an October 1 letter to Austin, every allusion to "Susie" is erased.

3

Friday forenoon –

Will you let me come dear Susie – looking just as I do, my dress soiled and worn, my grand old apron, and my hair – Oh Susie, time would fail me to enumerate my appearance, yet I love you just as dearly as if I was e'er so fine, so you wont care, will you? I am so glad dear Susie – that our hearts are always clean, and always neat and lovely, so not to be ashamed. I have been hard at work this morning, and I ought to be working now – but I cannot deny myself the luxury of a minute or two with you.

The dishes may wait dear Susie – and the uncleared table stand, *them* I have always with me, but *you*, I have "not always," *why* Susie, Christ hath saints ma*nie* – and I have *few*, but thee – the angels shant have Susie – no – no no!

Vinnie is sewing away like a *fictitious* seamstress, and I half expect some knight will arrive at the door, confess himself a *nothing* in presence of her loveliness, and present his heart and hand as the only vestige of him worthy to be refused.

Vinnie and I have been talking about growing old, today. Vinnie thinks *twenty* must be a fearful position for one to occupy – I tell her I dont care if I am young or not, had as lief be thirty, and you, as most anything else. Vinnie expresses her sympathy at my "sere and yellow leaf" and resumes her work, dear Susie, tell me how *you* feel – ar'nt there days in one's life when to be old dont seem a thing so sad –

I do feel gray and grim, this morning, and I feel it would be a comfort to have a piping voice, and a broken back, and scare little children.

Dont *you* run, Susie dear, for I wont do any harm, and I do love you dearly tho' I do feel so frightful.

Oh my darling one, how long you wander from me, how weary I grow of waiting and looking, and calling for you; sometimes I shut my eyes, and shut my heart towards you, and try hard to forget you because you grieve me so, but you'll never go away, Oh you never will – say, Susie, promise me again, and I will smile faintly – and take up my little cross again of sad – sad separation. How vain it seems to write, when one knows how to feel – how much more near and dear to sit beside you, talk with you, hear the tones of your voice – so hard to "deny thyself, and take up thy cross, and follow me –" give me strength, Susie, write me of hope and love, and of hearts that endured, and great was their reward of "Our Father who art in Heaven." I dont know how I shall bear it, when the gentle spring comes; if she should come and see me and talk to me of you, Oh it would surely kill me! While the frost clings to the windows, and the World is stern and drear; this absence is easier – the Earth mourns too, for all her little birds; but when they all come back again, and she sings and is so merry – pray, what will become of me? Susie, forgive me, forget all what I say, get some sweet little scholar to read a gentle hymn, about Bethleem and Mary, and you will sleep on sweetly and have as peaceful dreams, as if I had never written you all these ugly things. Never mind the letter Susie, I wont be angry with you if you dont give me any at all – for I know how busy you are, and how little of that dear strength remains when it is evening, with which to think and write. Only want to write me, only sometimes sigh that you are far from me, and that will do, Susie! Dont you think we are good and patient, to let you go so long; and dont we think you're a darling, a real beautiful hero, to toil for people, and teach them, and leave your own dear home? Because we pine and repine, dont think we forget the precious patriot at war in other lands! Never be mournful, Susie – be happy and have cheer, for how many of the long days have gone away since I wrote you – and it is almost noon, and soon the night will come, and then there is one less day of the long pilgrimage. Mattie is very smart, talks of you much, my darling; I must leave you now – "one little hour of Heaven," thank who did give it me, and will he also grant me one longer and more when it shall please his love – bring Susie home, ie! Love always, and ever, and true! Emily –

February 1852
Throughout Emily's letters to Susan, she combines a language of courtly love with terms of spiritual devotion. In 1915, Susan's daughter Martha Dickinson Bianchi described her Aunt Emily in the *Atlantic Monthly*, saying: "Her devotion to those she loved was that of a knight for his lady."

4

Wednesday morn

It's a sorrowful morning Susie – the wind blows and it rains; "into each life some rain must fall," and I hardly know which falls fastest, the rain without, or within – Oh Susie, I would nestle close to your warm heart, and never hear the wind blow, or the storm beat, again. Is there any room there for me, or shall I wander away all homeless and alone? Thank you for loving me, darling, and will you "love me more if ever you come home" ! it is enough, dear Susie, I know I shall be satisfied. But what can I do towards you? – dearer you cannot be, for I love you so already, that it almost breaks my heart – perhaps I can love you anew, every day of my life, every morning and evening – Oh if you will let me, how happy I shall be!

The precious billet, Susie, I am wearing the paper out, reading it over and o'er, but the dear thoughts cant wear out if they try, Thanks to Our Father, Susie! Vinnie and I talked of you all last evening long, and went to sleep mourning for you, and pretty soon I waked up saying "Precious treasure, thou art mine," and there you were all right, my Susie, and I hardly dared to sleep lest some one steal you away. Never mind the letter, Susie; you have so much to do; just write me every week one line, and let it be, "Emily, I love you," and I will be satisfied! Your own Emily

Upside down on first page

Vinnie's love – Mother's –

In margin on third page

Love to Hattie from us all. Dear Mattie is almost well.

about February 1852
The quote "into each life some rain must fall" is from Longfellow's "The Rainy Day," a poem that Emily and Susan shared with their friends.

5

Sunday morning –

Thank the dear little snow flakes, because they fall today rather than some vain weekday, when the world and the cares of the world would try so hard to keep me from my departed friend – and thank you, too, dear Susie, that you never weary of me, or never tell me so, and that when the world is cold, and the storm sighs e'er so piteously, I am sure of one sweet shelter, one covert from the storm! The bells are ringing, Susie, north, and east, and south, and your own village bell, and the people who love God, are expecting to go to meeting; dont you go Susie, not to their meeting, but come with me this morning to the church within our hearts, where the bells are always ringing, and the preacher whose name is Love – shall intercede there for us!

They will all go but me, to the usual meetinghouse, to hear the usual sermon; the inclemency of the storm so kindly detaining me; and as I sit here Susie, alone with the winds and you – I have the old king feeling even more than before, for I know not even the cracker man will invade this solitude, this sweet Sabbath of our's. And thank you for my dear letter, which came on Saturday night, when all the world was still; thank you for the love it bore me, and for it's golden thoughts, and feelings so like gems, that I was sure I gathered them in whole baskets of pearls! I mourn this morning, Susie, that I have no sweet sunset to gild a page for you, nor any bay so blue – not even a little chamber way up in the sky, as your's is, to give me thoughts of heaven, which I would give to you. You know how I must write you, down, down, in the terrestrial – no sunset here, no stars; not even a bit of twilight which I may poetize – and send you! Yet Susie, there will be romance in the letter's ride to you – think of the hills and the dales, and the rivers it will pass over, and the drivers and conductors who will hurry it on to you; and wont that make a poem such as can ne'er be written? I think of you dear Susie, now, I dont know how or why, but more dearly as every day goes by, and that sweet month of promise draws nearer and nearer; and I view July so differently from what I used to – once it seemed parched, and dry – and I hardly loved it any on account of it's heat and dust; but now Susie, month of all the year the best; I skip the violets – and the dew, and the early Rose and the Robins; I will exchange them all for that angry and hot noonday, when I can count the hours and the minutes before you come – Oh Susie, I often think that I will try to tell you how very dear you are, and how I'm watching for you, but the words wont come, tho' the tears will, and I sit down disappointed – yet darling, you know it all – then why do I seek to tell you? I do not know; in thinking of those I love, my reason is all gone from me, and I do fear sometimes that I must make a hospital for the hopelessly insane, and chain me up there such times, so I wont injure you.

Always when the sun shines, and always when it storms, and always always, Susie, we are remembering you, and what else besides remembering; I shall not tell you, because you know!

Were it not for dear Mattie, I dont know what we would do, but she loves you so dearly, and is never tired of talking about you, and we all get together and talk it oer and oer – and it makes us more resigned, than to mourn for you alone.

It was only yesterday, that I went to see dear Mattie, intending in my heart to stay a little while, only a very little one, because of a good many errands which I was going to do, and will you believe it, Susie, I was there an hour – and an hour, and half an hour besides, and would'nt have supposed it had been minutes so many – and what do you guess we talked about, all those hours long – what would you give to know – give me one little glimpse of your sweet face, dear Susie, and I will tell you all – we didn't talk of statesmen, and we didn't talk of kings – but the time was filled full, and when the latch was lifted and the oaken door was closed, why, Susie, I realized as never I did before, how much a single cottage held that was dear to me. It is sweet – and like home, at Mattie's, but it's sad too – and up comes little memory, and paints – and paints – and paints – and the strangest thing of all, her canvass is never full, and I find her where I left her, every time that I come – and who is she painting – Ah, Susie, "dinna choose to tell" – but it is'nt Mr Cutler, and it is'nt Daniel Boon, and I shant tell you any more – Susie, what will you say if I tell you that

Henry Root is coming to see me, some evening of this week, and I have promised to read him some parts of all your letters; now you wont care, dear Susie, for he wants so much to hear, and I shant read him anything which I know you would not be willing – just some little places, which will please him so – I have seen him several times lately, and I admire him, Susie, because he talks of *you* so frequently and beautifully; and I know he is so true to you, when you are far away – We talk more of you, dear Susie, than of any other thing – he tells me how wonderful you are, and I tell him how true you are, and his big eyes beam, and he seems so delighted – I know you would'nt care, Susie, if you knew how much joy it made – As I told him the other evening of all your letters to me, he looked up *very* longingly, and I knew what he would say, were he enough acquainted – so I answered the question his heart wanted to ask, and when some pleasant evening, before this week is gone, you remember home and Amherst, then know, Loved One – that *they* are remembering *you*, and that "two or three" are gathered in your name, loving, and speaking of you – and will you be there in the midst of them? Then I've found a beautiful, new, friend, and I've told him about dear Susie, and promised to let him know you so soon as you shall come. Dear Susie, in all your letters there are things sweet and many about which I would speak, but the time says no – yet dont think I forget them – Oh no – they are safe in the little chest which tells no secrets – nor the moth, nor the rust can reach them – but when the time we dream of – comes, *then* Susie, I shall bring them, and we will spend hours chatting and chatting of them – those precious thoughts of friends – how I loved them, and how I love them now nothing but Susie *herself* is *half* so dear. Susie, I have not asked you if you were cheerful and well – and I cant think why, except that there's something *perrennial* in those we dearly love, immortal life and vigor; why it seems as if any sickness, or harm, would flee away, would not dare do them wrong, and Susie, while you are taken from me, I class you with the angels, and you know the Bible tells us – "there is no sickness there." But, dear Susie, are you well, and peaceful, for I wont make you cry by saying are you happy? Dont see the blot, Susie. It's because I broke the Sabbath!

Upside down on first page

Susie, what shall I do – there is'nt room enough; not half enough, to hold what I was going to say. Wont you tell the man who makes sheets of paper, that I hav'nt the slightest respect for him!

In margin on first page

And when shall I have a letter – when it's convenient, Susie, not when tired and faint – ever!

In margin on second page

Emeline gets well so slowly; poor Henry; I guess he thinks true love's course does'nt run very smooth –

In margin on third page

Much love from Mother and Vinnie, and then there are some others who do not dare to send –

In margin on fourth page

Who loves you most, and loves you best, and thinks of you when others rest? T'is Emilie –

about February 1852

Precious stones and gold, love's riches, and Susan herself as a jewel become a pattern of imagery that continues throughout Emily's poetry. Her lamentation that she has no "sweet sunset to gild a page for you" may refer to Emily's inability to use gilt-edged stationery to make a gift of her writing. Mr. Cutler is the Amherst merchant, William Cutler, who married Susan's sister Harriet in 1842. In the margin on the second page, Emily refers to Emeline Kellogg and her future husband, Henry Nash. A letter to Austin written at the same time is mutilated when referring to "Susie."

6

Monday morning –

Will you be kind to me, Susie? I am naughty and cross, this morning, and nobody loves me here; nor would you love me, if you should see me frown, and hear how loud the door bangs whenever I go through; and yet it is'nt anger – I dont believe it is, for when nobody sees, I brush away big tears with the corner of my apron, and then go working on – bitter tears, Susie – so hot that they burn my cheeks, and almost schorch my eyeballs, but you have wept such, and you know they are less of anger than sorrow.

And I do love to run fast – and hide away from them all; here in dear Susie's bosom, I know is love and rest, and I never would go away, did not the big world call me, and beat me for not working.

Little Emerald Mack is washing, I can hear the warm suds, splash. I just gave her my pocket handkerchief – so I cannot cry any more. And Vinnie sweeps – sweeps, upon the chamber stairs; and Mother is hurrying round with her hair in a silk pocket handkerchief, on account of dust. Oh Susie, it is dismal, sad and drear eno' – and the sun dont shine, and the clouds look cold and gray, and the wind dont blow, but it pipes the shrillest roundelay, and the birds dont sing, but twitter – and there's nobody to smile! Do I paint it natural – Susie, so you think how it looks? Yet dont you care – for it wont last so always, and we love you just as well – and think of you, as dearly, as if it were not so. Your precious letter, Susie, it sits here now, and smiles so kindly at me, and gives me such sweet thoughts of the dear writer. When you come home, darling, I shant have your letters, shall I, but I shall have yourself, which is more – Oh more, and better, than I can even think! I sit here with my little whip, cracking the time away, till not an hour is left of it – then you are here! And Joy is here – joy now and forevermore!

Tis only a few days, Susie, it will soon go away, yet I say, go now, this very moment, for I need her – I must have her, Oh give her to me!

Mattie is dear and true, I love her very dearly – and Emily Fowler, too, is very dear to me – and Tempe – and Abby, and Eme', I am sure – I love them all – and I hope they love me, but, Susie, there's a great corner still; I fill it with that is gone, I hover round and round it, and call it darling names, and bid it speak to me, and ask it if it's Susie, and it answers, Nay, Ladie, Susie is stolen away!

Do I repine, is it all murmuring, or am I sad and lone, and cannot, cannot help it? Sometimes when I do feel so, I think it may be wrong, and that God will punish me by taking you away; for he is very kind to let me write to you, and to give me your sweet letters, but my heart wants more.

Have you ever thought of it Susie, and yet I know you have, how much these hearts claim; why I dont believe in the whole, wide world, are such hard little creditors – such real little misers, as you and I carry with us, in our bosoms everyday. I cant help thinking sometimes, when I hear about the ungenerous, Heart, keep very still – or someone will find you out!

I am going out on the doorstep, to get you some new – green grass – I shall pick it down in the corner, where you and I used to sit, and have long fancies. And perhaps the dear little grasses were growing all the while – and perhaps they heard what we said, but they cant tell! I have come in now, dear Susie, and here is what I found – not quite so glad and green as when we used to sit there, but a sad and pensive grassie – mourning o'er hopes. No doubt some spruce, young Plantain leaf won its young heart away, and then proved false – and dont you wish none proved so, but little Plantains?

I do think it's wonderful, Susie, that our hearts dont break, every day, when I think of all the whiskers, and all the gallant men, but I guess I'm made with nothing but a hard heart of stone, for it dont break any, and dear Susie, if mine is stony, your's is stone, upon stone, for you never yield any, where I seem quite beflown. Are we going to ossify always, say, Susie – how will it be? When I see the Popes and the Polloks, and the John-Milton Browns, I think we are liable, but I dont know! I am glad there's a big future waiting for me and you. You would love to know what I read – I hardly know what to tell you, my catalogue is so small.

I have just read three little books, not great, not thrilling – but sweet and true. "The Light in the Valley," "Only," and a "House upon a Rock" – I know you would love them all – yet they dont bewitch me any. There are no walks in the wood – no low and earnest voices, no moonlight, nor stolen love, but pure little lives, loving God, and their parents, and obeying the laws of the land; yet read, if you meet them, Susie, for they will do one good.

I have the promise of "Alton Lock" – a certain book, called "Olive," and the "Head of a Family," which was what Mattie named to you. Vinnie and I had "Bleak House" sent to us the other day – it is like him who wrote it – that is all I can say. Dear Susie, you were so happy when you wrote to me last – I am so glad, and you will be happy now for all my sadness, wont you? I cant forgive me ever, if I have made you sad, or dimmed your eye for me. I write from the Land of Violets, and from the Land of Spring, and it would ill become me to carry you nought but sorrows. I remember you, Susie, always – I keep you ever here, and when you are gone, then I'm gone – and we're 'neath one willow tree. I can only thank "the Father" for giving me such as you, I can only pray unceasingly, that he will bless my Loved One, and bring her back to me, to "go no more out forever. " Herein is Love." But that was Heaven – this is but Earth, yet Earth so like to heaven, that I would hesitate, should the true one call away. Dear Susie – adieu! Emilie –

Upside down on first page

Father's sister is dead, and Mother wears black on her bonnet, and has a collar of crape.

In margin on first page

A great deal of love from Vinnie, and she wants that little note.

In margin on second page

Austin comes home on Wednesday, but he'll only stay two days, so I fancy we shant

In margin on third page

go sugaring, as "we did last year." Last year is gone, Susie – did you ever think of that?

In margin on fourth page

Joseph is out south somewhere, a very great way off, yet we hear from him.

April 5, 1852
The reference to "Emerald" distinguishes Mrs. Mack, an Irish woman who works in the Dickinson household, from members of the family of Deacon David Mack. Emily mentions her friend Emily Fowler, and in the margin, she refers to Joseph Lyman, a friend of Emily's and Lavinia's. In Emily's caricatures of friends as literary celebrities, she seems to pun on the names of Alexander Pope and a near-contemporary Scottish divine. The books that are mentioned refer to *The Light in the Valley*, a memorial of Mary Elizabeth Stirling, *Only* and *A House Upon a Rock* by Matilda Anne Mackarness, *Alton Locke* by Charles Kingsley, *Head of a Family* and *Olive* by Dinah Maria Craik, and *Bleak House* by Charles Dickens. In the margins of this letter, Emily also refers to the March 30, 1852, death of her aunt Mary Newman, Edward Dickinson's sister.

7

Sunday afternoon

So sweet and still, and Thee, Oh Susie, what need I more, to make my heaven whole?

Sweet Hour, blessed Hour, to carry me to you, and to bring you back to me, long enough to snatch one kiss, and whisper Good bye, again.

I have thought of it all day, Susie, and I fear of but little else, and when I was gone to meeting it filled my mind so full, I could not find a chink to put the worthy pastor; when he said "Our Heavenly Father," I said "Oh Darling Sue"; when he read the 100th Psalm, I kept saying your precious letter all over to myself, and Susie, when they sang – it would have made you laugh to hear one little voice, piping to the departed. I made up words and kept singing how I loved you, and you had gone, while all the rest of the choir were singing Hallelujahs. I presume nobody heard me, because I sang so small, but it was a kind of a comfort to think I might put them out, singing of you. I a'nt there this afternoon, tho', because I am here, writing a little letter to my dear Sue, and I am very happy. I think of ten weeks – Dear One, and I think of love, and you, and my heart grows full and warm, and my breath stands still. The sun does'nt shine at all, but I can feel a sunshine stealing into my soul and making it all summer, and every thorn, a rose. And I pray that such summer's sun shine on my Absent One, and cause her bird to sing!

You have been happy, Susie, and now are sad – and the whole world seems lone; but it wont be so always, "some days must be dark and dreary"! You wont cry any more, will you, Susie, for my father will be your father, and my home will be your home, and where you go, I will go, and we will lie side by side in the kirkyard.

I have parents on earth, dear Susie, but your's are in the skies, and I have an earthly fireside, but you have one above, and you have a "Father in Heaven," where I have none – and a sister in heaven, and I know they love you dearly, and think of you every day.

Oh I wish I had half so many dear friends as you in heaven – I could'nt spare them now – but to know they had got there safely, and should suffer nevermore – Dear Susie!

I know I was very naughty to write such fretful things, and I know I could have helped it, if I had tried hard enough, but I thought my heart would break, and I knew of nobody here that cared anything about it – so I said to myself, "We will tell Susie about it." You dont know what a comfort it was, and you wont know, till the big cup of bitterness is filled brimfull, and they say, "Susie, drink it!" Then Darling, let me be there, and let me drink the half, and you will feel it all!

I am glad you have rested, Susie. I wish the week had been more, a whole score of days and joys for you, yet again, had it lasted longer, then had you not come so soon and I had been lonelier, it is right as it is! Ten weeks, they will seem short to you – for care will fill them, but to Mattie and me, long. We shall grow tired, waiting, and our eyes will ache with looking for you, and with now and then a tear. And yet we have hope left, and we shall keep her busy, cheering away the time. Only think Susie, it is vacation now – there shall be no more vacation until ten weeks have gone, and no more snow; and how very little while it will be now, before you and I are sitting out on the broad stone step, mingling our lives together! I cant talk of it now tho', for it makes me long and yearn so, that I cannot sleep tonight, for thinking of it, and you.

Yes, we did go sugaring, and remembered who was gone – and who was there last year, and love and recollection brought with them Little Regret, and set her in the midst of us.

Dear Susie, Dear Joseph; why take the best and dearest, and leave our hearts behind? While the Lovers sighed; and twined oak leaves, and the anti enamored ate sugar, and crackers, in the house, I went to see what I could find. Only think of it, Susie; I had'nt any appetite, nor any Lover, either, so I made the best of fate, and gathered antique stones, and your little flowers of moss opened their lips and spoke to me, so I was not alone, and bye and bye Mattie and me might have been seen sitting together upon a high – gray rock, and we might have been heard talking, were anyone very near! And did thoughts of that dear Susie go with us on the rock, and sit there 'tween us twain? Loved One, thou knowest!

I gathered something for you, because you were not there, an acorn, and some moss blossoms, and a little shell of a snail, so whitened by the snow you would think 'twas a cunning artist had carved it from alabaster – then I tied them all up in a leaf with some last summer's grass I found by a brookside, and I'm keeping them all for you.

I saw Mattie at church today, tho' could not speak to her. Friday evening I saw her, and talked with her besides. Oh I do love her – and when you come if we all live till then, it will be precious, Susie. You speak to me of sorrow, of what you have "lost and loved," say rather, of what you have loved and won, for it is much, dear Susie; I can count the big, true hearts by clusters, full of bloom, and bloom amaranthine, because eternal! Emilie –

In margin on first page

I have heard all about the journal, Oh Susie, that you should come to this! I want you to get it bound – at my expense – Susie – so when he takes you from me, to live in his new home, I may have some of you. I am sincere.

In margin on second page

Mother sends her best love to you. It makes her look so happy when I give your's to her. Send it always, Susie, and send your respects to father!

In margin on third page

And much from Vinnie. She was so happy at her note. After she finished reading it, she said, "I dont know but it's wrong, but I love Sue better –

In margin on fourth page

than Jane, and I love her and Mattie better than all the friends I ever had in my life." Vinnie hopes to be like you, and to do as you do.

Upside down, near "Loved One, thou knowest!" on fourth page

Hattie!

late April 1852
Susan is spending ten days of her spring vacation with her friend Harriet Hinsdale, and they are visiting Harriet's sister in Havre de Grace, Maryland. "Dear Joseph" again refers to Joseph Lyman, who recently left Amherst to seek his fortune in the South. Emily links Susan with Joseph because they are both far away. She also refers to her friend Jane Humphrey. As she has done in a previous letter, Emily once again quotes Longfellow's "The Rainy Day": "Some days must be dark and dreary." In offering to share all she owns with Susan, Emily echoes Ruth's words to Naomi from the *Book of Ruth*, a pledge that was frequently included in wedding ceremonies: "Entreat me not to leave thee, or to return from following after thee; for whether thou goest, I will go; and where thou lodgest, I will lodge; thy people *shall be* my people, and thy God my God; where thou diest, will I die, and there will I be buried: the Lord do so to me, and more also *if ought* but death part thee and me." (Ruth 1:16–17)

8

Wednesday –

Precious Sue – Precious Mattie!

All I desire in this life – all I pray for, or hope for in that long life to come!

Dear Mattie just left me, and I stand just where we stood smiling and chatting together a moment ago. Our last words were of you, and as we said Dear Susie, the sunshine grew so warm, and out peeped prisoned leaves, and the Robins answered Susie, and the big hills left their work, and echoed Susie, and from the smiling fields, and from the fragrant meadows came troops of fairy Susies, and asked "Is it me"? No, Little One, "Eye hath not seen, nor ear heard, nor can the heart conceive" my Susie, whom I love.

These days of heaven bring you nearer and nearer, and every bird that sings, and every bud that blooms, does but remind me more of that garden unseen, awaiting the hand that tills it. Dear Susie, when you come, how many boundless blossoms among those silent beds! How I do count the days – how I do long for the time when I may count the hours without incurring the charge of Femina insania! I made up the Latin – Susie, for I could'nt think how it went, according to Stoddard and Andrew!

I want to send you joy, I have half a mind to put up one of these dear little Robin's, and send him singing to you. I know I would, Susie, did I think he would live to get there and sing his little songs.

I shall keep everything singing tho', until Dear Child gets home – and I shant let anything blossom till then – either.

I have got to go out in the garden now, and whip a Crown-Imperial for presuming to hold it's head up, until you have come home, so farewell, Susie – I shall think of you at sunset, and at sunrise, again; and at noon, and forenoon, and afternoon, and always, and evermore, till this little heart stops beating and is still. Emilie

about May 1852
Emily refers to the New Testament: "Eye hath not seen, nor ear heard, neither have entered into the heart of man, the things which God hath prepared for them that love him." (I Corinthians 2.9) "Stoddard and Andrew" are Solomon Stoddard and Ethan Allen Andrews, the authors of *A Grammar of the Latin Language for Schools and Colleges.*

9

Friday morning –

They are cleaning house today, Susie, and I've made a flying retreat to my own little chamber, where with affection, and you, I will spend this my precious hour, most precious of all the hours which dot my flying days, and the one so dear, that for it I barter everything, and as soon as it is gone, I am sighing for it again.

I cannot believe, dear Susie, that I have stayed without you almost a whole year long; sometimes the time seems short, and the thought of you as warm as if you had gone but yesterday, and again if years and years had trod their silent pathway, the time would seem less long.

And now how soon I shall have you, shall hold you in my arms; you will forgive the tears, Susie, they are so glad to come that it is not in my heart to reprove them and send them home. I dont know why it is – but there's something in your name, now you are taken from me, which fills my heart so full, and my eye, too. It is not that the mention grieves me, no, Susie, but I think of each "sunnyside" where we have sat together, and lest there be no more, I guess is what makes the tears come. Mattie was here last evening, and we sat on the front door stone, and talked about life and love, and whispered our childish fancies about such blissful things – the evening was gone so soon, and I walked home with Mattie beneath the silent moon, and wished for you, and Heaven. You did not come, Darling, but a bit of Heaven did, or so it seemed to us, as we walked side by side and wondered of that great blessedness which may be our's sometime, is granted now, to some. This union, my dear Susie, by which two lives are one, this sweet and strange adoption wherein we can but look, and are not yet admitted, how it can fill the heart, and make it gang wildly beating, how it will take us one day, and make us all it's own, and we shall not run away from it, but lie still and be happy!

You and I have been strangely silent upon this subject, Susie, we have often touched upon it, and as quickly fled away, as children shut their eyes when the sun is too bright for them. I have always hoped to know if you had no dear fancy, illumining all your life, no one of whom you murmured in the faithful ear of night – and at whose side in fancy, you walked the livelong day; and when you come home, Susie, we must speak of these things.

How dull our lives must seem to the bride, and the plighted maiden, whose days are fed with gold, and who gather pearls every evening; but to the wife, Susie, sometimes the wife forgotten, our lives perhaps seem dearer than all others in the world; you have seen flowers at morning, satisfied with the dew, and those same sweet flowers at noon with their heads bowed in anguish before the mighty sun; think you these thirsty blossoms will now need naught but – dew? No, they will cry for sunlight, and pine for the burning noon, tho' it scorches them, scathes them; they have got through with peace – they know that the man of noon, is mightier than the morning and their life is henceforth to him. Oh, Susie, it is dangerous, and it is all too dear, these simple trusting spirits, and the spirits mightier, which we cannot resist! It does so rend me, Susie, the thought of it when it comes, that I tremble lest at sometime I, too, am yielded up.

Susie, you will forgive me my amatory strain – it has been a very long one, and if this saucy page did not here bind and fetter me, I might have had no end.

I have got the letter, Susie, dear little bud – and all – and the tears came again, that alone in this big world, I am not quite alone. Such tears are showers friend, thro' which when smiles appear, the angels call them rainbows, and mimic them in Heaven.

And now in four weeks more – you are mine, all mine, except I lend you a little occasionally to Hattie and Mattie, if they promise me not to lose you, and to bring you back very soon. I shall not count the days. I shall not fill my cups with this expected happiness, for perhaps if I do, the angels being thirsty, will drink them up – I shall only hope, my Susie, and that tremblingly, for havnt barques the fullest, stranded upon the shore?

God is good, Susie, I trust he will save you, I pray that in his good time we once more meet each other, but if this life holds not another meeting for us, remember also, Susie, that it has no parting more, wherever that hour finds us, for which we have hoped so long, we shall not be separated, neither death, nor the grave can part us, so that we only love! Your Emilie –

In margin on first page

Austin has come and gone; life is so still again; why must the storm have calms?

In margin on second page

I hav'nt seen Root this term, I guess Mattie and I, are not sufficient for him!

In margin on third page

When will you come again, in a week? Let it be a swift week!

In margin on fourth page

Vinnie sends much love, and Mother; and might I be so bold as to enclose a remembrance?

early June 1852
Emily's tone in this letter suggests that she was not aware of the intimacy Susan already shared with Austin. Just four months earlier, Susan had sent Austin a Valentine that included a private joke referring to another young man's gift of chestnuts to Susan, a gift that Susan and Austin ate together. Soon the word in Amherst was that "Austin D. and Susan Gilbert are constant, and the gossips say constantly together."

10

Friday afternoon –

I have but one thought, Susie, this afternoon of June, and that of you, and I have one prayer, only; dear Susie, that is for you. That you and I in hand as we e'en do in heart, might ramble away as children, among the woods and fields, and forget these many fears, and these sorrowing cares, and each become a child again – I would it were so, Susie, and when I look around me and find myself alone, I sigh for you again; little sigh, and vain sigh, which will not bring you home.

I need you more and more, and the great world grows wider, and dear ones fewer and fewer, every day that you stay away – I miss my biggest heart; my own goes wandering round, and calls for Susie – Friends are too dear to sunder, Oh they are far too few, and how soon they will go away where you and I cannot find them, dont let us forget these things, for their remembrance now will save us many an anguish when it is too late to love them! Susie, forgive me Darling, for every word I say – my heart is full of you, none other than you in my thoughts, yet when I seek to say to you something not for the world, words fail me; If you were here, and Oh that you were, my Susie, we need not talk at all, our eyes would whisper for us, and your hand fast in mine, we would not ask for language – I try to bring you nearer, I chase the weeks away till they are quite departed, and fancy you have come, and I am on my way through the green lane to meet you, and my heart goes scampering so, that I have much ado to bring it back again, and learn it to be patient, till that dear Susie comes. Three weeks – they cant last always, for surely they must go with their little brothers and sisters to their long home in the west!

I shall grow more and more impatient until that dear day comes, for till now, I have only mourned for you; now I begin to hope for you.

Dear Susie, I have tried hard to think what you would love, of something I might send you – I at last saw my little Violets, they begged me to let them go, so here they are – and with them as Instructor, a bit of knightly grass, who also begged the favor to accompany them – they are but small, Susie, and I fear not fragrant now, but they will speak to you of warm hearts at home, and of the something faithful, which "never slumbers nor sleeps" – Keep them 'neath your pillow, Susie, they will make you dream of blue-skies, and home, and the "blessed countrie"! You and I will have an hour with "Edward" and "Ellen Middleton", sometime when you get home – we must find out if somethings contained therein are true, and if they are, what you and me are coming to!

Now farewell, Susie, and Vinnie sends her love, and mother her's, and I add a kiss, shyly, lest there is somebody there!! Dont let them see, will you Susie? Emilie –

On fourth page

Why cant I be a Delegate to the great Whig Convention? – dont I know all about Daniel Webster, and the Tariff, and the Law? Then, Susie, I could see you, during a pause in the session – but I dont like this country at all, and I shant stay here any longer! "Delenda est" America, Massachusetts and all!

open me carefully –

June 11, 1852

Emily's father Edward Dickinson was a delegate to the national Whig convention, which met in Baltimore on June 16, 1852, and he delivered this letter to Susan. "Delenda est" is Latin for "blot out" or "obliterate" or "erase." Emily fantasizes about returning to childhood, then complains about woman's lower political and social status in nineteenth-century New England.

11

Sunday afternoon –

My Susie's last request; yes, darling, I grant it, tho' few, and fleet the days which separate us now – but six more weary days, but six more twilight evens, and my lone little fireside, my silent fireside is once more full.

"We are seven, and one in heaven," we are three next Saturday, if I have mine and heaven has none.

Do not mistake, my Susie, and rather than the car, ride on the golden wings where you will ne'er come back again – do not forget the lane, and the little cot that stands by it, when people from the clouds will beckon you, and smile at you, to have you go with them – Oh Susie, my child, I sit here by my window, and look each little while down towards that golden gateway beneath the western trees, and I fancy I see you coming, you trip upon the green grass, and I hear the crackling leaf under your little shoe; I hide behind the chair, I think I will surprise you, I grow too eager to see you. I hasten to the door, and start to find me that you are not there. And very, very often when I have waked from sleep, not quite waked, I have been sure I saw you, and your dark eye beamed on me with such a look of tenderness that I could only weep, and bless God for you.

Susie, will you indeed come home next Saturday, and be my own again, and kiss me as you used to?

Shall I indeed behold you, not "darkly, but face to face" or am I fancying so, and dreaming blessed dreams from which the day will wake me? I hope for you so much, and feel so eager for you, feel that I cannot wait, feel that now I must have you – that the expectation once more to see your face again, makes me feel hot and feverish, and my heart beats so fast – I go to sleep at night, and the first thing I know, I am sitting there wide awake, and clasping my hands tightly, and thinking of next Saturday, and "never a bit" of you.

Sometimes I must have Saturday before tomorrow comes, and I wonder if it w'd make any difference with God, to give it to me today, and I'll let him have Monday, to make him a Saturday; and then I feel so funnily, and wish the precious day would'nt come quite so soon, till I could know how to feel, and get my thoughts ready for it.

Why, Susie, it seems to me as if my absent Lover was coming home so soon – and my heart must be so busy, making ready for him.

While the minister this morning was giving an account of the Roman Catholic system, and announcing several facts which were usually startling, I was trying to make up my mind w'h of the two was prettiest to go and welcome you in, my fawn colored dress, or my blue dress. Just as I had decided by all means to wear the blue, down came the minister's fist with a terrible rap on the counter, and Susie, it scared me so, I hav'nt got over it yet, but I'm glad I reached a conclusion! I walked home from meeting with Mattie, and incidentally quite, something was said of you – and I think one of us remarked that you would be here next Sunday; well – Susie – what it was I dont presume to know, but my gaiters seemed to leave me, and I seemed to move on wings – and I move on wings now, Susie, on wings as white as snow, and as bright as the summer sunshine – because I am with you, and so few short days, you are with me at home. Be patient then, my Sister, for the hours will haste away, and Oh so soon!

Susie, I write most hastily, and very carelessly too, for it is time for me to get the supper, and my mother is gone and besides, my darling, so near I seem to you, that I disdain this pen, and wait for a warmer language. With Vinnie's love, and my love, I am once more

Your Emilie –

June 27, 1852
Emily refers to her mother, who is in Boston visiting Austin and probably staying with her sister's family, the Norcrosses. Susan is expected to arrive in Amherst in early July, and Austin is to return at the month's end. Emily refers to Wordsworth's poem "We Are Seven" in the second paragraph, changing two children in heaven to one. The "three next Saturday" will be Susan, Emily, and Vinnie. No written record has been preserved of Susan's homecoming from Baltimore on July 3, nor of Emily's feelings concerning the reunion and Austin's return to Amherst on July 26. How Emily experienced the events of that summer and fall, with Austin and Susan "constantly together" is unclear.

12

Friday noon.

Dear Friend.

I regret to inform you that at 3. oclock yesterday, my mind came to a stand, and has since then been stationary.

Ere this intelligence reaches you, I shall probably be a snail. By this untoward providence a mental and moral being has been swept ruthlessly from her sphere. Yet we should not repine – "God moves in a mysterious way, his wonders to perform, he plants his foot upon the sea, and rides upon the storm," and if it be his will that I become a bear and bite my fellow men, it will be for the highest good of this fallen and perishing world.

If the gentleman in the air, will please to stop throwing snowballs, I may meet you again, otherwise it is uncertain. My parents are pretty well – Gen Wolf is here – we're looking for Major Pitcairn in the afternoon stage.

We were much afflicted yesterday, by the supposed removal of our Cat from time to Eternity.

She returned, however, last evening, having been detained by the storm, beyond her expectations.

I see by the Boston papers that Giddings is up again – hope you'll arrange with Corwin, and have the North all straight.

Fine weather for sledding – have spoken for 52 cord black walnut. We need some paths our way, shant you come out with the team?

Yours till death – Judah

early December 1852
In the second paragraph, Emily quotes William Cowper's "Light Shining Out of Darkness" from memory, altering one line. Edward Dickinson has just been elected to Congress as the Whig candidate, and Emily nicknames his visitors after General Wolfe, who died victorious at Quebec, and Major Pitcairn, who was fatally wounded at Bunker Hill. In 1848, Joshua Reed Giddings broke with the Whigs because the party endorsed the Fugitive Slave Law, which Thomas Corwin, Fillmore's Secretary of the Treasury, also opposed.

13

Thursday afternoon –

The sun shines warm, dear Susie, but the sweetest sunshine's gone, and in that far off Manchester, all my blue sky is straying this winter's afternoon. Vinnie and I are here – just where you always find us when you come in the afternoon to sit a little while – We miss your face today, and a tear fell on my work a little while ago, so I put up my sewing, and tried to write to you. I had rather have talked, dear Susie – it seems to me a long while since I have seen you much – it is a long while Susie, since we have been together – so long since we've spent a twilight, and spoken of what we loved, but you will come back again, and there's all the future Susie, which is as yet untouched! It is the brightest star in the firmament of God, and I look in it's face the oftenest.

I ran to the door, dear Susie – I ran out in the rain, with nothing but my slippers on, I called "Susie, Susie," but you did'nt look at me; then I ran to the dining room window and rapped with all my might upon the pane, but you rode right on and never heeded me.

It made me feel so lonely, that I could'nt help the tears, when I came back to the table, to think I was eating breakfast, and you were riding away – but bye and bye I thought that the same ugly coach which carried you away, would have to bring you back again in but a little while, and the spite pleased me so that I did'nt cry any more till the tear fell of which I told you. And now, my absent One, I am hoping the days away, till I shall see you home – I am sewing as fast as I can, I am training the stems to my flowers, I am working with all my might, so as to pause and love you, as soon as you get home.

How fast we will have to talk then – there will be those farewell gaieties – and all the days before, of which I have had no fact, and there will be your absence, and your presence, my Susie dear, sweetest, and brightest, and best of every and all the themes. It is sweet to talk, dear Susie, with those whom God has given us, lest we should be alone – and you and I have tasted it, and found it very sweet; even as fragrant flowers, o'er which the bee hums and lingers, and hums more for the lingering.

I find it very lonely, to part with one of mine, with mine especially, and the days will have more hours while you are gone away.

They played the trick yesterday – they dupe me again today.

Twelve hours make one indeed – Call it twice twelve, three times twelve, and add, and add, and add, then multiply again, and we will talk about it.

"At Dover dwells George Brown Esq – Good Carlos Finch and David Fryer" – Oh Susie! How much escapes me, mine; whether you reached there safely, whether you are a stranger – or have only just gone home – Whether you find the friends as you fancied you should find them, or dearer than you expected?

All this, and more, Susie, I am eager to know, and I shall know soon, shant I? I love to think I shall.

Oh Susie, Susie, I must call out to you in the old, old way – I must say how it seems to me to hear the clock so silently tick all the hours away, and bring me not my gift – my own, my own!

Perhaps you cant read it, Darling, it is incoherent and blind; but the recollection that prompts it, is very distinct and clear, and reads easily. Susie, they send their love – my mother and my sister – thy mother and thy sister, and the Youth, the Lone Youth, Susie, you know the rest!

Emilie –

Tell me when you write Susie, if I shall send my love to the Lady where you stay!

February 24, 1853
Emily quotes a calendar game included in Longfellow's *Kavanagh*: "At Dover dwells George Brown, Esquire, / Good Christopher Finch, and Daniel Friar." In this game, one could determine on which day the first of every month of the year fell.

14

Saturday morning –

I know dear Susie is busy, or she would not forget her lone little Emilie, who wrote her just as soon as she'd gone to Manchester, and has waited so patiently till she can wait no more, and the credulous little heart, fond even tho' forsaken, will get it's big black inkstand, and tell her once again how well it loves her.

Dear Susie, I have tried so hard to act patiently, not to think unkind thoughts, or cherish unkind doubt concerning one not here, I have watched the stages come in, I have tried to look indifferent, and hum a snatch of tune when I heard Father and Austin coming, and knew how soon they'd bring me a dear letter from you, or I should look in the hat, and find it all empty – and here comes Saturday, and tomorrow the world stands still, and I shall have no message from my dear Susie!

Why dont you write me, Darling? Did I in that quick letter say anything which grieved you, or made it hard for you to take your usual pen and trace affection for your bad, sad Emilie?

Then Susie, you must forgive me before you sleep tonight, for I will not shut my eyes until you have kissed my cheek, and told me you would love me.

Oh it has been so still, since when you went away, nothing but just the ticking of the two ceaseless clocks – swiftly the "Little mystic one, no human eye hath seen," but slowly and solemnly the tall clock upon the mantel – you remember <u>that</u> clock, Susie. It has the oddest way of striking twelve in the morning, and six in the afternoon, just as soon as you come. I am trying to teach it a few of the proprieties of life, now you are gone away, and the poor thing does indeed seem quite obedient, and goes slowly eno', but as soon as you're back again, Susie, it will be the same graceless one it ever used to be, and only gallop with accelerated speed, to make up for resting now.

Dear Susie, it is harder to live alone than it was when you were in Baltimore, and the days went slowly, <u>then</u> – they go e'en slower than they did while you were in the school – or else I grow impatient, and cannot brook as easily absence from those I love. I dont know which it is – I only know that when you shall come back again, the Earth will seem more beautiful, and bigger than it does now, and the blue sky from the window will be all dotted with gold – though it may not be evening, or time for the stars to come.

It is pleasant to talk of you with Austin – and Vinnie and to find how you are living in every one of their hearts, and making it warm and bright there – as if it were a sky, and a sweet summer's noon. Austin has gone this morning – the last little thing I did for him was while they were at breakfast, to write on four envelopes for him to send to you –

It made me smile, Susie, to think how Little Argus was cheated after all – and I smiled again, at thinking of something holier, of something from the skies, come Earthward.

Dear Susie, I dont forget you a moment of the hour, and when my work is finished, and I have got the tea, I slip thro' the little entry, and out at the front door, and stand and watch the West, and remember all of mine – yes, Susie – the golden West, and the great, silent Eternity, forever folded there, and bye and bye it will open it's everlasting arms, and gather us all – all – Good bye, dear Susie – they all send you their love – Emilie –

Susie – will you give my love to Mrs Bartlett, and tell her the fortnight is out next Wednesday, and I thought she m't like to know!

March 5, 1853
Susan's courtship with Austin is intensifying at this time, and Susan is sending him letters. Emily writes to Susan frequently. On March 5, Austin arrived in Cambridge to attend Harvard Law School, and Emily addressed four envelopes for him to send to Susan. "Little mystic one" may be an allusion to "The Life Clock," translated from German and printed in both the *Hampshire Gazette* and *Northampton Courier* in the late 1840s: "There is a little mystic clock, / No human eye hath seen, / That beateth on and beateth on / From morning until e'en."

15

Write! Comrade – write!
On this wondrous sea
Sailing silently,
Ho! Pilot, ho!
Knowest thou the shore
Where no breakers roar –
Where the storm is oer?

In the peaceful west
Many the sails at rest –
The anchors fast –
Thither I pilot thee –
Land Ho! Eternity!
Ashore at last!
Emilie –

March 1853
This is the first poem that Emily is known to have sent to Susan.

16

Dear Susie –

I'm so amused at my own ubiquity that I hardly know what to say, or how to relate the story of the wonderful correspondent. First, I arrive from Amherst, then comes a ponderous tome from the learned Halls of Cambridge, and again by strange metamorphosis I'm just from Michigan, and am Mattie and Minnie and Lizzie in one wondering breath –

Why, dear Susie, it must'nt scare you if I loom up from Hindoostan, or drop from an Appenine, or peer at you suddenly from the hollow of a tree, calling myself King Charles, Sancho Panza, or Herod, King of the Jews – I suppose it is all the same.

"Miss Mills," that is, Miss Julia, never dreamed of the depths of my clandestiny, and if I stopped to think of the figure I was cutting, it would be the last of me, and you'd never hear again from your poor Jeremy Bentham –

But I say to my mind, "tut, tut," "Rock a bye baby" conscience, and so I keep them still!

And as for the pulling of wool over the eyes of Manchester, I trust to the courtesy of the Recording Angel, to say nothing of that. One thing is true, Darling, the world will be none the wiser, for Emilie's omnipresence, and two big hearts will beat stouter, as tidings from me come in. I love the opportunity to serve those who are mine, and to soften the least asperity in the path which ne'er "ran smooth," is a delight to me. So Susie, I set the trap and catch the little mouse, and love to catch him dearly, for I think of you and Austin – and know it pleases you to have my tiny services. Dear Susie, you are gone – One would hardly think I had lost you to hear this revelry, but your absence insanes me so – I do not feel so peaceful, when you are gone from me –

All life looks differently, and the faces of my fellows are not the same they wear when you are with me. I think it is this, dear Susie; you sketch my pictures for me, and 'tis at their sweet colorings, rather than this dim real that I am used, so you see when you go away, the world looks staringly, and I find I need more vail – Frank Peirce thinks I mean berage vail, and makes a sprightly plan to import the "article," but dear

Susie knows what I mean. Do you ever look homeward, Susie, and count the lonely hours Vinnie and I are spending, because that you are gone?

Yes, Susie, very lonely, and yet is it very sweet too to know that you are happy, and to think of you in the morning, and at eventide, and noon, and always as smiling and looking up for joy – I could not spare you else, dear Sister, but to be sure your life is warm with such a sunshine, helps me to chase the shadow fast stealing upon mine – I knew you would be happy, and you know now of something I had told you.

There are lives, sometimes, Susie – Bless God that we catch faint glimpses of his brighter Paradise from occasional Heavens here!

Stay, Susie; yet not stay! I cannot spare your sweet face another hour more, and yet I want to have you gather more sheaves of joy – for bleak, and waste, and barren, are most of the fields found here, and I want you to fill the garner. Then you may come, dear Susie, and from our silent home, Vinnie and I shall meet you. There is much to tell you, Susie, but I cannot bring the deeds of the rough and jostling world into that sweet inclosure; they are fitter fonder, here – but Susie, I do bring you a Sister's fondest love – and gentlest tenderness; little indeed, but "a'," and I know you will not refuse them. Please remember me to your friend, and write soon to your lonely – Emilie –

Upside down on first page

Vinnie sends you her love – She would write, but has hurt her hand – Mother's love too – Oh Susie!

March 12, 1853

Emily refers to Austin as the philosopher and jurist Jeremy Bentham. Julia Mills is the close friend of Dora Spenlow in *David Copperfield*. Erasures of affectionate references to "Susie" continue in Emily's letters to Austin of this period. On March 23, Susan and Austin become engaged.

17

It's hard to wait, dear Susie, though my heart is there, and has been since the sunset, and I knew you'd come – I'd should have gone right down, but Mother had been at work hard, as it was Saturday, and Austin had promised to take her to Mrs Cobb's, as soon as he got home from Palmer – then she wanted to go, and see two or three of the neighbors, and I wanted to go to you, but I thought it would be unkind – so not till tomorrow, Darling – and all the stories Monday – except short sketches of them at meeting tomorrow night. I have stories to tell – very unusual for me – a good many things have happened – Love for you Darling – How can I sleep tonight? Ever Emilie –

So precious, my own Sister, to have you here again. Somebody loves you more – or I were there this evening –

Mother sends her love – She spoke of it this morning, what a day Susie would have –

about October 1853

There are few existing letters from Emily to Susan for the next eight months. During this time Emily writes frequently to Austin in Cambridge, sending him news from home and often elaborating on time spent with Susan. Her tone is generally cheerful as she and all of the Dickinsons welcome Susan into the family as Austin's future wife, and Emily and Susan see each other nearly every day.

18

Sabbath Day –

I'm just from meeting, Susie, and as I sorely feared, my "life" was made a "victim." I walked – I ran – I flew – I turned precarious corners – One moment I was not – then soared aloft like Phoenix, soon as the foe was by – and then anticipating an enemy again, my soiled and drooping plumage might have been seen emerging from just behind a fence, vainly endeavoring to fly once more from hence. I reached the steps, dear Susie – I smiled to think of me, and my geometry, during the journey there – It would have puzzled Euclid, and it's doubtful result, have solemnized a Day.

How big and broad the aisle seemed, full huge enough before, as I quaked slowly up – and reached my usual seat!

In vain I sought to hide behind your feathers – Susie – feathers and Bird had flown, and there I sat, and sighed, and wondered I was scared so, for surely in the whole world was nothing I need to fear – Yet there the Phantom was, and though I kept resolving to be as brave as Turks, and bold as Polar Bears, it did'nt help me any. After the opening prayer I ventured to turn around. Mr Carter immediately looked at me – Mr Sweetser attempted to do so, but I discovered nothing, up in the sky somewhere, and gazed intently at it, for quite a half an hour. During the exercises I became more calm, and got out of church quite comfortably. Several roared around, and, sought to devour me, but I fell an easy prey to Miss Lovina Dickinson, being too much exhausted to make any farther resistance.

She entertained me with much sprightly remark, until our gate was reached, and I need'nt tell you Susie, just how I clutched the latch, and whirled the merry key, and fairly danced for joy, to find myself at home! How I did wish for you – how – for my own dear Vinnie – how for Goliah, or Samson – to pull the whole church down, requesting Mr Dwight to step into Miss Kingsbury's, until the dust was past!

Prof Aaron Warner, late propounder of Rhetoric to youth of Amherst College, gave us the morning sermon. Now Susie, you and I, admire Mr Warner, so my felicity, when he arose to preach, I need not say to you. I will merely remark that I shall be much disappointed if the Rev Horace Walpole does'nt address us this evening.

You can see how things go, dear Susie, when you are not at home. If you stay another Sunday I hav'nt any doubt that the "Secretary of War" will take charge of the Sabbath School – yet I would not alarm you!

The singing reminded me of the Legend of "Jack and Gill," allowing the Bass Viol to be typified by Gill, who literally tumbled after, while Jack – i e the choir, galloped insanely on, "nor recked, nor heeded" him.

Dear Sister, it is passed away, and you and I may speak of dear things, and little things – some of our trifles Susie – There's Austin – he's a trifle – and trifling as it is that he is coming Monday, it makes my heart *[ink blot covers "beat"]* faster – Vinnie's a trifle too – Oh how I love such trifles. Susie, under that black spot, technically termed a blot, the word beat may be found – My pen fell from the handle – occasioning the same, but life is too short to transcribe or apologize – I dont doubt Daniel Webster made many a blot, and I think you said, you made one, under circumstances quite aggravating! But of Austin and Vinnie – One is with me tomorrow noon, and I shall be so happy –

The one that returns, Susie, is dearer than "ninety and nine" that did not go away.

To get you all once more, seems vague and doubtful to me, for it would be so dear. Did you ever think, Susie, that there had been no grave here? To me there are three, now. The longest one is Austin's – I must plant brave trees there, for Austin was so brave – and Susie, for you and Vinnie I shall plant each a rose, and that will make the birds come.

Sister, I hav'nt asked if you got to Manchester safely, if all is happy, and well, and yet I'm sure it is – if it were not, you would have told me. Susie, the days and hours are very long to me, but you must not come back until it is best and willing.

Please remember me to your friends, with respect and affection, leaving only affection for you –

from your own Emily –

In margin on first page

Remember the hint, Susie!

In margin on third page

Mother asks if I've given her love.

January 15, 1854
Susan is away visiting her sister's in-laws, Mary and Samuel Bartlett, in Manchester, New Hampshire, and Austin is due home almost immediately for a six week stay. Professor Aaron Warner resigned from Amherst College because the trustees did not give him the opportunity to rebut criticisms of his work.

19

Monday evening.

Susie – it is a little thing to say how lone it is – anyone can do it, but to wear the loneness next your heart for weeks, when you sleep, and when you wake, ever missing something, <u>this</u>, all cannot say, and it baffles me.

I could paint a portrait which would bring the tears, had I canvass for it, and the scene should be <u>solitude</u>, and the figures – solitude – and the lights and shades, each a solitude.

I could fill a chamber with landscapes so lone, men should pause and weep there; then haste grateful home, for a loved one left. Today has been a fair day, very still and blue. Tonight, the crimson children are playing in the West, and tomorrow will be colder.

In all I number you. I want to think of you each hour in the day. What you are saying – doing – I want to walk with you, as seeing yet unseen. You say you walk and sew alone. <u>I</u> walk and sew alone. I dont see much of Vinnie – she's mostly, dusting stairs!

We go out very little – once in a month or two, we both set sail in silks – touch at the principal points, and then put into port again – Vinnie cruises about some to transact the commerce, but coming to anchor, is most that I can do. Mr and Mrs Dwight are a sunlight to me, which no night can shade, and I still perform weekly journeys there, much to Austin's dudgeon, and my sister's rage.

I have heard it said "persecution kindles" – think it kindled me! They are sweet and loving, and one thing, dear Susie, always ask for you. Sunday Afternoon – I left you a long while

Susie, that is, in pen and ink – my heart kept on. I was called down from you to entertain some company – went with a sorry grace, I fear, and trust I acted with one. There is a tall – pale snow storm stalking through the fields, and bowing here, at my window – shant let the fellow in!

I went to church all day in second dress, and boots. We had such precious sermons from Mr Dwight. One about unbelief, and another Esau. Sermons on unbelief ever did attract me. Thanksgiving was observed throughout the state last week! Believe we had a Turkey, and two kinds of Pie. Otherwise, no change. Father went Thanksgiving night. Austin goes tomorrow, unless kept by storm. He will see you, Darling! What I cannot do. Oh could I! We did not attend the Thanksgiving "Soiree" – owing to our sadness at just parting with father –

Your sister will give particulars.

Abby is much better – rode horseback every day until the snow came, and goes down street now just like other girls – Abby seems more gentle, more affectionate, than she has.

Eme Kellogg wonders she does not hear from you. I gave your message to her, and bring you back the same. Eme is still with Henry, tho' no outward bond has as yet encircled them. Edward Hitchcock and baby – and Mary, spent Thanksgiving here. I called upon Mary – she appears very sweetly, and the baby is quite becoming to her. They all adore the baby. Mary inquired for you with a great deal of warmth, and wanted to send her love when I wrote.

Susie – had that been you – well – well! I must stop, Sister. Things have wagged, dear Susie, and they're wagging still. "Little Children, love one another." Not all of life to live, is it, nor all of death to die.

In margin on first page

Susie – we all love you – Mother – Vinnie – me. Dearly!

Upside down on first page

I have not heard from Mat for months. "They say that absence conquers." It has vanquished me.

In margin on second page

Your Sister Harriet is our most intimate friend.

In margin on third page

Mother and Vinnie send their love. Austin must carry his.

In margin on fourth page

The last night of the term, John sent his love to you.

November 27 to December 3, 1854
Thanksgiving night, Edward Dickinson returns to Washington for the second session of the thirty-third Congress. On December 4, Austin departs for Chicago and Grand Haven, Michigan to visit his future brothers-in-law. He returns to Amherst at the beginning of the new year, 1855, and Susan stays in Michigan until late February. John is Emily's cousin, John Graves, an Amherst College student. The letter's last line refers to the last two lines of a stanza from James Montgomery's hymn, "O where shall rest be found": " 'Tis not the whole of life to live; Nor all of death to die."

20

Sabbath Day.

I am sick today, dear Susie, and have not been to church. There has been a pleasant quiet, in which to think of you, and I have not been sick eno' that I cannot write to you. I love you as dearly, Susie, as when love first began, on the step at the front door, and under the Evergreens, and it breaks my heart sometimes, because I do not hear from you. I wrote you many days ago – I wont say many *weeks*, because it will look sadder so, and then I cannot write – but Susie, it troubles me.

I miss you, mourn for you, and walk the Streets alone – often at night, beside, I fall asleep in tears, for your dear face, yet not one word comes back to me from that silent West. If it is finished, tell me, and I will raise the lid to my box of Phantoms, and lay one more love in; but if it *lives* and *beats* still, still lives and beats for *me*, then say me *so*, and I will strike the strings to one more strain of happiness before I die. Why Susie – think of it – you are my precious Sister, and will be till you die, and will be still, when Austin and Vinnie and Mat, and you and I are marble – and life has forgotten us!

Vinnie and I are going soon – either this week or next – father has not determined. I'm sure I cannot go, when I think that you are coming, and I would give the whole world if I could stay, instead.

I cant believe you are coming – but when I think of it, and tell myself it's so, a wondrous joy comes over me, and my old fashioned life capers as in a dream. Sue – I take the words of that Sweet Kate Scott, I have never seen – and say "it is too blissful." I never will be "so busy" when you get back to me, as I used to be. I'll get "my spinning done," for Susie, it steals over me once in a little while, that as fingers fly and I am so busy, a far more wondrous Shuttle shifts the subtler thread, and when that's web is spun, indeed my spinning will be done. I think with you, dear Susie, and Mat by me again, I shall be still for joy. I shall not fret or murmur – shall not care when the wind blows, shall not observe the storm – "Such, and so precious" are you.

Austin told me about you when he came from the West – though many little things I wanted most to know, he "had not noticed." I asked him how you looked, and what you wore, and how your hair was fixed, and what you said of me – his answers were quite limited – "you looked as you always did – he did'nt know what you wore – never did know what people wore – you said he must tell me everything," which by the way dear Child, he has not done to this day, and any portion of which, I would savor with joy, might I but obtain it. Vinnie inquired with promptness "if you wore a Basque" – "it seemed to him," he said, "you did have on a black thing."

Ah Susie – you must train him 'twill take full many a lesson in the fashion plate, before he will respect, and speak with proper deference of this majestic garment. I have some new clothes, Susie – presume I shall appear like an embarrassed Peacock, quite unused to its plumes. Dear Susie – you will write to me when I am gone from home – Affy, Emilie –

Upside down on first page

Mother and Vinnie send much love – they will be delighted to see you. My dearest love to Mat.

In margin on first page

I asked Austin if he had any messages – he replied he –

In margin on second page

had not! The good for nothing fellow! I presume he will

In margin on third page

fill a fools Cap with protestations to you, as soon

In margin on fourth page

as I leave the room! Bats think Foxes have no eyes – Ha Ha!!

late January 1855
Emily's early 1855 letter makes clear how all-consuming her love for Susan is, and how enamored Emily is of Susan's appearance. Emily's frustration is obvious, since Austin has "sanctuary privileges" and can see Susan when he wishes, yet he appears to be oblivious of his good fortune. The "step at the front door" where "love first began" is a reference to the house on South Pleasant Street in which the Dickinsons lived from 1840 to 1855. Sometimes called the "Mansion," this house is no longer standing.

21

Wednesday morning.

Sweet and soft as summer, Darlings, maple trees in bloom and grass green in the sunny places hardly seems it possible this is winter still; and it makes the grass spring in this heart of mine and each linnet sing, to think that you have come.

Dear Children – Mattie – Sue for one look at you, for your gentle voices, I'd exchange it all. The pomp – the court – the etiquette – they are of the earth – will not enter Heaven.

Will you write to me – why hav'nt you before? I feel so tired looking for you, and still you do not come. And you love me, come soon – this is *not* forever, you know, this mortal life of our's. Which had you rather I wrote you – what I am doing here, or who I am loving *there*?

Perhaps I'll tell you both, but the "last shall be first, and the first last." I'm loving you at home – I'm coming every hour to your chamber door. I'm thinking when awake, how sweet if you were with me, and to talk with you as I fall asleep, would be sweeter still.

I think I cannot wait, when I remember you, and that is *always*, Children. I shall love you more for this sacrifice.

Last night I heard from Austin – and I think he fancies we are losing sight of the things at home – Tell him "not so," Children – Austin is mistaken. He says we forget "the Horse, the Cats, and the geraniums" – have not remembered Pat – proposes to sell the farm and move west with mother – to make boquets of my plants, and send them to his friends – to come to Washington in his Dressing gown and mortify me and Vinnie.

Should be delighted to see him, even in "dishabille," and will promise to *notice* him whenever he will come. The *cats* I will confess, have not so absorbed my attention as they are apt at home, yet do I still remember them with tender emotion; and as for my sweet flowers, I shall know each leaf and every bud that bursts, while I am from home. Tell Austin, never fear! My thoughts are far from idle, concerning e'en the *trifles* of the world at home, but all is jostle, here – scramble and confusion, and sometimes in writing home I cant stop for detail, much as I would love. Vinnie met the other evening, in the parlor here a certain Mr Saxton, who inquired of her for his Amherst cousins. Vinnie told him joyfully, all she knew of you, and another evening, took me down to him.

We walked in the hall a long while, talking of you, my Children, vieing with each other in compliment to those we loved so well. I told him of you both, he seemed very happy to hear so much of you. He left Washington yesterday morning. I have not been well since I came here, and that has excused me from some gaieties, tho' at that, I'm gayer than I was before. Vinnie is asleep this morning – she has been out walking with some ladies here and is very tired. She says much of you – wants so much to see you. Give my love to your sister – Kiss Dwightie for me – my love for Abbie and Eme, when you see them, and for dear Mr & Mrs Dwight.

On top of first page

Tell Mother and Austin they need'nt flatter themselves we are forgetting them – they'll find themselves much mistaken before long. We think we shall go to Philadelphia next week, tho' father has'nt decided. Eliza writes most every day, and seems

In margin on second page

impatient for us. I dont know how long we shall

In margin on third page

stay there, nor how long in New York. Father has not de[ci]

In margin on fourth page

ded. Shant you write, when this gets to you? Affy – E –

Washington, February 28, 1855

Susan received this letter when she returned to Amherst from Michigan. Emily and Lavinia are in Washington for three weeks, from mid-February until early March. From there they travel to Philadelphia to visit their cousins the Colemans. Eliza Coleman, two years younger than Emily, became a close friend when the girls were in their midteens. "Dwightie," to whom Emily sends a kiss, is the youngest child of Susan's sister Harriet Cutler, with whom Susan and Martha are living.

By 1855, Susan and Austin had been engaged for more than a year. Yet it would be another sixteen months before they married and settled in the Evergreens. There Susan would live next door to Emily for the next thirty years.

SECTION TWO

Sue, Dear Sue, Sweet Sue, Sister

EARLY MIDDLE WRITINGS, MID-1850S TO MID-1860S

BETWEEN THE MID-1850s and mid-1860s, Emily's correspondence to Susan unequivocally acknowledges that their emotional, spiritual, and physical communion is vital to her creative insight and sensibilities. In fact, Emily will call Susan "imagination" itself.

During this period, the structure of their lives changes dramatically. The Dickinson family moves from the "Mansion" on South Pleasant Street in Amherst back to the renovated Homestead on Main Street.

Susan's engagement to Austin lasts three years, and the wedding, having been postponed by Susan on several occasions, finally takes place at the house of Susan's aunt Sophia Arms Van Vranken in Geneva, New York, on July 1, 1856. Austin is the only Dickinson in attendance. No letters exist from the period of the wedding, a fact that seems surprising given Emily's previous attentiveness. Not even a letter of congratulations remains. Again, it is possible that letters or letter-poems from this period were written, sent, and destroyed or lost. With financial assistance from Susan's brothers, Edward Dickinson builds the Evergreens, next door to the Homestead, and Susan and Austin settle there and raise their family.

In the late 1850s, Emily begins making her manuscript books, or fascicles. This common nineteenth-century practice enabled people to create their own special collections of favorite poems, essays, or stories. In fact, several years earlier, Susan had compiled a fascicle, including works by writers such as James Russell Lowell, Julia A. Fletcher, and Edgar Allen Poe. Emily's fascicles differ, however, because they are comprised of her own poems, and they total forty separate books at the time of her death in 1886.

During the period when Emily begins to gather her poems into fascicles, she writes three missives, now known as the "Master" letters, to a fictional or real addressee(s). Emily also places three love poems to "Dollie" (Susan's nickname) in her manuscript books. These "Dollie" poems are deeply romantic and erotic, and it is unclear whether Emily ever actually gives them to Susan, or if Susan receives them and destroys them because they are "too personal and adulatory ever to be printed."[1] Emily does send two letter-poems addressed "Dollie" to Susan, and they appear in the following pages. Emblematic of the ongoing passion Emily feels for Susan, these documents reflect an ardor that is sustained throughout Susan's engagement to Austin and the unavoidable shift in Susan's availability once she undertakes her wifely duties.

After Susan moves to the Evergreens, she becomes immersed in social engagements, entertaining a wide range of literary and political figures over the next twenty years, including essayist and philosopher Ralph Waldo Emerson, novelist Harriet Beecher Stowe, landscape-architect Frederick Olmsted, and abolitionist and suffragist Wendell Phillips. Emily attends many of the Evergreens gatherings, but she secludes herself more often and devotes her energies and time to writing and contemplation.

From the late 1850s on, Emily shares her poems with Susan, regularly sending drafts and inviting feedback. It is likely that this relationship is reciprocal, and that Susan sends Emily her own poems for critiques as well. One example of this process is preserved in the following exchange of various versions of Emily's poem "Safe in their Alabaster Chambers."

Throughout this period, Susan sends a selection of Emily's poems to various newspapers and magazines for printing, and she writes excitedly of "our Fleet" when the *Springfield Republican* prints what is probably her own poem, "The Shadow of Thy Wing," just below a version of "Safe in their Alabaster Chambers." Over the next several years,

Emily publishes eight poems in *Drum Beat, Round Table,* the *Brooklyn Daily Union,* the *Springfield Republican,* and the *Boston Post.* In April 1862, *Atlantic Monthly* editor, Thomas Wentworth Higginson, publishes "Letter to a Young Contributor," and Emily sends him the first of many letters, along with four poems.

Emily spends several months in the Boston area in 1864 and 1865. During these eight- and seven-month periods, she receives medical care for her eyes and lives with her cousins Louise (Loo) and Fanny Norcross in a boarding house in Cambridgeport.

By the mid-1860s, Emily has written over a thousand poems. Susan has given birth to her son Ned (b. 1861) and her daughter Martha (b. 1866). Emily's correspondence to Susan continues to reflect on a great array of subjects, from the ordinary details of life in the Homestead and the Evergreens households to monumental spiritual considerations, literature, and the birth of Susan's first child. Some of the missives are playful while others indicate the strain of profound differences of opinion between the two women. Emily's writings to Susan expand from conventional letters to what Susan refers to as "letter-poems" as she later compiles her book of Emily's writings. These "letter-poems" are letters that look and sound like poems; they are also poems addressed to Susan that read like letters, or messages. During this time, Emily appears to take the calligraphic design and placement of the text on the page more and more into account. To show this gradual transformation, the missives in the following three sections of *Open Me Carefully* replicate many characteristics of Emily's placement of words and lines on the page as closely as possible.

While Dickinson's expressions of love for Susan mature over the decades, they do not become less intense, and the transformation from early exuberance to the direct, often humorous, and contemplative tone in these middle letters reflects the magnitude of Emily's passion and respect for her beloved friend.

22

Tuesday morning –

Sue – you can go or stay – There is but one alternative – We differ often lately, and this must be the last.

You need not fear to leave me lest I should be alone, for I often part with things I fancy I have loved, – sometimes to the grave, and sometimes to an oblivion rather bitterer than death – thus my heart bleeds so frequently that I shant mind the hemorrhage, and I only add an agony to several previous ones, and at the end of day remark – a bubble burst!

Such incidents would grieve me when I was but a child, and perhaps I could have wept when little feet hard by mine, stood still in the coffin, but eyes grow dry sometimes, and hearts get crisp and cinder, and had as lief burn.

Sue – I have lived by this.

It is the lingering emblem of the Heaven I once dreamed, and though if this is taken, I shall remain alone, and though in that last day, the Jesus Christ you love, remark he does not know me – there is a darker spirit will not disown it's child.

Few have been given me, and if I love them so, that for idolatry, they are removed from me – I simply murmur gone, and the billow dies away into the boundless blue, and no one knows but me, that one went down today. We have walked very pleasantly – Perhaps this is the point at which our paths diverge – then pass on singing Sue, and up the distant hill I journey on.

I have a Bird in spring
Which for myself doth sing –
The spring decoys.
And as the summer nears –
And as the Rose appears,
Robin is gone.

Yet do I not repine
Knowing that Bird of mine
Though flown_
Learneth beyond the sea
Melody new for me
And will return.

Fast in a safer hand
Held in a truer Land
Are mine_
And though they now depart,
Tell I my doubting heart
They're thine.

In a serener Bright,
In a more golden light
I see
Each little doubt and fear,
Each little discord here
Removed.

Then will I not repine,
Knowing that Bird of mine
Though flown

Shall in a distant tree
Bright melody for me
Return.
E –

mid-1850s

"The Jesus Christ you love, remark he does not know me" suggests that the differences expressed in this letter may have been over spiritual matters. While Emily would soon remove herself from the ceremonies of organized religion altogether, Susan struggled with the place of orthodoxy in her life. Known to honor certain religious conventions, Susan once assured her brothers that she only wrote letters on the Sabbath in the case of overriding necessity. For Emily, who kept the Sabbath "staying at Home," the pomp and pageantry of High Church was as foreign as "Firmament to Fin." As late as September 1898, Susan considered converting to Catholicism.

23

A slash of Blue –
A sweep of Gray –
Some scarlet patches
on the way,
Compose an Evening Sky –
A little purple – slipped
between –
Some Ruby Trowsers
hurried on –
A Wave of Gold –
A Bank of Day –
This just makes out
the Morning Sky –

1850s

This is one of several poems from which the address "Sue" was later erased.

24

Dear Susie – I send
you a little air –
The "Music of the Spheres."
They are represented above
as passing thro' the sky.

mid-1850s

This may be an example of a letter-poem inspired by the elaborate poetry games that Emily and Susan play throughout their correspondence. On this missive, written in her more casual "rough draft" hand, Emily sketches ascending musical notations and clouds, perhaps joking about the "Pythagorean maxim" to "avoid eating beans, which cause flatulence" that Melville refers to in *Moby Dick*. She may also be teasing Susan, the math teacher, about Pythagoreanism, or poking fun at her own style of writing, of feeding people on air.

25

These are the days when Birds come back –
A very few – a Bird or two –
To take a final look.

These are the days when skies resume
The old – old Sophistries of June –
A blue and gold mistake.

Oh fraud that cannot cheat the Bee –
Almost thy plausibility
Induces my belief.

Till ranks of seeds their witness bear –
And swiftly thro' the altered air
Hurries a timid leaf.

Oh Sacrament of summer days !
Oh Last Communion in the Haze –
Permit a child to join.

Thy sacred emblem to partake –
Thy consecrated bread to take
And thine immortal wine!

1850s
Emily's poem echoes a poem by Susan, "There are three months of the Spring," suggesting a call-and-response relationship in their writing life.

26

Besides the Autumn poets sing
A few prosaic days
A little this side of the snow
And that side of the Haze.
A few incisive Mornings –
A few ascetic Eves –
Gone – Mr Bryant's "Golden Rod"
And Mr Thomson's "Sheaves."
Still, is the bustle in the brook –
Sealed, are the spicy valves –
Mesmeric fingers softly touch
The Eyes of many Elves –
Perhaps a squirrel may remain –
My sentiments to share –
Grant me Oh Lord a
sunny mind –
Thy windy will to bear!

Emilie –

1850s

Letter-poems take a variety of forms, including signed poems. In this letter-poem, Emily refers to poems by William Cullen Bryant, who lived in nearby Cummington, and the Scottish poet James Thomson. The address "Sue" was erased from the verso.

27

Pigmy Seraphs – gone astray –
Velvet people from Vevay –
Belles from some lost summer
day –
Bees exclusive Coterie –
Paris could not lay the fold
Belted down with Emerald!
Venice could not show a cheek
Of a tint so lustrous meek.
Never such an Ambuscade
As of briar and leaf displayed
For my little damask maid.
I had rather wear her grace
Than an Earl's distinguished
face –
I had rather dwell like her
Than be Duke of Exeter –
over –

Next page

Royalty eno' for Me
To subdue the Bumblebee.

Emily –

1850s
Previous editors have not noted that this poem was addressed to Susan.

28

Thursday Eve

Susie –

You will forgive me, for I never visit. I am from the fields, you know, and while quite at home with the Dandelion, make but sorry figure in a Drawing – room – Did you ask me out with a bunch of Daisies, I should thank you, and accept – but with Roses – "Lilies" – "Solomon" himself – suffers much embarrassment! Do not mind me Susie – If I do not come with feet, in my heart I come – talk the most, and laugh the longest – stay when all the rest have gone – kiss your cheek, perhaps, while those honest people quite forget you in their Sleep!

Thank you for your frequent coming, and the flowers you bring – thank you for the glad laugh, which I heard this morning, tho' I did not see you.

I will keep them all till I reach my other Susie, whose sweet face you bring afresh, every day you come.

Affy –
Emilie –

late 1850s
To describe her place in society, Emily draws on a mock hierarchy of flowers — daisies at the bottom, roses and lilies at the top. Throughout this correspondence, she uses the symbols of the rose and the lily to represent Susan and herself. She identifies with King Solomon and his riches, and her description of her own social interaction when her heart is so inclined — "talking the most and laughing the longest" — will be echoed decades later by her niece, who declared that with an appreciative audience her "Aunt Emily [would] talk more and funnier."

29

Sunday.

I hav'nt any paper, dear, but faith continues firm – Presume if I met with my "deserts," I should receive nothing. Was informed to that effect today by a "dear pastor." What a privilege it is to be so insignificant! Thought of intimating that the "Atonement" was'nt needed for such atomies! I think you went on Friday. Some time is longer than the rest, and some is very short. Omit to classify Friday – Saturday – Sunday! Evenings get longer with the Autumn – that is nothing new! The Asters are pretty well. "How are the other blossoms?" "Pretty well, I thank you."

Vinnie and I are pretty well. Carlo – comfortable – terrifying man and beast, with renewed activity – is cuffed some – hurled from piazza frequently, when Miss Lavinia's "flies" need her action elsewhere.

She has the "patent action," I have long felt!

I attended church early in the day. Prof Warner preached. Subject – "little drops of dew."

Este[y] took the stump in the afternoon. Aunt Sweetser's dress would have startled Sheba. Aunt Bullard was not out – presume she stayed at home for "self examination." Accompanied by father, they visited the grave yard, after services. These are stirring scenes! Austin supped with us. "Appears well." Ah – Dobbin – Dobbin – you little know the chink which your dear face makes.

We would'nt mind the sun, dear, if it did'nt set – How much you cost – how much Mat costs – I will never sell you for a piece of silver. I'll buy you back with red drops, when you go away. I'll keep you in a casket – I'll bury you in the garden – and keep a bird to watch the spot – perhaps my pillow's safer – Try my bosom last – That's nearest of them all, and I should hear a foot the quickest, should I hear a foot – The thought of the little brown plumes makes my eye awry. The pictures in the air have few visitors.

You see they come to their own and their own do not receive them, "Power and honor" are here today, and "dominion and glory"! I shall never tell!

You may tell, when "the seal" is opened; Mat may tell when they "fall on their faces" – but I shall be lighting the lamps then in my new house – and I cannot come.

God bless you, if he please! Bless Mr John and Mrs Mat – Bless two or three others!

I wish to be there – Shall I come? If I jump, shall you catch me. Hav'nt the conceit to jump! Vinnie is asleep – and must dream her message. Good night, little girls!

Since there are two varieties, we will say it softly – Since there are snowier beds, we'll talk a little every night, before we sleep in these!

Love Emilie –

September 26, 1858
In late September, Susan went to Geneva, New York, to visit her sister Martha, now wife of John Williams Smith. "Aunt Sweetser" and "Aunt Bullard" are Edward Dickinson's sisters, in town for a Dickinson family reunion. Emily's dog Carlo, possibly a Newfoundland, was first mentioned in an 1850 Valentine spoof, so the dog is now at least eight years old. Allusions in the third paragraph from the end are to Revelation 7:11: "And all the angels stood round about the throne, and *about* the elders and the four beasts, and fell before the throne on their faces, and worshipped God." Captain Dobbin is the steadfast, devoted lover of Amelia Sedley in Thackeray's *Vanity Fair*.

30

One Sister have I in our house –
And one, a hedge away.
There's only one recorded,
But both belong to me.

One came the road that I came –
And wore my last year's gown –
The other as a bird her nest,
Builded our hearts among.

She did not sing as we did –
It was a different tune –
Herself to her a Music
As Bumble bee of June.

Today is far from Childhood –
But up and down the hills
I held her hand the tighter –
Which shortened all the miles –

And still her hum
The years among,
Deceives the Butterfly;
Still in her Eye
The Violets lie
Mouldered this many May.

I spilt the dew –
But took the morn –
I chose this single star
From out the wide night's numbers –
Sue _ forevermore!

Emilie –

late 1850s

Written after Austin and Susan took up residence in the Evergreens, this letter-poem is torn above the folding crease on the third page. The tear is probably not a mutilation unless it signals Susan's removal of expressions "too personal and adulatory to be printed." However, the fascicle version of this poem was entirely inked over. It is quite possible that someone (probably Mabel Loomis Todd) found this poem's unabashed expression of affection offensive and tried to blot it out. This mutilation parallels those in the earlier letters, as well as the erasure of "Sue" as the addressee of erotic verses such as "Her breast is fit for pearls."

31

Darling.
The feet of people walking home –
With gayer Sandals go –
The Crocus, till she rises
The Vassal of the snow –

The lips at Hallelujah
Long years of practise bore –
Till bye and bye, these Bargmen
Walked singing, on the shore –

Pearls are the Diver's farthings –
Extorted from the Sea_
Pinions – the Seraph's wagon –
Pedestrian once – as we –

Night is the Morning's Canvas –
Larceny_Legacy –
Death, but our rapt attention
To Immortality –

My figures fail to tell me
How far the Village lies
Whose Peasants are the Angels –
Whose Cantons dot the skies –

My Classics vail their faces –
My faith that dark adores –
Which from its' solemn Abbeys
Such Resurrection pours –

Lovingly,
Emilie –

late 1850s
With both households well established and prospering, Emily sends many poems to Susan, some as messages, and some for her evaluation and critical response. During this time, the poet was making her manuscript books, or fascicles, and she had begun a significant lifelong relationship with another recipient of many poems, Samuel Bowles, editor of the *Springfield Republican*. Bowles and his wife Mary were also friends of Susan and Austin, who probably met him in the mid-1850s when Bowles began to cover the Amherst College commencements. The *Republican* was considered one of the most influential newspapers in the country. Both Dickinson households read the paper every day, and Emily often comments on the news in the notes she sends to Susan.

32

Frequently the woods are pink –
Frequently are brown.
Frequently the hills undress
Behind my native town.
Oft a head is crested
I was wont to see –
And as oft a cranny
Where it used to be –
And the Earth_ [world_] they tell me –

On it's Axis turned!
Wonderful Rotation!
By but Twelve performed!

late 1850s
As neighbors, the two women often passed notes and poems in face-to-face encounters, the folded paper small enough to tuck handily into a pocket. Emily frequently sends Susan poems that she also shares with other readers. Yet she comfortably offers Susan drafts, like this one, in addition to finished poems. Here "world" is crossed out and "Earth" inscribed above it.

33

There is a word
Which bears a sword
Can pierce an armed man –
It hurls it's barbed syllables
And is mute again –
But where it fell
The Saved will tell
On patriotic day,
Some Epauletted Brother
Gave his breath away!

Wherever runs the breathless sun –
Wherever roams the day –
There is it's noiseless onset –
There is it's victory!

Behold the keenest marksman –
The most accomplished shot!
Time's sublimest target
Is a soul "forgot"!
Emily –

late 1850s

34

Thro' lane it lay – thro' bramble –
Thro' clearing, and thro' wood –
Banditti often passed us
Upon the lonely road –
The wolf came peering curious –
The owl looked puzzled down –
The Serpent's satin figure
Glid stealthily along –
The tempests touched our garments –
The Lightning's poinards gleamed –
Fierce from the crag above us
The hungry Vulture screamed –
The Satyr's fingers beckoned –
The Valley murmured "Come" –
These were the mates –
This was the road
These Children fluttered home.

"Emily – "

late 1850s
The "hungry Vulture" may refer to Kate Anthon, a lifelong friend of Susan's whom Emily refers to as "Condor Kate" in a letter written a few years later.

35

My Wheel is in the dark.
I cannot see a spoke –
Yet know it's dripping feet
Go round and round.

My foot is on the Tide –
An unfrequented road
Yet have all roads
A "Clearing" at the end.

Some have resigned the Loom –
Some – in the busy tomb
Find quaint employ.
Some with new – stately feet
Pass royal thro' the gate
Flinging the problem back, at you and I.

late 1850s

36

I never told the buried gold
Upon the hill that lies –
I saw the sun, his plunder done –
Crouch low to guard his prize –

He stood as near
As stood you here –
A pace had been between –
Did but a snake bisect the brake
My life had forfeit been.

That was a wondrous booty –
I hope 'twas honest gained –
Those were the fairest ingots
That ever kissed the spade.

Whether to keep the secret –
Whether to reveal –
Whether while I ponder
Kidd may sudden sail –

Could a shrewd advise me
We might e'en divide –
Should a shrewd betray me –
"Atropos" decide_

late 1850s
"Atropos" refers to one of the three Fates in Greek mythology.

37

The morns are meeker than they were –
The nuts are getting brown –
The berry's cheek is plumper –
The Rose is out of town –

The Maple wears a gayer scarf –
The field – a Scarlet gown –
Lest I sh'd seem old fashioned
I'll put a trinket on!

Emilie –

late 1850s
A yellowed ribbon that once held a flower is woven through this letter-poem. The paper is cut so that the ribbon, precisely trimmed, does not cover the text of the poem.

38

"Navy" Sunset!

The guest is gold and Crimson –
An Opal guest, and gray –
Of Ermine is his doublet –
His Capuchin gay –
He comes to town at nightfall –
He stops at every door –
Who looks for him at morning –
I pray him too – explore
The Lark's pure territory –
Or, the Lapwing's shore!

Emilie –

late 1850s

39

A little over Jordan,
As Genesis record,
An Angel and a Wrestler
Did wrestle long and hard.

Till, morning touching mountain,
And Jacob waxing strong,
The Angel begged permission
To breakfast and return.

Not so, quoth wily Jacob
And girt his loins anew,
"Until thou bless me, stranger!"
The which acceded to:

Light swung the silver fleeces
Peniel hills among,
And the astonished Wrestler
Found he had worsted God!

late 1850s

Whatever the religious differences between Emily and Susan, the image of the biblical figures Jacob and the angel would have resonated profoundly for both of them. Throughout the correspondence, biblical characters and events are often emblematic of Emily's internal and external observations. As Susan's daughter, Martha Dickinson Bianchi, put it, "her [Aunt Emily's] mind dared earth and heaven," and "apocrypha and apocalypse met in her."

40

"Sown in dishonor"?
Ah' Indeed!
May <u>this</u> dishonor be?
If I were <u>half</u> so fine, myself,
I'd notice nobody!

"Sown in corruption"?
By no means!
Apostle is Askew!
Corinthians 1.15. narrates
A Circumstance, or two!

late 1850s

The quotations refer to the New Testament: "So also is the resurrection of the dead. It is sown in corruption; it is raised in incorruption: It is sown in dishonor; it is raised in glory; it is sown in weakness; it is raised in power." (1 Corinthians 15:42-43)

41

Some Rainbow – coming from the Fair!
Some Vision of the World Cashmere
I confidently see!
Or else a Peacock's purple train
Feather by feather – on the plain –
Fritters itself away!

The dreamy Butterflies bestir!
Lethargic pools resume the whirr
Of last year's sundered tune –
From some old Fortress on the Sun
Baronial Bees march – one by one –
In murmuring platoon!

The Robins stand as thick today
As flakes of snow did, yesterday –
On fence, and roof – and twig –
The Orchis binds her feather on
For her old lover – Don the Sun.
Revisiting the Bog.

over –

Without Commander_Countless – still –
The Regiments of Wood and Hill
In bright detachments stand!

Behold! Whose Multitudes are these?
The Children of whose Turbaned seas –
Or what Circassian Land!
Emily.

Dear Sue –
I havnt "paid you an
attention" for some time.
Girl.

late 1850s

42

Success is counted sweetest
By those who ne'er succeed.
To comprehend a nectar
Requires sorest need.
Not one of all the purple Host
Who took the flag today
Can tell the definition so Clear
of Victory –
As he defeated – dying –
On whose forbidden Ear
The distant strains of triumph
Burst agonized and Clear.

late 1850s
This was first printed during the Civil War in the *Brooklyn Daily Union.* It is likely that Susan passed the poem along to the editor Reverend Richard Salter Storrs, who was a guest at the Evergreens. In 1878 Helen Hunt Jackson, a writer and close friend of Emily's, included this poem in the collection *A Masque of Poets,* without identifying the poet. Many readers attributed it to Ralph Waldo Emerson.

43

Ambition cannot find him!
Affection does'nt know
How many leagues of Nowhere
Lie between them now!
 Yesterday, undistinguished!
  Eminent Today
   For our mutual honor,
    Immortality!

late 1850s

A small cut in the paper suggests that Emily attached a ribbon or a flower to this poem.

44

Low at my problem bending –
Another problem comes –
Larger than mine – Serener –
Involving statelier sums –
I check my busy pencil,
My Ciphers steal away '
Wherefore my baffled fingers
 Thine Extremity?

late 1850s

45

A throe upon the features –
A hurry in the breath –
An extacy of parting
Denominated Death.
An anguish at the mention
Which when to patience grown,
I've known permission given
To rejoin it's own.

late 1850s
Dickinson repeatedly attempted to capture the moment of death in her poems.

46

Who never lost, is
unprepared
A Coronet – to find.
Who never thirsted,
Flagons, and Cooling Tamarind.
Who never climbed the
weary league –
Can such a foot Explore
The purple Territories
On Pizarro's shore?
How many legions overcome –
The Emperor will say?
How many Colors taken
over –

new page

On Revolution Day?
How many Bullets bearest?
Hast thou the Royal Scar!
Angels! Mark "Promoted"
On this soldier's brow!

Emily –

late 1850s
During the late 1850s, Dickinson's integration of letter writing and poetry begins to affect the form of her poems. Many that she sends to Susan are in her rough-draft handwriting, and presented in a single stanza, suggesting that the poems are works-in-progress.

47

She died at play '
Gambolled away
Her lease of spotted hours,
Then sank as gaily as a Turk
Upon a Couch of flowers.

Her ghost strolled softly o'er the hill
Yesterday, and today.
Her vestments as the silver fleece –
Her countenance, as spray,

Emily '

late 1850s

48

Exultation is the going
Of an inland soul to sea,
Past the houses – past the headlands –
Into deep Eternity ,

Bred as we, among the mountains,
Can the sailor understand
The divine intoxication
Of the first league out from land?

late 1850s

49

Our lives are Swiss,
So still – so cool –
Till some odd afternoon
The Alps neglect their curtains
And we look further on.
Italy stands the other side.
While like a guard between –
The solemn Alps.
The siren Alps
Forever intervene.

late 1850s

In her literary play, Emily often appears to allude to Elizabeth Barrett Browning, "that Foreign Lady" whom she associated with Italy and who "enchanted" her so.

50

Her breast is fit for pearls,
But I was not a "Diver" –
Her brow is fit for thrones
But I have not a crest,
Her heart is fit for home –
I – a Sparrow – build there
Sweet of twigs and twine
My perennial nest.

Emily –

1850s

This poem, and the following one, are written in pencil, in Emily's rough-draft hand. "Sue" was carefully erased from the verso. In Mabel Loomis Todd's 1894 edition of *Letters*, she placed this poem in the Samuel Bowles correspondence, suggesting that Emily had sent "Her breast is fit for pearls" to Samuel in honor of his wife, Mary. Loomis Todd may well have been attempting to make Emily's correspondence with Mary Bowles look more extensive, since Dickinson wrote the Bowles few joint letters. By falsely attributing the poem, Loomis Todd accomplished two objectives: she disguised a love poem to Susan, and she made Emily's correspondence to Bowles (with whom she is said to have been in love) appear more inclusive of his wife.

51

As Watchers hang upon the East,
As Beggars revel at a feast
By savory Fancy spread –
As brooks in deserts babble sweet
On ear too far for the delight,
Heaven beguiles the tired.

As that same watcher, when the East
Opens the lid of Amethyst
And lets the morning go –
That Beggar, when an honored Guest,
Those thirsty lips to flagons pressed,
Heaven to us, if true.

Emilie –

late 1850s

52

The sun kept stooping – stooping – low –
The Hills to meet him – rose –
On his part – what Transaction!
On their part – what repose!

Deeper and deeper grew the stain
Upon the window pane –
Thicker and thicker stood the feet
Until the Tyrian

Was crowded dense with Armies –
So gay – so Brigadier –
That I felt martial stirrings
Who once the Cockade wore –

Charged – from my Chimney Corner –
But nobody was there!

Emily –

late 1850s

53

Except to Heaven – she is nought.
Except for Angels – lone.
Except to some wide-wandering Bee –
A flower superfluous – blown.

Except for winds – provincial –
Except for Butterflies
Unnoticed as a single dew
That on the Acre lies –

The smallest Housewife in the grass –
Yet take her from the lawn
And somebody has lost the face
That made Existence – Home –

Emily.

early 1860s

54

The Bumble of a Bee –
A Witchcraft, yieldeth me.
If any ask me "Why – "
'Twere easier to die
Than tell!

The Red upon the Hill
Taketh away my will –

If Anybody sneer,
  Take care, for God is near –
  That's All!

The Breaking of the Day –
Addeth to my Degree –
If any ask me "how" –
Artist who drew me so –
Must tell!

Emily '

early 1860s

55

Just lost, when I was saved!
Just heard the world go by!
Just girt me for the onset with eternity,
When breath drew back,
And on the other side
I heard recede the disappointed tide!

Therefore, as one returned, I feel,
Odd secrets of "the Line" to tell!
Some sailor skirting novel shores –
Some pale "reporter" from the awful doors
Before the Seal!

Next time to stay!
Next time the things to see
By ear unheard,
Unscrutinized by eye –
Next time to tarry,

While the ages steal –
Tramp the slow centuries,
And the cycles wheel!

early 1860s
First published in the *Independent* on March 12, 1891, and titled "Called Back," this is among the poems that Susan submitted for publication shortly after Emily's death.

56

Will Susan – please lend
Emily – "Life in the Iron Mills" –
and accept Blossom
        from Emily –

spring 1861
Here, Emily requests Susan's copy of the April 1861 issue of the *Atlantic Monthly*, which contained Rebecca Harding Davis's *Life in the Iron Mills*.

57

Is it true, dear Sue?
Are there two?
I should'nt like to come
For fear of joggling Him!
If you could shut him up
In a Coffee Cup,
Or tie him to a pin
Till I got in –
Or make him fast

To "Toby's" fist
Hist! Whist! I'd come!
Emily –

about June 19, 1861
This letter-poem was written after the birth of Susan's first child, Edward (Ned). In earlier published versions, "If you could shut him up" is mistranscribed as "If I could shut him up . . . ," inaccurately suggesting that Emily was jealous of the newborn. "Toby" is the cat, and "Coffee Cup" may playfully refer to Susan's love of coffee.

58

from Susan

Emily –
All's well –

Never mind Emily – to-morrow
will do just as well – Don't bother –
I'm "not an hard master" – You
know Maggie is out, and I don't like
to leave my fold – There were two or
three little things I wanted to talk
with you about without witnesses
but to-morrow will do just as
well – Has girl read Republican?
It takes as long to start our
Fleet as the Burnside.

March 1862
On March 1, 1862, the *Springfield Republican* printed an early version of "Safe in their Alabaster Chambers" entitled "The Sleeping." It is likely that the poem printed in the *Republican* beneath "The Sleeping," entitled "The Shadow of Thy Wing," was written by Susan. Both poems were published anonymously. In one of the few surviving letters from Susan to Emily, Susan excitedly in-

scribes the greeting, "All's well" in one quarter of the fold, and then compares their mutual enterprise — making their poetry known to the public — to the Civil War general Burnside's siege and the capture of Roanoke Island in February 1862.

59

The Sleeping.

Safe in their alabaster chambers,
Untouched by morning,
And untouched by noon,
Sleep the meek members of the Resurrection,
Rafter of satin, and roof of stone.

Light laughs the breeze
In her castle above them,
Babbles the bee in a stolid ear,
Pipe the sweet birds in ignorant cadences:
Ah! What sagacity perished here!
Pelham Hill, June, 1861.

March 1, 1862
This is Emily's poem that Susan refers to reading in the *Springfield Republican.*

60

Safe in their Alabaster Chambers,
Untouched by Morning –
And untouched by Noon –
Lie the meek members of
the Resurrection –
Rafter of Satin – and Roof of
Stone –

Grand go the Years – in the
Crescent – above them –
Worlds scoop their Arcs –
And Firmaments – row –
Diadems – drop – and Doges –
Surrender –
Soundless as dots – on a
Disc of Snow –

Perhaps this verse would
please you better – Sue –
Emily '

about 1861
Emily sends Susan another version of the poem, and appends a note showing that Susan is familiar with the poem and does not like the second verse.

61

from Susan

I am not suited
dear Emily with the second
verse – It is remarkable as the
chain lightening that blinds us
hot nights in the Southern sky
but it does not go with the
ghostly shimmer of the first verse
as well as the other one – It just
occurs to me that the first verse
is complete in itself it needs

no other, and can't be coupled –
Strange things always go alone – as
there is only one Gabriel and one
Sun – You never made a peer
for that verse, and I guess you[r]
kingdom does'nt hold one – I
always go to the fire and get warm
after thinking of it, but I never
can again – The flowers are sweet
and bright and look as if they
would kiss one – ah, they expect
a humming-bird – Thanks for
them of course – and not thanks
only recognition either – Did it
ever occur to you that is all there
is here after all – "Lord that I
may receive my sight"__
Susan is tired making bibs for
her bird – her ring-dove – he will
paint my cheeks when I am old
to pay me –

Sue –

about 1861
This rare sample of a correspondence, marked "Pony Express," from Susan to Emily may have been preserved because it was sent back to Susan with another draft of the poem, and then kept by Susan's daughter Martha. Susan refers to a second stanza of "Safe in their Alabaster Chambers," which may be the one printed in the *Republican*, or another version that Emily bound into an early fascicle. A decade later, Thomas Higginson's paraphrase of Emily's definition of poetry echoes Susan's note: "If I read a book [and] it makes my whole body so cold no fire ever can warm me I know that is poetry."

62

Is this, frostier?

Springs – shake the Sills –
But – the Echoes – stiffen –
Hoar – is the Window – and
numb – the Door –
Tribes of Eclipse – in Tents
of Marble –
Staples of Ages – have
buckled – there –

Dear Sue –
Your praise is good –
to me – because I know
it knows – and suppose –
it means –
Could I make you and
Austin – proud – sometime – a
great way off – 'twould give
me taller feet –
Here is a crumb – for the
"Ring dove"- and a spray '
for his Nest, a little while
ago – just – "Sue"–
Emily'

about 1861

Susan's daughter, Martha Dickinson Bianchi, attached a note to the folder that contained this poem: "In reply to Mamma's criticism of one stanza – " After Emily's death, when Susan was compiling her book of Emily's writings, she jotted down Emily's words of thanks from memory, "'If some day far off I / should make you glad I / should have taller feet' Emily."

63

from Susan

Private
I have intended to
write you Emily to-day but the
quiet has not been mine I send
you this, lest I should seem to
have turned away from a kiss –
If you have suffered this past
summer I am sorry I
Emily bear a sorrow that I
never uncover – – If a nightingale
sings with her breast against
a thorn, why not we [!]
When I can, I shall write —
Sue –

early 1860s
This message probably accompanied a gift of some sort — "I send you this." Martha Dickinson Bianchi described her mother and her aunt watching and waiting for a few private moments in a day when they could talk, deliver letters face-to-face, and exchange favored reading materials. These exchanges usually took place in the "Northwest Passage," the back hallway of the Homestead.

64

The face I carry with
me – last –
When I go out of Time –

To take my Rank – by – in
the West –
That face – will just be thine –

I'll hand it to the Angel –
That – Sir – was my Degree –
In Kingdoms – you have heard
the Raised –
Refer to – possibly .

He'll take it – scan it – step
aside –
Return – with such a Crown
As Gabriel – never capered at –
And beg me put it on –

And then – he'll turn me round
and round –
To an admiring sky –
As One that bore her Master's name –
Sufficient Royalty!

1860s
This poem, associated with the fascicles, has the address "Sue" erased from the verso.

65

Could I – then –
shut the door –
Lest my beseeching
face – at last –
Rejected – be – of Her?

early 1860s

Write! Comrade, write!

On this wondrous sea
Sailing silently,
Ho! Pilot, ho!
Knowest thou the shore
Where no breakers roar –
Where the storm is o'er?

In the peaceful west
Many the sails at rest –
The anchors fast –
Thither I pilot thee –
Land Ho! Eternity!
Ashore at last!

Emilie –

Write! Comrade – write! *March 1853* (15):44

Sweet Sue,
There is
no first, or last,
in Forever -
It is Centre, there,
all the time -
To believe - is enough,
and the right of
supposing -
Take back that
"Bee" and "Buttercups" -
I have no Field
for them, though

Sweet Sue, / There is / no first, or last, *1864* (102):130

for the Woman
whom I prefer,
Here is Festival -
When my Hands
are Cut, Her
fingers will be
found inside.
Our beautiful Neigh-
bor "moved" in May -
It leaves an
Unimportance
Take the key to
the Lily, now, and
I will lock the Rose.

Susan's Idolater keeps / a Shrine for Susan. *late 1860s* (127):156

I must wait
a few Days
before seeing
you – You are
too momentous.
But remember
it is idolatry,
not indifference.
Emily.

I must wait /a few Days *late 1870s* (202):220

That Susan
lives - is a
Universe which
neither going
nor coming
could displace.

That Susan / lives – is a / Universe *spring 1880* (219):232

Thanks
for the
profligate
little Book
that tasted
of all
Cigars

Susan is a
vast and sweet
Sister, and
Emily hopes to
deserve her,
but not now –

Susan is a / vast and sweet / Sister, *early 1880s* (220):232

To be Susan
is Imagination,
To have been
Susan, a Dream -
What depths
of Domingo
in ~~that~~ torrid
Spirit!
Emily

To be Susan / is Imagination, *1880s* (233):242

66

When Etna
basks and purrs
Naples is more
afraid
Than when she
shows her Garnet Tooth –
Security is loud –

1862 or later
Emily refers to Mount Etna in eastern Sicily, the highest active volcano in Europe.

67

Savior! I've no one else
to tell –
And so I trouble thee.
I am the one forgot
thee so –
Dost thou remember
me?
Nor, for myself, I
came so far –
That were the little
load –
I brought thee the
imperial Heart
I had not strength
to hold –
The Heart I carried

in my own –
Till mine too heavy
grew –
Yet – strangest – heavier
since it went –
Is it too large for
you?

early 1860s

68

Blazing in Gold – and
Quenching – in Purple!
Leaping – like Leopards – [in] to
the Sky –
Then – at the feet of the
old Horizon –
Laying it's spotted face – to die!

Stooping as low as the
kitchen window –
Touching the Roof –
And tinting the Barn –
Kissing it's Bonnet to
the Meadow –
And the Juggler of
Day – is gone!

early 1860s
Susan's copy of this poem was "lost," though it is likely that she sent it to the editors of the *Republican* or *Drum Beat* where it was printed in 1864. Emily's cousin Perez Cowan, a student at Amherst College from 1862 to 1866,

transcribed this poem from memory in an 1891 letter, noting that Susan had given it to him when he was in Amherst. This indicates that Susan was transcribing Emily's poems and giving them as gifts from an early date.

69

Dear Sue –
I'm thinking
on that other morn –
When Cerements – let
go –
And Creatures – clad
in Victory –
Go up – by two – and
two!
Emily.

early 1860s

70

Dear Sue.
Your – Riches –
taught me – poverty!
Myself, a "Millionaire"
In little – wealths – as
Girls can boast –
Till broad as "Buenos Ayre" –
You drifted your Dominions –
A Different – Peru –

And I esteemed – all –
poverty –
For Life's Estate – with you!

Of "Mines" – I little know –
my self –
But just the names – of Gems –
The Colors – of the
Commonest –
And scarce of Diadems –
So much – that did
I meet the Queen –
Her glory – I should know –
But this – must be
a different Wealth –
To miss it – beggars – so!

I'm sure 'tis "India" – all
day –
To those who look on
you –
Without a stint – without
a blame –
Might I – but be the Jew!
I know it is "Golconda" –
Beyond my power to
dream –
To have a smile – for
mine – each day –
How better – than a Gem!

At least – it solaces –
to know –
That there exists – a Gold –

Altho' I prove it, just
in time –
Its' distance – to behold!
Its' far – far – Treasure – to
surmise –
And estimate – the Pearl –
That slipped – my simple fingers –
thro'
While yet – a Girl –
at School!

Dear Sue –
You see I remember –
Emily.

early 1860s

71

I reason –
Earth is short –
And Anguish – absolute –
And many – hurt –
But, what of that?
I reason –
We should
die –
The best – Vitality –
Could not excel Decay –
But – What of that?
I reason –
That in "Heaven" –

Somehow – it will be even –
Some new Equation – given –
But – what of that!

early 1860s
As Emily increasingly copies poems into manuscript books, she includes more poems in letters, and sends poems as letters, using the arrangement of lines on the page to reflect the content of her messages and observations.

72

Sue –
  Give little Anguish –
Lives will fret –
Give Avalanches –
And they'll slant –
Straighten – look cautious
for their Breath –
But make no syllable –
like Death –
Who only shows his
Marble Disc –
Sublimer sort – than
Speech –
        Emily –

early 1860s

73

I send two Sunsets –
Day and I – in com –
petition – ran –
I finished Two, and
several Stars
While He – was making
One –
His own is ampler –
but as I
Was saying to a friend –
Mine – is the more
Convenient
To Carry in the Hand ,

Emily –

1860s

74

For Largest Woman's
Heart I knew –
'Tis little I can do –
And yet the Largest
Woman's Heart
Could hold an Arrow – too –
And so, instructed by
my own,
I tenderer, turn me to.

Emily.

early 1860s

75

It sifts from Leaden
Sieves –
It powders all the Wood.
It fills with Alabaster
Wool
The Wrinkles of the Road –

It makes an Even
Face
Of Mountain, and of
Plain –
Unbroken Forehead
from the East
Unto the East again –

It reaches to the Fence –
It wraps it Rail by Rail
Till it is lost in Fleeces –
It deals Celestial Vail

To Stump, and Stack –
and Stem –
A Summer's Empty Room –
Acres of Joints, where
Harvests were,
Recordless, but for them –

It Ruffles Wrists
of Posts
As Ankles of a
Queen –
Then stills it's Artisans –

like Ghosts –
Denying they have been –
Emily –

early 1860s

76

Her – "last Poems" –
Poets ended –
Silver perished with her
Tongue –
Not on Record bubbled
Other –
Flute, or Woman, so
divine –
Not unto its' Summer –
Morning
Robin – uttered – half – the
tune –
Gushed too free for the
adoring –
From the Anglo-Florentine –
Late – the Praise –
'Tis dull – conferring
On a Head too high
to crown –
Diadem – or Ducal Showing –
Be its' Grave – sufficient
Sign –
Yet, if We – No Poet's
Kinsman –

Suffocate – with easy Wo –
What and if Ourself
a Bridegroom –
Put Her down – in Italy?

Emily –

early 1860s
Emily sends this letter-poem to Susan after the death of Elizabeth Barrett Browning, whom she and Susan deeply admired.

77

Defeat – whets Victory –
they say –
The Reefs in Old
Gethsemane –
Endear the Coast –
beyond !
'Tis Beggars – Banquets –
can define –
'Tis Parching – vitalizes
Wine –
Faith bleats – to
understand !

Emily '

early 1860s

78

Nature – sometimes
sears a Sapling –
Sometimes – scalps
a Tree –
Her Green People
recollect it –
When they do not
die –
Fainter Leaves – to
further Seasons
Dumbly testify –
We – who have
the Souls
Die oftener – not
so vitally –

Emily.

early 1860s

79

Distance – is not
the Realm of Fox
Nor by Relay of
Bird
Abated – Distance is
Until thyself, Beloved

Emily '

early 1860s

Susan remembered this letter-poem when making notes for her book of Emily's writings. On a sheet of paper are: "'A spring of intellectuality [?]' – Pater" and "'Distance! Tis till thyself, Beloved' – E." It is likely that she was writing down her favorite first lines or aphorisms.

80

He fumbles at your Soul
As Players at the Keys
Before they drop full
Music on –
He stuns you by degrees –
Prepares your brittle Nature
For the Etherial Blow
By fainter Hammers –
further heard –
Then nearer – Then so slow
Your Breath has time to
straighten –
Your Brain – to bubble Cool –
Deals – One – imperial –
Thunder bolt –
That scalps your
naked Soul –

When Winds take Forests
in their Paws –
The Universe – is still –
Emily.

early 1860s

81

There came a Day at Summer's full,
Entirely for me –
I thought that such was for the Saints,
Where Resurrections – be –

The Sun, as common, went abroad,
The flowers, accustomed, blew,
As if no sail the solstice passed
That maketh all things new –

The time was scarce profaned, by speech –
The symbol of a word
Was needless, as at Sacrament,
The Wardrobe – of our Lord –

Each was to
Each – the Sealed
Church,
Permitted to commune
this – time –
Lest we too awkward
show
At Supper of "the Lamb"

The Hours slid past – as Hours will,
Clutched tight, by greedy hands –
So faces on two Decks, look back,
Bound to opposing lands –

And so when all the time had leaked,
Without external sound
Each bound the Other's Crucifix –
We gave no other Bond –

Sufficient troth, that we should rise –
Deposed – at length, the Grave –
To that new Marriage,
Justified – through Calvaries of Love –

1862
This poem was later titled "Renunciation" by Susan. Omitting the fourth stanza, she submitted it to *Scribner's Magazine* after Emily's death, and the poem was published in August 1890. After the publication Emily's sister, Lavinia, who had a fascicle copy of the poem, objected to Susan's presumption. However, Susan maintained that she had the right to publish any poems that Emily had sent to her. This poem was also among the work that Emily sent to Thomas Higginson in 1862.

82

Essential Oils are
wrung –
The Attar from the
Rose
Is not expressed
by Suns – alone –
It is the gift of
Screws –
The General Rose
decay –
While this – in
Lady's Drawer
Make Summer, when
the Lady lie
In Spiceless Sepulchre.
Emily –

early 1860s

83

I showed her Hights
she never saw –
"Would"st climb," I said?
She said – "Not so" –
"With me -" I said –
With me?
I showed her Secrets –
Morning's Nest –
The Rope the Nights
were put across –
And now – "Would'st
have me for a Guest"?
She could not find her Yes –

And then, I brake
My life – And Lo,
A Light, for her,
did solemn glow,
The larger, as her
face withdrew –
And could she, further,
"No"?

Emily –

early 1860s

Emily changes the pronouns in another version of this poem, which she included in the fascicles: "He showed me Hights I / never saw – ."

84

The difference between
Despair
And Fear, is like
the One
Between the instant
of a Wreck
And when the
Wreck has been.
The Mind is
smooth –
No Motion – Contented
as the Eye
Upon the Forehead
of a Bust –
That knows it
cannot see.
Emily '

1860s

85

Like Some Old fashioned
Miracle
When Summertime is done –
Seems Summer's Recollec –
tion
And the Affairs of June

As infinite Tradition
As Cinderella's Bays –
Or little John – of
Lincoln Green –
Or Blue Beard's
Galleries –

Her Bees have a fictitious Hum –
Her Blossoms, like
a Dream –
Elate us – till we
Almost weep –
So plausible – they seem –

Her Memories like
Strains – Review –
When Orchestra is
dumb –
The Violin in Baize
replaced –
And Ear – and Heaven –
numb –

Emily –

early to mid-1860s

86

The Soul unto itself
Is an imperial friend –
Or the most agonizing Spy
An Enemy – could send –
Secure against it's own –
No treason it can fear –

Itself – it's Sovreign – of itself
The Soul should stand in awe –
Emily –

mid-1860s
The address, "Sue," was erased from the verso of this letter-poem.

87

The Soul's Superior
instants
Occur to Her – alone –
When friend – and
Earth's occasion
Have infinite withdrawn –

Or She – Herself – as-
cended
To too remote a Hight
For lower Recognition
Than Her Omnipotent –

This Mortal Abolition
Is seldom – but as fair
As Apparition – subject
To Autocratic Air –

Eternity's disclosure
To favorites – a few –
Of the Colossal
Substance
Of Immortality

Emily.

mid-1860s

88

Ah' Teneriffe!
Retreating Mountain!
Purples of Ages – pause
for you.

Sunset – reviews her Sapphire
Regiment –
Day – drops you her Red
Adieu!

Still – Clad in your Mail
of ices –
Thigh of Granite – and
thew – of Steel –
Heedless – alike – of pomp –
or parting

Ah' Teneriffe!
I'm kneeling – still –

Emily '

mid-1860s
"Teneriffe" is the volcanic island in the Canary Islands, and most likely refers to the poetic and painterly portrayals of Elizabeth Barrett Browning, John Ruskin, and Byron.

89

"Nature" is what
we See –
The Hill – the

Afternoon –
Squirrel – Eclipse –
the Bumble bee –
Nay – Nature is
Heaven –
Nature is what
we hear –
The Bobolink –
the Sea –
Thunder – the
Cricket –
Nay – Nature is
Harmony –
Nature is what
we know –
Yet have no art
to say –
So impotent Our
Wisdom is
To her Simplicity
Emily

mid-1860s

90

No Romance sold
unto
Could so enthrall
a Man
As the perusal of
His Individual One –

'Tis Fiction's – to dilute
to Plausibility
Our Novel – When 'tis
small enough
To Credit – 'Tis'nt true!
Emily –

mid-1860s

91

One need not be
a Chamber – to be
Haunted –
One need not
be a House –
The Brain has
Corridors – surpassing
Material Place –
Far safer, of a
Midnight Meeting
External Ghost
Than its' interior
Confronting –
That Cooler Host –

Far safer, through
an Abbey gallop,
The Stones a'chase –
Than Unarmed,
One's a'self encounter –
In lonesome Place –

Ourself behind
Ourself, Concealed –
Should startle most –
Assassin hid in
Our Apartment
Be Horror's least

The Body – borrows
a Revolver –
He bolts the Door –
O'erlooking a
Superior Spectre –
Or More –

Emily –

mid-1860s

92

Excuse me – Dollie –

The Love a Child can
show – below –
Is but a Filament – I
know –
Of that Diviner – Thing –
That faints upon the face
of Noon –
And smites the Tinder
in the Sun –
And hinders – Gabriel's – Wing!

'Tis This – in Music –
hints – and sways –
And far abroad – on
Summer Days –
Distils – uncertain – pain –
'Tis This – afflicts us
in the East –
And tints the Transit
in the West –
With Harrowing – Iodine!

'Tis This – invites – appalls –
endows –
Flits – glimmers – proves –
dissolves –
Returns – suggests – convicts –
enchants –
Then – flings in Paradise!

Emily –

mid-1860s
Emily refers to Susan using her nickname, "Dollie."

93

The Overtakelessness
of Those
Who have accom –
plished Death –
Majestic is to Me
beyond

The Majesties of
Earth –
The Soul her
"Not at Home"
Inscribes upon the
Flesh,
And takes a fine
aerial gait
Beyond the Writ
of Touch –

Emily –

mid-1860s
This poem, a previously unpublished version, is addressed to "Dollie" on the verso.

94

Least Bee that
Brew –
A Honey's worth
The Summer multiply –
Content Her smallest
fraction help

mid-1860s
This poem was handled extensively by Susan and her children. There is a game on the verso, which the children played by drawing sets of boxes in rows and entering letters that spelled their names. One of the names is "Matty Dickinson," Susan's second child, Martha, born in 1866. These marks suggest that some years after Susan received this poem it was being used by her children. Pinholes in the manuscript suggest that this occurred as Susan was working on her scrapbooks.

95

To be alive, is
power –
Existence – in itself –
Without a further
function –
Omnipotence – Enough –
To be alive and
Will –
'Tis able as a God –
The Further of
Ourselves, be What –
Such being Fin-
itude?
Emily '

1860s

96

Nor myself to Him,
by accent
Forfeit probity.
Weariness of Him, were
quainter
Than Monotony
Knew a particle, of
Space's
Vast society –
Neither if He visit other –

Do He dwell or nay
Know I – just instinct
esteem Him
Immortality – Emily.

mid-1860s

These lines constitute the last two and a half stanzas of the fascicle version of Emily's poem, "Conscious am I in my Chamber."

97

Content of fading
is enough for me
Fade I unto Divinity -
And Dying – Lifetime – ample
as the eye
Her least attention raise
on Me.

mid-1860s

98

Ungained – it may be
By a Life's low Venture –
But then
Eternity enable the
endeavoring
Again –
Springfield

mid-1860s

It is possible that Emily's signature, "Springfield," may refer to their mutual friend Samuel Bowles, editor of the *Springfield Republican*, or it may refer to the newspaper itself and the publication of her poems.

99

Soil of Flint, if
Steady tilled –
Will refund the Hand –
Seed of Palm, by
Lybian Sun
Fructified in Sand –

Emily –

mid-1860s

100

Two – were immortal –
twice –
The privilege of few –
Eternity – obtained – in
Time –
Reversed – Divinity –
That Our ignoble
Eyes
The Quality – perceive
Of Paradise Superlative —
Thro' Their – Comparative.

mid-1860s

101

I could not drink
it, Sue,
Till you had tasted
first –
Though cooler than
the Water – was
The Thoughtfulness of
Thirst,
Emily.

mid-1860s

102

Sweet Sue,
There is
no first, or last,
in Forever –
It is Centre, there,
all the time –
To believe – is enough,
and the right of
supposing –
Take back that
"Bee" and "Buttercup" –
I have no Field
for them, though
for the Woman
whom I prefer,

Here is Festival –
When my Hands
are Cut, Her
fingers will be
found inside –
Our beautiful Neigh-
bor "moved" in May –
It leaves an
Unimportance.
Take the Key to
the Lily, now, and
I will lock the Rose –

1864
In February 1864, Emily went to Boston to consult an ophthalmologist. In late April, she returned to Boston for eye treatments and stayed until November. During these seven months she lived with her Norcross cousins, ages twenty-two and sixteen, in a boarding house in Cambridgeport. Loo and Fannie had been orphaned by the death of their father in 1863, and their mother, Mrs. Dickinson's sister Lavinia, in 1861. The "beautiful Neigh- / bor" refers to Nathaniel Hawthorne who died on May 19, 1864. Emily suggests that his "moving" is unimportant because his spirit thrives in his literary productions. The "Lily" and the "Rose" have special significance in the spiritual, erotic exchange between Emily and Susan. These, not the daisy, are now the signature flowers in the correspondence, and they measure a shift in dynamics, a maturation of the bond between the two women. Emily regularly identifies or otherwise connects the lily (faith) and the rose (blood, beauty, and love) with Susan.

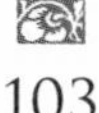

103

at Centre of
the Sea –
I am glad Mrs.
Gertrude lived –
I believed she

would – Those that
are worthy of Life
are of Miracle,
for Life is Miracle,
And Death, as
harmless as a Bee –
except to those
who run _
It would be best to
  see you – it would
be good to see the
Grass, and hear the
Wind blow the wide
way in the Orchard –
Are the Apples
ripe – Have the
Wild Geese crossed –
Did you save the
seed to the
Pond Lily?
Love for Mat, and
John, and the
Foreigner – And
kiss little Ned
in the seam in
the neck, entirely
for Me –
The Doctor is
very kind –
I find no Enemy –
Till the Four o'Clocks
strike Five, Loo
will last, she says.
Do not cease, Sister.

Should I turn in
my long night, I should
murmur "Sue"?
Emily.

September 1864
References to the "Doctor" and "Loo" suggest that this is another letter-poem that Emily sends to Susan while she is in the Boston area undergoing medical treatments for her eye condition. "Mrs. Gertrude" refers to Susan's friend Gertrude Vanderbilt, who was wounded by a gunshot when she came to the rescue of her maid, who was being attacked by a former suitor. "Mat" is Susan's sister Martha, and "John" is her brother-in-law.

104

The Soul selects
her own Society
Then shuts the
Door
To her divine
Majority
Present no more –

on verso

Love reckons by
itself – alone –
"As large as I" –
relate the Sun
To One who never
felt it blaze –
Itself is all the
like it has –

mid-1860s

The handwriting used for both poems is from the mid-1860s; however, one is in ink and one in pencil, suggesting that they were probably written at different times. The numerous folds of this manuscript indicate that the sheet was passed back and forth between Susan and Emily.

105

So set its' Sun in
Thee
What Day be dark
to me –
What Distance, far,
So I the Ships
may see
That touch, how
seldomly,
Thy Shore?
Emily.

mid-1860s

106

Her Grace is all
she has,
And that, so
least displays,
One Art, to
recognize, must be,
Another Art, to
praise –
Emily '

mid-1860s

107

We pass, and
she abides.
We conjugate
Her Skill.
While She – creates
and federates
Without a syllable,

mid-1860s

108

The Luxury to
apprehend
The Luxury 'twould
be
To look at Thee
a single time
An Epicure of Me
In whatsoever
Presence makes
Till for a further
food
I scarcely recollect
to starve
  So first am I
supplied –
The Luxury to
meditate

The Luxury it was
To banquet on
thy Countenance
A Sumptuousness
bestows
On plainer Days,
whose Table, far
As Certainty – can see –
Is laden with a
single Crumb –
The Consciousness –
of Thee.

Emily.

mid-1860s

109

Given in Marriage
unto Thee
Oh thou Celestial
Host –
Bride of the
Father and the
Son,
Bride of the
Holy Ghost.
Emily –

mid-1860s

110

Dear Sue –
Unable are the
Loved – to die –
For Love is immortality –
Nay – it is Deity –
Emily.

March 1865
This letter-poem was sent to Susan after the death of her sister, Harriet Cutler, on March 16, 1865. This is one of the many instances in which Emily's poems are bestowed as spiritual gifts for Susan's solace.

111

Sister,
We both are
Women, and there
is a Will of God –
Could the Dying
confide Death,
there would be no
Dead – Wedlock
is shyer than Death.
Thank you for
Tenderness –
I find it is the only
food that the Will
takes, nor that

from general fingers.
I am glad you go –
It does not remove
you. I seek you
first in Amherst,
then turn my
thoughts without
a Whip – so well
they follow you –
An Hour is a Sea
Between a few, and me –
With them would Harbor
be –

early December 1865
It is likely that Susan is visiting her sister Martha Smith in Geneva, New York, when Emily writes this letter-poem. Martha's two-year-old daughter, named Susan, died on November 2. This may also refer to the December 2 death of Emily and Susan's friend Susan Phelps.

112

Ample make this Bed.
Make this Bed
with Awe –
In it, wait till
Judgment Break
Excellent, and Fair –

Be it's Mattress
straight –
Be it's Pillow
round –
Let no Sunrise'

Yellow noise
Interrupt this
Ground –

mid-1860s

113

You must let me
go first, Sue, because
I live in the Sea
always and know
the Road –
I would have drowned
twice to save
you sinking, dear,
If I could only
have covered your
Eyes so you would'nt
have seen the Water –

mid-1860s
On a slip of paper attached to this letter-poem is a note by Martha Dickinson Bianchi: "One of the first scraps sent over – ." However, Emily had been writing to Susan for approximately fifteen years. It is possible that Susan's daughter misdated the note to protect her mother and aunt from public scrutiny of their intimate correspondence.

114

The Missing All –
prevented Me
From missing minor
Things '
If nothing larger
than a World's
Departure from a
Hinge,
Or Sun's extinction –
be observed –
'Twas not so large
that I
Could lift my Forehead
from my work
For Curiosity –
Emily.

mid-1860s

115

Gratitude – is not
the mention
Of a Tenderness,
But its' still
appreciation
Out of Plumb of
Speech.
Emily '

mid-1860s

116

The Dust behind
I strove to join
Unto the Disk
before –
But Sequence
ravelled out of
Sound
Like Balls upon
a Floor –

mid-1860s

117

Except the smaller
size
No Lives are Round –
These – hurry to a Sphere –
And show – and end –

The Larger – slower grow –
And later hang –
The Summers of Hesperides
Are long –
Emily –

mid-1860s

In Greek mythology, "Hesperides" refers to the Daughters of the West, who, with the aid of a dragon, watch over the Garden of the Golden Apples at the western end of the earth. Pencil scratches cover the front and back of this letter-poem. Drawings of a little cow or dog are probably by Susan's son Ned, who was five or six at the time.

118

Perception of an
Object costs
Precise the Objects'
loss –
Perception in itself
a Gain
Replying to its'
Price –
The Object Absolute –
is nought –
Perception sets it
fair
And then upbraids
a Perfectness
That situates
so far.
Emily –

mid-1860s

119

The Definition of
Beauty, is
That Definition
is none –
Of Heaven, Easing
Analysis,
Since Heaven
and He
Are One.

Emily –

mid-1860s

Emily changes "Beauty" to "Melody" and uses the lines "The Definition of Melody – is – / That Definition is none –" in the poem, "By my Window have / I for Scenery." The repetition of lines throughout this literary liaison shows how central revision or re-seeing is to Emily's creative process as she contemplates beauty, despair, love, neighborly affiliations, madness, desire — indeed, as she ponders all of life's experiences.

SECTION THREE

The Incidents of Love

LATE MIDDLE WRITINGS, MID-1860S TO MID-1870S

FROM THE MID-1860s to the mid-1870s, the collaborative nature of the literary, emotional bond is evident, for Emily's correspondence with Susan continues to include letter-poems, poems, and poems-in-progress. Many of the following missives include allusions to shared literary pleasures coupled with references to Emily and Susan's involvement in family concerns and in the daily business of their households. By the early 1870s, it is often the children and the household servants who carry the messages from Emily in the Homestead to Susan, next door.

The writings of this period call into question the biographical commonplace that Emily did not see Susan for years at a time. In fact, the contact between the two is deeply intimate and sustained. The letter-poems allude to unkempt appearance, shared cups of coffee, and private interludes, which Susan's daughter Martha described as taking place in the back hallway of the Homestead. Not only were the two regularly in each other's company at home, they were occasionally together in public. Flora White, a friend of Martha Dickinson Bianchi, remembered meeting Emily in the spring of 1872 at the Congregational Church, where Susan was a member. She described Susan seating Emily, remarking that Susan's quiet words to her beloved friend "seemed smilingly protective."[1]

During the 1860s and 1870s, the relationship between Emily and Susan deepens, matures, and solidifies. Both Emily and Susan have several correspondents with whom they exchange letters and poems, and discuss books and the details of their daily lives. However, no other correspondence of Emily's approaches that to Susan for its sheer volume, duration, and diversity. Many of the messages to Susan remain informal, inspired by emotion, an observation, a household concern, and the basic need to communicate in the most ordinary way with the object of love, comfort, and intellectual and creative inspiration.

As indicated in the Notes at the end of *Open Me Carefully*, in addition to sending poems to Susan, Emily sends work to Thomas Wentworth Higginson, Samuel Bowles, Elizabeth Holland, Fanny and Loo Norcross, Helen Hunt Jackson, and others. However, we can only assume that a love poem sent to the beloved has a very different impact from a version of the same poem sent to a friend or an editor.

A number of the following documents are written on scrap paper, which indicates the level of comfort and informality between the two women. Susan's "X's" and other notations are usually placed on the verso of a letter-poem or poem, and signal her editorial work as she later compiles her book of Emily's writings. Pinholes can be seen on the paper, suggesting that the messages are conveyed inside clothing or perhaps attached to gifts of bread, cake, fruit, or preserved in one of Susan's scrapbooks. Unlike letters and poems that Emily sends to other recipients, those preserved by Susan are often worn, suggesting Susan's numerous readings and re-readings. On the verso of one of the poems in this section ("The Crickets / sang"), Susan wrote a pair of stanzas of her own.

During the early 1870s, Austin replaces Edward Dickinson as treasurer of Amherst College, and Edward is elected to the General Court of Massachusetts. Susan takes annual autumn vacations with her children to visit her sister Martha and her brother-in-law John Smith in Geneva, New York. Susan also travels to Swampscott, Massachusetts, in the summer of 1873, and Emily writes to her there as the family vacations at the beach. As is evident throughout the correspondence, Emily's love and desire for Susan, and her playfulness with her, continue in the various stages of their lives. In one letter sent to Swampscott, Emily compares her feelings for Susan with Dante's passionate love of Beatrice, Jonathan Swift's love of Stella, and Mirabeau's love of Sophie de Ruffey.

On June 16, 1874, while serving a term in the State Legislature, Emily's father collapses and dies in his room at a Boston hotel. The following year, on the eve of the first anniversary of his death, Emily's mother suffers a debilitating stroke, requiring that Lavinia and Emily take over the household responsibilities for the Homestead as well as nurse their mother. Because no letters or letter-poems to Susan reflect on the death of Emily's father and the illness of her mother, it is likely that Emily and Susan speak face-to-face about these profound events, and that throughout these trying times Susan consoles Emily in person. Two months after Emily's mother falls ill, Susan gives birth to her third child, Gilbert (Gib).

120

Title divine, is mine.
The Wife without
the Sign –
Acute Degree
Conferred on Me –
Empress of Calvary –
Royal, all but the
Crown –
Betrothed, without
the Swoon
God gives us Women –
When You hold
Garnet to Garnet –
Gold – to Gold –
Born – Bridalled –
Shrouded –
In a Day –
Tri Victory –
"My Husband" –
Women say
Stroking the Melody –
Is this the Way –

Emily –

mid-1860s

121

It passes and we
stay.
A quality of loss
Affecting our
Content
As Trade had
suddenly encroached
Upon a Sacrament

Emily.

mid-1860s
Emily uses these lines to end her poem, "A Light exists in Spring." This poem appears to have been sent to Susan as a message as well as for her critical evaluation.

122

The Crickets
sang
And set the
Sun
And Workmen
finished One by
One
Their Seam the
Day upon –

The low Grass
loaded with the
Dew

The Twilight
stood, as Strangers
 do
With Hat in
Hand, polite and
new
To stay as if,
or go –

A Vastness, as
a Neighbor, came,
A Wisdom, without
Face, or Name,
A Peace, as
Hemispheres at
Home
And so the
Night became –
  Emily '

on verso in pencil, by Susan

 I was all ear
And took in strains that
 might create a seal
Under the lids of death

upside down

Despair is treason
 toward Man
And blasphemy
 to Heaven.

mid-1860s
Emily and Susan found one another's work mutually inspirational.

123

We do not know the time
we lose –
The awful moment is
And takes its' fundamental
place
Among the Certainties –

A firm appearance still
inflates
The card – the chance –
the friend –
The spectre of solidities
Whose substances are sand –

mid-1860s

124

[The] A Diamond on
[A]
the Hand
To Custom Common
grown
Subsides from its'
significance
The Gem were
best unknown '
Within a Seller's
Shrine
How many sight

and sigh
And cannot, but
for
are mad with fear
That any other buy.
Lest some one else
should
Lest Richer People
buy –

late 1860s
This poem and the next are among the drafts sent to Susan, indicating that the exchange in the creation of "Safe in their Alabaster Chambers" was indeed routine.

125

I fit for them –
I seek the Dark
Till I am thorough
fit.
The labor is a sober
one
With the austerer
sweet ' an – this '
With this sufficient
Sweet

That abstinence of mine
me
produce
A purer food for them,
if I succeed,

If not I had
The transport of
the Aim.

late 1860s

126

Going is less, Sister,
long gone from you,
yet We who take
all with Us, leave
not much behind '
Busy missing you '
I have not tasted
Spring – Should
there be other Aprils,
We will perhaps dine –
Emily '

late 1860s
It is possible that Emily writes this when Susan travels to Stamford, Connecticut, in April 1868 to visit her friends Joseph and Laura Lyman, authors of *The Philosophy of Housekeeping*.

127

Susan's Idolater keeps
a Shrine for Susan.

late 1860s

128

Dear Sue'
Just say one
word,
"Emily has not
grieved me"
Sign your name
to that and
I will wait for
  the rest –

late 1860s

The text of this letter-poem continues onto the verso, with the address, "Sue." When the sheet is unfolded, it appears that Susan has signed her name to this agreement.

129

That my
sweet Sister
remind me
to thank her
for herself
is valuablest.
      Emily '

late 1860s

130

The murmuring of
Bees, has ceased
But murmuring of
some
Posterior, prophetic,
Has simultaneous come.
The lower metres
of the Year
When Nature's laugh
is done
The Revelations of
the Book
Whose Genesis was June.
Appropriate Creatures
to her Change
The Typic Mother
sends
As Accent fades
to interval
With separating
Friends
Till what we
speculate, has been
And thoughts we
will not show '
More intimate with
us become
Than Persons,
that we know.
Emily.

late 1860s

131

There is another Loneliness
That many die without,
Nor want or friend occasions it,
Or circumstance or lot.

But nature sometimes, sometimes thought
And who so it befall
Is richer than could be divulged;
By mortal numeral.

late 1860s

132

A Mine there is
no Man would own
But must it be
conferred,
Demeaning by
Exclusive Wealth
A Universe beside –

Potosi never to
be spent
But hoarded in
the Mind
What Misers
wring Their
hands Tonight

For Indies in
the Ground!
Emily '

late 1860s
Emily refers to the Bolivian city, "Potosi," and the East "Indies," which were associated with great wealth. In December 1868, Samuel Bowles was arrested for libel and jailed for a night, while his friends rallied for him. Two days later, Emily's father Edward wrote a letter to Bowles saying that he would rather have been there that night "than to have owned the mines of Potosi."

133

Exhiliration is the Breeze
That lifts us from
the Ground
And leaves us in
another place
Whose statement is
not found –

Returns us not,
but after time
We soberly descend
A little newer for
the term
Upon Enchanted Ground –

Best Witchcraft is
Geometry
To the Magician's Mind –

His Ordinary Acts
are feats
To thinking of mankind .

late 1860s

The arrangement of these poems, separated with a line, resembles pages in the fascicles where Emily draws lines between poems. Susan does the same in manuscript copies of her own poems. Here Emily sends a sheet with drafts for Susan's evaluation.

134

The things of
which we want
the proof are those
we knew before –

late 1860s

135

Dont do such
things, dear Sue –
The "Arabian
Nights" unfit
the Heart for
its' Arithmetic –
Emily –

late 1860s

136

Too cold is this
To warm with Sun –
Too stiff to bended
be,
To joint this Agate
were a work – feat –
Outstaring Masonry –
Defying – Appalling – Abashing
Beyond machinery –

How went the Agile
Kernel out
Contusion of the Husk
Nor Rip, nor wrinkle
indicate
But just an Asterisk.

late 1860s

137

Rare to the Rare – .
Her sovreign People
Nature knows as
well
And is as fond
of signifying
As if fallible –
Emily –

late 1860s

138

The Frost of
Death was on the
Pane,
"Secure your Flower"
said he.
Like Sailors
fighting with a Leak
We fought
Mortality.

Our passive Flower
we held to Sea –
   To Mountain,
To the Sun –
Yet even on his
Scarlet shelf
To crawl the
Frost begun –

We pried him
back
Ourselves we
wedged
Himself and her
between.
Yet easy as the
narrow Snake
He forked his
way along

Till all her
helpless beauty
bent

And then our
wrath begun –
We hunted him
to his Ravine
We chased him
to his Den –

We hated Death
and hated Life
And nowhere
was, to go –
Than Sea and
continent there
is
A larger – it
is Woe
Emily –

late 1860s
This was among the poems that Susan copied, which suggests that she planned to include it in her book of Emily's writings or that she intended to send it to a friend or an editor for printing.

139

The Duties of the
Wind are few,
To cast the ships
at Sea,
Establish March,
the Floods escort
And usher Liberty.
Emily –

late 1860s

Martha Dickinson Bianchi pasted this poem onto the half-title page of *The Single Hound* when she presented the book to her friend Laura Scull of Langhorne, Pennsylvania. Her inscription reads: "To Laura – In memory of our Immortals – with Martha's love – 1914."

140

To pile like
Thunder to
its' close
Then crumble
grand away
While Everything
created hid
This – would
be Poetry –

Or Love – the
two coeval come –
We both and
neither prove –
Experience either
and consume –
For None see
God and live –
Emily

1866 or later
Susan copied "None see God and live" into one of her journals.

141

A Spider sewed
at Night
Without a Light
Upon an Arc of
White.

If Ruff it was
of Dame
Or Shroud of Gnome
Himself himself
inform '

Of Immortality
His Strategy
Was Physiognomy.

Emily.

late 1860s
"Physiognomy" is the attempt to understand the character and spiritual qualities of an individual through the study of facial features. Martha Dickinson Bianchi made a point of mentioning that during the years when Susan and Emily were in their thirties, "My Mother was blessedly busy in her home," and one could see "Aunt Emily's light across the snow in the Winter gloaming, or burning late when she remained up all night, to protect her plants from chill." For "days and even weeks," the light was a "mute greeting between them supplemented only by their written messages." Emily sent or recited this poem to Loo and Fanny Norcross, and the Norcross sisters then sent the poem to Thomas Higginson.

142

The Face we
choose to miss –
Be it but for
a Day
As absent as
a Hundred
Years,
When it has rode
away '

on verso, in Susan's handwriting

The face we
  choose to miss
Be it but for
    a day
As absent as
A hundred years
When it has
 rode away –
          Emily.

late 1860s

In a penciled note, Susan's daughter Martha Dickinson Bianchi wrote: "The other side is Aunt Emily's own original m.s. This side is a copy in my mother's hand – ."

143

Safe Despair
it is that
raves –
Agony is
frugal –
Puts itself
severe away
For its' own
perusal –
Garrisoned no
Soul can be
In the front
of Trouble –
Love is one –
not aggregate –
Nor is Dying
double –
Emily .

1866 or later

144

To take away our
Sue leaves but a
lower World, her
firmamental quality
our more familiar
Sky.

It is not Nature –
dear, but those
that stand for
Nature.
The Bird would be
a soundless thing
without Expositor.
Come Home and
see your Weather.
The Hills are full
of Shawls, and I
am going every
Day to buy myself
a Sash.
Grandma moans for
Neddie, and Austin's
face is soft as
Mist when he
hears his name.
Tell "Dexter" I
miss his little
team.
I humbly try to fill
your place at the
Minister's, so faint
a competition, it
only makes them
smile.
Mattie is stern and
lovely_literary, they
tell me – a graduate
of Mother Goose
and otherwise ambi-
tious.

We have a new
man whose name
is Tim.
Father calls him
"Timothy" and the
Barn sounds like
the Bible.
Vinnie is still on
her "Coast Survey"
and I am so
hurried with Parents
that I run all
Day with my Tongue
abroad, like a
Summer Dog.
Tell Mattie for me
glad little Girl
is safe, and
congratulate minor
little Girl on her
priceless Mama.
Susan's
Emily.

autumn 1869
During the fall of 1869, Susan is visiting her sister Martha in Geneva, New York. Emily refers to her sister Lavinia ("Vinnie"), who is in Boston through the autumn. "Mattie" is Susan's three-year-old daughter, Martha. The "minor / little Girl" refers to Susan's infant niece, Elizabeth Throop Smith. The minister Emily alludes to is probably J.L. Jenkins, pastor of Amherst's Congregational Church.

145

The Props assist the
House
Until the House is
built
And then the Props
withdraw
And adequate, erect,
The House support
itself
And cease to recollect
The Augur and the
Carpenter –
Just such a retrospect
Hath the perfected
Life –
A past of Plank
and Nail
And slowness – then
the Scaffolds drop
Affirming it a Soul.
Emily.

late 1860s

146

I bet with every
Wind that blew
Till Nature

in chagrin
Employed a
Fact to visit
me
And scuttle
my Balloon –

late 1860s to 1870s

147

My Sue –
Loo and
Fanny will come
tonight, but need
that make a
difference?
Space is as the
Presence –

A narrow Fellow
in the Grass
Occasionally rides –
You may have
met him?
Did you not
His notice instant is –

The Grass divides
as with a Comb –
A Spotted Shaft
is seen,
And then it closes

at your Feet
And opens
further on_

He likes a
Boggy Acre_
A Floor too
cool for Corn_
But when a
Boy and Barefoot
I more than
once at Noon

Have passed
I thought a
Whip Lash
Unbraiding in the
Sun
When stooping
to secure it
It wrinkled
and was gone_

Several of
Nature's People
I know and they
know me
I feel for
them a transport
Of Cordiality

But never met
this Fellow
Attended or
alone
Without a

tighter Breathing
And Zero at
the Bone.

Emily.

about 1870
Loo and Fanny, Emily's cousins, are arriving in Amherst for a visit. The poem that Emily includes here was printed in the *Springfield Daily Republican* on February 14, 1866. It is possible that Emily now sends Susan the poem to replace the copy that Susan sent to the newspaper. From this letter-poem, it is clear that the two women are seeing each other face-to-face. In a letter postmarked March 17, 1866, Emily worried that Higginson would come across the poem in the *Republican* and think that she had been duplicitous concerning her intentions not "to print."

148

Who were
"the Father and
the Son"
[I] We pondered
when a Child –
And what had
they to do with
[me] us
And when [in]
[Terror] portentous told
With inference [alarming] appalling
By [Distance] Childhood fortified
[Through Accents
terrible as Death
To one that
never died]
[I] We thought, at

least they are
no worse
Than they have
been described.

Who are "the
Father and the
Son"
Did [I] we demand
Today
"The Father
and the Son"
himself
Would doubtless
[Answer me] specify –

But had they
[had] the felicity [readiness]
When [I] we desired
to know,
We better
Friends had
been, perhaps,
1 3
Than time to
4 2
be ensue –

We start – to
learn that We
believe
But once –
Entirely –
Belief, it does
not fit so well

When altered
frequently –

We blush,
that Heaven
if We [behold –] achieve
Event ineffable –
We shall
have shunned
until Ashamed
To own the
Miracle –

1870 or later
This ink draft has many penciled changes and is further documentation of Emily and Susan working over poems.

149

Best Witchcraft
is Geometry
To a Magician's
eye –
Emily –

early 1870s
This is a revision of a portion of a letter-poem sent to Susan in the late 1860s. The paper includes a cut that was probably intended for a flower. On the back of the letter is a shopping list written by Susan, which includes "ink" and "satin ribbon."

150

Oh Matchless
Earth , We
underrate the
chance to
dwell in Thee

early 1870s
Susan quotes these lines in a letter she writes to the *Springfield Republican* in 1906.

151

We meet
no Stranger
but Ourself.

early 1870s

152

Were not Day
of itself memo-
rable, dear Sue's
remembrance would
make it so
Emily.

early 1870s

153

The Wind begun to
knead the Grass
As Women do a Dough –
He flung a Hand full
at the Plain
A Hand full at the Sky.
The Leaves unhooked
themselves from Trees
And started all abroad –
The Dust did scoop
itself like Hands
And throw away the
Road –
        The Wagons
quickened on the Streets
The Thunders gossiped
low
The lightning showed
a Yellow Head
And then a livid Toe –
The Birds put up
the Bars to Nests
The Cattle flung to
Barns
Then came one
drop of Giant Rain
        And then as if
the Hands
That held the Dams
had parted hold
The Waters Wrecked

the Sky
But Overlooked my
Father's House
Just Quartering a Tree
Emily –

early 1870s

154

Lest any doubt
that we are glad
that they were born
Today
Whose having lived
is held by us
in noble Holiday
Without the date,
like Consciousness
or Immortality '
Emily '

early 1870s
In *Face to Face,* Martha Dickinson Bianchi notes that this was sent "To Sue with flowers on her birthday."

155

Trust is better
than Contract, for
One is still, but
the other moves.
Emily '

early 1870s

156

Has All – a
codicil?
Emily –

early 1870s

157

To see you
unfits for staler
meetings.
I dare not
risk an intemperate
moment before
a Banquet of
Bran.

early 1870s

158

To miss you, Sue,
is power.
The stimulus
of Loss makes
most Possession
mean.
To live lasts
always, but to
love is firmer
than to live.
No Heart that
broke but further
went than
Immortality.
The Trees keep
House for you
all Day and
the Grass looks
chastened.
A silent Hen
frequents the
place with
superstitious
Chickens – and
still Forenoons
a Rooster knocks
at your outer
Door.
To look that
way is Romance.
The Novel "out,"

pathetic worth
attaches to the
Shelf.
Nothing has gone
but Summer, or
no one that you
knew.
The Forests
are at Home –
the Mountains
intimate at
Night and arrogant
at Noon, and
lonesome Fluency
abroad, like
suspending Music.
Of so divine
a Loss
We enter but
the Gain,
Indemnity for
Loneliness
That such a
Bliss has been.
Tell Neddie
that we miss
him and cherish
"Captain Jinks."
Tell Mattie
that Tim's Dog
calls Vinnie's Pussy
names and I dont
discourage him.
She must come

Home and chase
them both and
that will make
it square.
For Big Mattie
and John, of
course a strong
remembrance.
I trust that
you are warm.
I keep your
faithful place.
Whatever throng
the Lock is
firm upon your
Diamond Door.
Emily.

September 1871
"Captain Jinks" refers to the horse marines in a popular song, and apparently was Emily's nickname for Ned, who enjoyed the family's horses. "Big Mattie" is Susan's sister, Martha Smith, and "John" is Martha's husband.

In the early 1870s, Ned, nearly ten, and Mattie, almost five, were old enough to travel and vacation with Susan. July 1871 was a difficult month: both children had the measles, and Ned, suffering from physical weakness and general ill health, was being treated by a doctor in Springfield, Massachusetts. Mary Bowles, who hosted Susan during these visits, reported in a letter to her son that "poor little Ned is having a hard time & does not look really so hale as when he was here last – and he does his best to keep up . . . they come down next week and I told Mrs D – that she had better bring Mattie with her and stay a little time for she too looked used up." Early in the fall the children accompanied Susan on her annual trip to Geneva, New York, to visit their aunt and uncle.

159

A prompt – executive
Bird is the Jay –
Bold as a Bailiff's
Hymn –
Brittle and Brief
in quality –
Warrant in every
Line –

Sitting a Bough
like a Brigadier
Confident and straight –
Much is the mien
of him in March
As a Magistrate –
Emily –

early 1870s
Susan also found blue jays a worthy topic for her own poems and wrote about a jay's "low loving notes" in "Amor" (1884).

160

My God – He sees
thee –
Shine thy best –
Fling up thy
Balls of Gold
Till every Cubit
play with thee
And every Crescent

hold –
Elate the Acre
at his feet –
Upon his Atom
swim –
Oh Sun, but
just a Second's
right
In thy long
Race with him!
Emily '

early 1870s

161

When I hoped,
I feared –
Since I hoped
I dared
Everywhere alone
As a Church
remain –
Spectre cannot
harm
Serpent cannot
charm
He is Prince of
Harm
Who hath suffered
him.
Emily '

early 1870s

162

Our Own
possessions,
though Our Own –
'Tis well to
hoard anew –
Remembering
the Dimensions
Of Possibility.

Emily –

early 1870s

163

Of Death
the Sharpest
function
That just
as we discern
The Excellence
defies us
Securest gathered
then
The Fruit
perverse to
plucking
But leaning
to the Sight
With the

Extatic limit
Of unobtained
Delight.

early 1870s

164

Sister
          Our parting
was somewhat
interspersed and
I cannot con-
clude which
went.
I shall be
cautious not to
so as to miss
no one.
Vinnie drank
your Coffee
and has looked
a little like you
since, which
is nearly a
comfort.
Austin has had
two calls and
is very tired _
One from
Professor Tyler,

and the other
from Father.
I am afraid
they will call
here.
Bun has run
away _
Dísaffection_
doubtless – as to
the Supplies.
Ned is a better
Quarter Master
than his vagrant
Papa.
The little Turkey
is lonely and
the Chickens
bring him to call.
His foreign
Neck in familiar
Grass is quaint
as a Dromedary.
I suppose the
Wind has
chastened the
Bows on Mattie's
impudent Hat
and the Sea
presumed as
far as he dare
on her Stratified
Stockings.
If her Basket

wont hold the
Boulders she
picks, I will
send a Bin.
Ned is much
lamented and
his Circus Airs
in the Rowen
will be doubly
sweet.
Bela Dickinson's
son is the only
Basso remaining.
It rains every
pleasant Day now
and Dickens'
Maggie's Lawn
will be green
as a Courtier's.
Love for your
Brother and
Sister _ please_
and the dear
Lords.
Nature gives
her love –
Twlight touches
Amherst with
his yellow Glove.
Miss me
sometimes, dear –
Not on most
occasions, but

the Seldoms
of the Mind.
Emily –

early 1870s
During summer months, Emily writes to Susan as Susan vacations with her family. This letter may have been sent to Long Branch, New Jersey, or to Swampscott, Massachusetts, where the next letter was sent.

165

Part to whom
Sue is precious
gave her a note
Wednesday, but as
Father omitted the
"Ocean House"
presume it is
still groping in
the Swampscott
Mail –
We remind her
we love her –
Unimportant fact,
though Dante
did'nt think so,
nor Swift, nor
Mirabeau.
Could Pathos
compete with
that simple
statement
"Not that we

loved him but
that he loved
us"?
Emily –

summer 1873
Emily refers to Dante's passionate love of Beatrice, Jonathan Swift's love of Stella, and Mirabeau's love of Sophie de Ruffey. The closing quotation is from 1 John 4:10: "... not that we loved God, but that he loved us."

166

The Butterfly
in honored Dust
Assuredly will lie
But none will
man's
pass the Catacomb
So chastened as
the Fly –
Emily '

mid-1870s
Emily probably intended this poem for her niece's and nephew's pleasure as well as for Susan's.

167

Without the
annual parting
I thought to
shun the

Loneliness that
parting ratifies.
How artfully
in vain!
Your Coffee
cooled un-
touched except
by random
Fly.
A one Armed
Man conveyed
the flowers.
Not all my
modest schemes
have so perverse
a close.
My love to
"Captain Jenks"
who forbore
to call.
If not too
uncongenial
to the Divine
Will, a Kiss
also for
Mattie.
"God is a
jealous God."
I miss the
Turkey's quaint
face – once
my grave
Familiar, also
the former

Chickens, now
forgotten Hens.
"Pussum" cries
I hear, but
it is too
select a grief
to accept solace.
Tell Mattie
Tabby caught
a Rat and it
ran away.
Grandpa caught
it and it
stayed.
He is the best
Mouser.
The Rabbit
winks at me
all Day, but
if I wink
back, he
shuffles a
Clover.
What Rowen
he leaves,
Horace will
pick for the
Cow.
This is the
final Weather.
The transport
that is not
postponed is
is stopping

with us all.
But Subjects
hinder talk.
Silence is all
we dread.
There's Ransom
in a Voice –
But Silence
is Infinity.
Himself have
not a face.

Love for
John and
Mattie.
Sister.

autumn 1873
Letters from this period show that Emily and Susan are in the habit of having coffee together. Susan is now visiting her sister Martha in Geneva, New York, as she did most autumns. In the quotation, Dickinson paraphrases Exodus: "I the Lord thy God am a jealous God." (20:5)

168

Dear Sue –
I would
have liked to
be beautiful and
tidy when you
came –
You will excuse
me, wont you,
I felt so sick.

How it would
please me if
you would come
once more, when
I was palatable.
Emily

mid-1870s

169

Had this one
Day not been ,
Or could it
cease to be
How smitten ,
how superfluous ,
Were every
other Day !

Lest Love
should value
less
What Loss
would value
more
Had it the
stricken privi -
lege ,
It cherishes
before .
Emily .

mid-1870s

170

Dear Sue '
It is
sweet you
are better .
I am greedy
to see you.
Your note was
like the Wind.
The Bible
chooses that
you know to
define the
Spirit .

A Wind that
rose though
not a Leaf
In any Forest
stirred,
But with
itself did cold
engage
Beyond the
realm of Bird.

A Wind
that woke
a lone Delight
Like Separation's
Swell –

mid-1870s

171

Trifles – like
Life – and
the Sun, we
Acknowledge
in Church,
but the Love
that demeans
them , having
no Confede –
rate , dies
without a
Term .

Emily'

mid-1870s

172

Never mind
dear –
Trial as a
Stimulus far
exceeds Wine
though it would
hardly be
prohibited as a
Beverage.

Emily.

mid-1870s

173

Two Lengths
has every Day –
It's absolute
extent
And Area
superior
By Hope or
  Horror lent –

Eternity will
be
Velocity or
Pause
At Fundamental
Signals
From Fundamental
Laws.

To die is
not to go –
On Doom's
consummate
Chart
No Territory
new is Staked –
Remain thou
as thou Art .

mid-1870s

Emily penciled a draft of the second stanza of this poem on the triangular flap of an envelope: "Eternity will / be / Velocity or Pause / Precisely as / the Candidate / Preliminary / was – / character." Martha Dickinson Bianchi notes that Susan kept this piece pinned to her workbox.

174

I think that the Root of
the Wind is Water –
It would not sound
so deep
Were it a Firmamental
Product –
Airs no Oceans keep –
Mediterranean intonations –
To a Current's Ear –
There is a maritime
conviction
In the Atmosphere –

1870s

175

Not One by
Heaven defrauded
stay –
Although he seem
to steal
He restitutes in
some sweet way
Secreted in his will –

1870s

176

To lose what we
never owned
might seem an
eccentric Bereavement
but Presumption
has its' Affliction
as actually as
Claim –

Emily

mid-1870s

177

The incidents of
Love
Are more than
its' Events –
Investment's best
Expositor
Is the minute
Per Cents –
Emily –

mid-1870s

SECTION FOUR

To Be Susan Is Imagination

LATE WRITINGS, MID-1870S TO MAY 1886

FROM THE MID-1870s until Emily's own death on May 15, 1886, the correspondence from Emily to Susan features dramatic personal statements and remarkable manuscript art. The quotations at the beginning of this section raise intriguing questions of literary identity. Single-line messages from various Shakespeare plays may be part of parlor or calendar games or they may indicate Emily's use of characters as diverse as Anthony and Horatio to convey her deepest desires to Susan. Certainly, the numerous letter-poems and poems that Emily sends to Susan during the end of Emily's life discount the popular claim that the two women had nothing to do with each other in these final years. The following writings feature many allusions to seeing and hearing Susan in the flesh, and they testify to her taking care of Emily during her illness.

The period begins shortly after the birth of Susan's youngest child Gib, and it reaches a tragic climax when the child dies from typhoid fever on October 5, 1883, at the age of eight. Susan's daughter Martha makes it clear that Emily's total seclusion occurs after — not before — Gib's death, which corrects the standard account that October 1883 is the only time Emily ventures to see Susan. According to Martha, Emily visits Susan and her niece and nephews regularly, and she is a distinct presence across the great lawn, either as a light burning late into the night or as a figure waving from the window. Martha describes her Aunt Emily as the "confederate in every contraband desire, the very Spirit of 'Never, Never Land'"[1]

A few weeks after Gib's death, Austin begins an affair with Mabel Loomis Todd, who moved to Amherst with her husband in 1881.

Originally a friend of Susan's, Mabel never meets Emily face-to-face, but she later presents herself as an authority on Emily's life and work and becomes the first editor of a printed volume of Dickinson's poetry. In fact it is Mabel Loomis Todd who sets in motion many of the fallacies that have since become Dickinson legend.

After the death of her son, Susan goes into seclusion, overwhelmed with grief. Emily also removes herself from public contact at this time, yet she continues to console Susan through her writing, her devotion and love as palpable as always.

This period in Emily's correspondence to Susan is marked by numerous other losses, beginning with the 1877 death of Elizabeth Lord, family friend and visitor to the Dickinson houses, and the 1878 death of Samuel Bowles, editor of the *Springfield Republican*. J.G. Holland, family friend, publisher and editor of *Scribner's,* dies in October 1881, and Emily's friend and spiritual confidant Charles Wadsworth dies in April 1882. In November of the same year, Emily's mother, Emily Norcross Dickinson, dies. Then in March 1884, Emily loses her friend Judge Otis Phillips Lord, and her literary friend and correspondent Helen Hunt Jackson dies in August 1885.

Austin suffers from malaria in 1883, and Emily falls ill immediately after Gib's death. Her health deteriorates in 1884, and she is eventually diagnosed with kidney ailments known as Bright's disease. Over the next year, she moves in and out of remission, and it is Susan who nurses Emily through her last days. In grief and illness, Emily writes profusely, and the letter-poems and poems she sends to Susan are profound, passionate, and encoded with feelings, memories, and literary allusions.

On May 15, 1886, Emily Dickinson dies at home. In the hours that follow, Susan prepares Emily's body for burial. She then writes an obituary for the *Springfield Republican* publicly declaring her admiration and love for her friend, neighbor, and sister-in-law, whom she will quote as a literary authority for the rest of her life. In her tributary essay, Susan presents Emily as a writer as well as a compassionate human being, and she pays homage to her originality, her brilliance, and her devotion to those she loved.

178

"Egypt – thou
knew'st " –

mid-1870s

Emily and Susan circulate literary quotations as commentary on events and relationships. Here Emily borrows from Shakespeare, using a line from Antony's speech to Cleopatra (III, xi, 56-61):

> Egypt, thou knew'st too well,
> My heart was to thy rudder tied by the strings,
> And thou shouldst tow me after. O'er my spirit
> Thy full supremacy thou knew'st, and that
> Thy beck might from the bidding of the gods
> Command me.

This may be part of a game based on their mutual love for Shakespeare, or from a daily Shakespeare calendar.

179

"For Brutus,
as you know,
was Caesar's
Angel."

mid-1870s

Again Emily quotes Shakespeare, this time using lines from *Julius Caesar* (III, ii, 183). Emily once wrote to an editor at the *Springfield Republican*: "He has found his Future who has found Shakespeare."

180

"Doth forget
that ever
he heard
the name
of Death."

mid-1870s
These are lines from Shakespeare's *Coriolanus* (III, i, 256-258):

> His heart's his mouth:
> What his breast forges, that his tongue must vent;
> And, being angry, does forget that ever
> He heard the name of death.

In this speech, Menenius Agrippa defends his friend Coriolanus. Emily's "talking in Shakespeare" reflects the literary consecration of her relationship with Susan.

181

Emily and all
that she has
are at Sue's
service , if of
any comfort
to Baby.
Will send
Maggie , if you

will accept
her –
Sister –

early August 1875

At the age of forty-four, Susan gives birth to her third child, Thomas Gilbert Dickinson (Gib). This letter-poem celebrates his arrival on August 1, 1875. "Maggie" is Margaret Maher. Born in Ireland in 1841, Maggie began working for the Dickinsons in 1869. She was especially protective of and trusted by Emily.

182

Only Woman
in the World ,
Accept a
Julep '

mid-1870s

183

A little
Madness in
the Spring
Is wholesome
even for the
King '
But God be
with the Clown –
Who ponders
this tremendous

scene,
This whole
Experiment of
Green,
As if it
were his own!

mid-1870s

184

Thank you,
dear, for the
"Eliot"
She is the
Lane to the
Indies , Columbus
was looking for.
Emily '

1870s
Emily thanks Susan for George Eliot's latest novel, *Daniel Deronda*. In a letter to Thomas Higginson, Emily writes that " 'Sue' smuggled it under my Pillow."

185

Not when we know,
the Power accosts,
The Garment of
Surprise
Was all our timid

Mother wore
At Home – in
Paradise –

mid-1870s

186

The Rat
is the
concisest
Tenant.
He pays no
Rent .
Repudiates
the Obligation –
On Schemes
intent

Balking our
Wit
To Sound
or Circumvent
Hate cannot
harm
A Foe so
reticent –
Neither Decree
prohibit him
Lawful as
Equilibrium.

mid-1870s

187

"Faithful to
the End"
Amended
From the
Heavenly
Clause
Constancy with
a Proviso
Constancy
Abhors –

mid-1870s

188

Susan knows
she is a Siren –
and that at a
word from her,
Emily would
forfeit Righteousness –
Please excuse
the grossness
of this Morning –
I was for a
moment disarmed –
This is the
World that opens

and shuts, like
the Eye of the
Wax Doll –

1876 or later

189

The healed Heart
shows it's shallow
scar
With confidential
moan –
Not mended by
Mortality
Are Fabrics truly
torn –
To go its'
convalescent way
So shameless is
to see
More genuine
were Perfidy
Than such
Fidelity –

1876 or later

190

’Tis not the
swaying frame
we miss ’
It is the
steadfast Heart,
That had it
beat a thousand
years,
With Love alone
had bent,
It’s fervor the
Electric Oar,
That bore it
through the Tomb,
Ourselves, denied
the privilege,
Consolelessly
presume –

1876 or later
The top two-thirds of the first leaf of this poem is cut away. It is possible that Susan may have removed something she considered too confidential, or that she may have placed lines of verse in one of her scrapbooks.

191

The Treason
of an Accent
Might vilify

the Joy –
To breathe –
corrode the
rapture
Of Sanctity
to be –

mid-1870s

192

The long sigh
of the Frog
Upon a Summer's
Day
Enacts intoxication
Upon the Revery –
But his receding
Swell
Substantiates a Peace
That makes the
Ear inordinate
For corporal
release –

mid-1870s

193

The ignominy
to receive – is

eased by the
reflection that
interchange of
infamies – is
either's Antidote.
Emily.

mid-1870s

194

Sue – This
is the last
flower –

To wane
without
disparagement
In a dissembling
hue
That will not
let the Eye
decide
If it abide
or no
is Sunset's –
perhaps – only. Emily

mid-1870s

195

To own a
Susan of
my own
Is of itself
a Bliss –
Whatever
Realm I
forfeit, Lord,
Continue
me in this!
Emily.

late 1870s

196

But Susan is
a Stranger yet –
The Ones who
cite her most
Have never scaled
her Haunted House
Nor compromised
her Ghost –

To pity those who
know her not
Is helped by the
regret
That those who

know her know
her less
The nearer her
they get –
Emily –

late 1870s

197

My Maker –
let me be
Enamored most
of thee –
But nearer
this
I more should
miss –

late 1870s

198

March is
the Month
of Expectation.
The Things
we do not
know –
The Persons
of prognostication

Are coming
now –
We try to
show becoming
firmness –
But pompous
Joy
Betrays us, as
his first
Betrothal
Betrays a
Boy.

—

late 1870s

199

Crisis is sweet and
yet the Heart
Upon the hither side
Has Dowers of Prospective
Surrendered by the Tried –
Withheld to the arrived –

Upside down

Witheld to the arrived –
Defamed – denied

In margin beside preceding lines

To Denizen denied
Inquire of the proudest
fullest
Rose closing
Triump
Which rapture – Hour –
Moment
she preferred
And she [would] will point
undoubtedly
tell you sighing – answer

The Transport of the

Bud – rapture rescinded
To her surrendered Bud
The Hour of her Bud –
session of
And she will point you
longingly
fondly – sighing
receding
To her rescinded Bud
Departed –
Receipted Bud
Expended

late 1870s

200

(115)
The inundation of
the Spring
+ Enlarges every
Soul –   +submerges
It sweeps the
tenement – [or s] away
But leaves the
Water whole –

In which the
Soul at first
+ estranged – + alarmed
Seeks +faintly for
its' Shore – + softly
But acclima-   gropes
ted – pines no more
For [its'] Peninsula –
    that
+ submerged –

+ [seeks furtive
    For its' shore]

sideways, on bottom right

Loses sight
Of aught
    aught Peninsular –

late 1870s
Plus signs and various alternatives for her final word choice indicate Emily's writing and revision process. Once again, the exchange of drafts suggests that Emily works on poems in various stages with Susan, showing unfinished work and welcoming Susan's reactions and feedback.

201

Where we
owe but a
little, we pay.
Where we
owe so much
it defies
Money, we
are blandly
insolvent.
Adulation is
inexpensive
Except to him
who accepts
it.
It has cost
him – Himself.
Emily.

late 1870s

202

I must wait
a few Days
before seeing
you – You are
too momentous.

But remember
it is idolatry,
not indifference.
Emily.

late 1870s

203

Susan –
Whoever blesses,
you always
bless – the last –
and often made
the Heaven of
Heavens – a sterile
Stimulus –
Cherish Power –
dear –
Remember that
stands in the
Bible between the
Kingdom and
the Glory, because
it is wilder
than either of
them –
Emily –

late 1870s

204

Susan –
The sweetest
acts both exact
and defy, gratitude,
so silence is all
the honor there is –
but to those who
[c]an estimate silence,
it is sweetly
enough –
In a Life that
stopped guessing,
you and I should
not feel at home

late 1870s

This letter-poem is torn at the bottom of the second leaf, and it is likely that the signature was removed by Susan to offer as a gift or to paste into a scrapbook, a common practice in the nineteenth century.

205

To the faithful
Absence is
condensed presence.
To others, but
there <u>are</u> no
others –

late 1870s

206

Sue – to be
lovely as you
is a touching
Contest, though
like the Siege
of Eden, impracticable,
Eden never
capitulates –
Emily '

1876 or later

207

Susan– I dreamed
of you, last
night, and send
a Carnation to
indorse it –
Sister of Ophir –
Ah Peru –
Subtle the Sum
That purchase
you –

1876 or later

In this late handwriting, Emily's "Y" looks like an "S," so that "you" in the second and final lines looks like "Sou," or Sue. "Ophir" is a biblical land rich in gold and precious stones (1 Kings 10:11).

208

In petto –

A Counterfeit –
a Plated Person –
I would not be –
Whatever Strata
of Iniquity
My Nature underlie –
Truth is good
Health – and
Safety, and the
Sky.
How meagre, what
an Exile – is a Lie,
And Vocal – when
we die –
Lothrop –

late 1870s
Emily signs this letter-poem "Lothrop," referring to the Amherst minister, Charles Dexter Lothrop, who was accused of domestic abuse by his three daughters. "In petto" means "in confidence." Both Susan and Austin were involved with the events of this case from 1876 through 1879, supporting the claims of the daughters and defending Samuel Bowles and the *Republican*'s reporting of the case. Emily speaks in the voice of the perpetrator, who was later excommunicated from the First Congregational Church in Amherst.

209

Sister spoke
of Springfield –
The beginning of
"Always" is more
dreadful than
the close – for
that is sustained
by flickering
identity –
His nature was
Future –
He had not yet
lived –
David's route was
simple – "I shall
go to him" –
Emily '

January 1878
"Springfield" refers to Samuel Bowles, who died on January 16, 1878. Emily sent this letter-poem to Susan after the funeral of their dear friend. In it she alludes to the Book of Samuel in the Old Testament, when, after the death of his son, David says: "But now he is dead, wherefore should I fast? can I bring him back again? I shall go to him, but he shall not return to me." (2 Samuel 12:23)

210

Those not live
yet
Who doubt to
live again –
"Again" is of
a twice
But this – is one –
The Ship beneath
the Draw
Aground – is he?
Death – so – the Hyphen
of the Sea –
Deep is the
Schedule
Of the Disk
to be –
Costumeless Consciousness,
That is he –

Easter.

late 1870s

Susan wrote "To read to friends" at the bottom of this letter-poem. Susan's interest in sharing Emily's poetry with others included the introduction of Emily's work to Mabel Loomis Todd, the editor of the first printed volume of Emily's poetry and Austin's lover. In an 1882 diary entry, written one year before the affair with Austin began, Loomis Todd jotted, "Went in the afternoon to Mrs. Dickinson's. She read me some strange poems by Emily Dickinson. They are full of power."

211

So gay a
Flower
Bereaves the
Mind
As if it were
a Woe –
Is Beauty an
Affliction – then?
Tradition
ought to know –

late 1870s

212

Emily is sorry for
Susan's Day –
To be singular
under plural
circumstances , is
a becoming heroism –
Opinion is a
flitting thing,
But Truth , outlasts
the Sun –
If then we cannot
own them both –

Possess the oldest
One –
Emily '

late 1870s

213

So sorry for
Sister's hardships –
"Make me thy
wrack when I come
back, but spare
me when I gang."
Emily '

late 1870s

214

Mrs Delmonico's
things were very
nice – Art has
a "Palate," as well
as an Easel –
Susan breaks
many Commandments,
but one she obeys –
"Whatsoever ye do,
do it unto the
Glory" –
Susan will be

saved –
Thank her –
Emily –

late 1870s

For Emily, Susan's delectable dinners make it seem as if Delmonico's, a fashionable New York restaurant, is right next door. The reference to Paul's injunction, "Whether therefore ye eat, or drink, or whatsoever ye do, do all to the glory of God" (1 Corinthians 10:31), uses New Testament rhetoric to describe the heights of taste achieved by Susan's dinners. The recipes that are among Susan's papers describe "A February Dinner" that includes "Caviar & toast, bermuda onion / Oysters on half-shell; horseradish; brown bread & butter / Clear soup, with noodle puffs / Timbales of salmon w/mayonnaise hearts / Creamed celery in cheese shell / Crown roast of lamb w/French peas; potato hearts / Ginger sherbet / Breast of roast duck w/orange slices & dressed chicory / Large ice-cream heart w/frozen roses; fancy cakes / Brie cheese, toasted wafers; coffee."

215

Susan –
A little overflowing
word
That any, hearing,
had inferred
For Ardor or
for Tears,
Though Generations
pass away,
Traditions ripen
and decay,
As eloquent
appears –
Emily –

late 1870s

216

The Sweets of
Pillage, can be known
To no one but
the Thief –
Compassion for
Integrity
Is his divinest
Grief –

1876 or later
It is likely that Emily sends this poem to Susan and to her niece and nephews, especially Ned. In the fall of 1880, Ned becomes a student at Amherst College, and pursues a partial course of study while living at home due to protracted health problems, including general weakness and epilepsy. Emily sends him several poems and notes during this time, including one in which she teases him about "that Pie you stole – well, this is that Pie's brother."

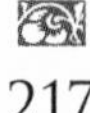

217

The Moon upon
her fluent Route
Defiant of a Roád –
The Star's
Etruscan Argument
Substantiate a God –

If Aims impel
these Astral Ones
The ones allowed
to know
Know that which

makes them as
forgot

As Dawn
forgets them –
now –

1870s to 1880s

218

The Devil – had he
fidelity
Would be the best
friend –
Because he has
ability –
But Devils cannot
mend –
Perfidy is the
Virtue
That would but he
resign
The Devil – + without
question
Were thoroughly
divine
– so amended –
were durably divine –

late 1870s to 1880s

219

That Susan
lives – is a
Universe which
neither going
nor coming
could displace –

---

spring 1880

During the spring of 1880, Susan and Austin are both unwell. Austin is suffering from malaria, a disease that he has already succumbed to twice, and Susan is described by a friend as "unstrung and nervous." To regain her strength, she travels to Providence, Rhode Island, for a two-week stay, and then she meets Austin and Ned in Boston. It is likely that Emily sends this letter-poem to Susan upon her return to Amherst.

220

Susan is a
vast and sweet
Sister, and
Emily hopes to
deserve her,
but not now –

Written sideways on top of page

Thanks
for the
profligate
little Box

that lacked
only
Cigars.

early 1880s

221

"Thank you"
ebbs – between us,
but the Basis
of thank you,
is sterling and
fond –
Emily'

early 1880s

222

Susan – I would
have come out
of Eden to open
the Door for you
if I had known
you were there.
You must knock
with a Trumpet
as Gabriel does,
whose Hands are
small as yours –

I knew he knocked
and went away –
I did'nt dream
that you did –
Emily'

early 1880s
Emily refers to the archangel Gabriel. Martha Dickinson Bianchi pointed out that her aunt sometimes addressed her mother as "You from whom I never run away." By apologizing for not being able to see Susan on one occasion, Emily suggests that there are other occasions when she will see her, indicating that Emily and Susan enjoyed face-to-face contact until the end of Emily's life.

223

Memoirs of Little
Boys that live –
"Were'nt you chasing
Pussy," said Vinnie
to Gilbert?
"No – she was chasing
herself" –
"But was'nt she
running pretty
fast"? "Well, some
slow and some
fast" said the
beguiling Villain –
Pussy's Nemesis
quailed –
Talk of "hoary
Reprobates"!
Your Urchin is
more antique in

wiles than the
Egyptian Sphinx –
Have you noticed
Granville's Letter
to Lowell?
"Her Majesty" has
contemplated you,
and reserves
her decision!

Emily'

early 1880s
Emily presents a playful exchange between her sister Lavinia and her youngest nephew, Gib, while alluding to James Russell Lowell, who served as minister to England in 1880, the year in which the second Earl of Granville took over the Foreign Office.

224

Susan.
To thank one
for Sweetness, is
possible, but for
Spaciousness, out
of sight –
The Competition of
Phantoms is

On separate page

inviolate –
Emily '

early 1880s

225

"Boast not"
myself "of Tomorrow"
for I "knowest
not what a"
Noon "may bring
forth" –

early 1880s

Emily adapts an exhortation from Solomon in the Old Testament: "Boast not thyself of tomorrow; for thou knowest not what a day may bring forth." (Proverbs 27:1) "Noon" or "day" often signifies a climactic event throughout Emily's letters and poems. It is possible that the phrases in this letter-poem are part of a word game that Emily and Susan are in the midst of playing or that the phrases represent a playful encoding of desire.

226

It was like
a breath from
Gibraltar to hear
your voice again,
Sue – Your
impregnable
syllables need
no prop, to stand –
The Loaf
for Ned, I will
send Wednesday
evening, unless
he prefer before –
If he would,

let him whisper
to me –
Emily'

early 1880s

227

How inspiriting
to the clandestine
Mind those Words
of Scripture,
"We thank thee
that thou hast
hid these things" –

Candor – my
tepid friend –
Come not to
play with me –
The Myrrhs, and
Mochas, of the
Mind
Are it's
iniquity –
Emily'

1880s

Though Emily rejects formal religion, she frequently uses the language of the Old Testament and the New Testament in a metaphorical way, to express social commentary as well as emotional and spiritual observations. This letter-poem alludes to Matthew (11:25): "At that time Jesus answered and said, I thank thee, O Father, Lord of heaven and earth, because thou hast hid these things from the wise and prudent, and hast revealed them unto babes."

228

I send My
Own, two answers –
Not one of
them so spotless
nor so strong
as her's – Sinew
and Snow in
one –
Thank her for
all the promise –
I shall perhaps
need it –
Thank her
dear power
for having come,
An Avalanche
of Sun! Emily –

1880s

This letter-poem echoes Emily's poem "I send Two Sunsets," which she wrote in the 1860s, twenty years earlier.

229

Dear Sue –
With the
Exception of
Shakespeare, you
have told me of
more knowledge

than any one living –
To say that sincerely
is strange praise –

early 1880s

230

Had "Arabi"
only read
Longfellow, he'd
have never been
caught –
          Khedive.

"Shall fold their
Tents like the
Arabs, and as
silently steal
away" ————

September 1882
"Arabi" refers to the Egyptian rebel Ahmed Arabi Pasha, who was defeated at Tel-el-Kebir, on September 13, 1882. Khedive served as the Turkish viceroy of Egypt from 1867 to 1914. Emily uses Longfellow's "The Day Is Done" to comment on current events.

231

No Brigadier
throughout the
year

So civic as the
Jay –
A Neighbor and
a Warrior too –
With shrill felicity
Pursuing Winds
That censure us
A Febuary Day –
The Brother of
the Universe
Was never blown
away –
The Snow and
he are intimate –
I've often seen
them play
When Heaven looked
upon us all
With such severity
I felt apology
were due to
an insulted Sky
Whose pompous
frown was nutriment
To their Temerity –
The Pillow of
this daring Head
Is pungent
Evergreens –
His Larder – terse
and Militant –
Unknown – refreshing
things –
His Character

a Tonic,
His Future a
Dispute –
Unfair an
Immortality
That leaves
this Neighbor
out___
Emily '

spring 1883

232

Will my great
Sister accept
the minutiae of
Devotion, with ti-
midity that it is
no more?
Susan's Calls are
like Antony's
Supper –
"And pays his
Heart for what
his Eyes eat,
only ' "
Emily '

1880s

The quotation from Shakespeare depicts the moment when Enobarbus describes Antony gazing with longing at Cleopatra: "And for his ordinary, pays his heart, / For what his eyes eat only." (*Antony and Cleopatra*, II, ii, 225-226)

233

To be Susan
is Imagination,
To have been
Susan, a Dream –
What depths
of Domingo
in that torrid
Spirit!
Emily '

1880s
Emily refers to Santo Domingo, well-known for its rum and for the bloody slave revolt that ushered in the nineteenth century.

234

Dear Sue –
The Vision
of Immortal
Life has been
fulfilled –
How simply at
the last the
Fathom comes!
The Passenger
and not the
Sea, we find
surprises us –
Gilbert rejoiced
in Secrets –

His Life was
panting with them –
With what menace
of Light he cried
"Dont tell, Aunt
Emily"! Now my
ascended Playmate
must instruct me.
Show us, prattling
Preceptor, but the
way to thee!
He knew no
niggard moment –
His Life was
full of Boon –
The Playthings of
the Dervish were
not so wild
as his –
No Crescent was
this Creature –
He traveled from
the Full –
Such soar, but
never set –
I see him in
the Star, and
meet his sweet
velocity in every-
thing that flies –
His Life was
like the Bugle,
which winds
itself away,

his Elegy an
Echo – his Requiem
Ecstacy –
Dawn and
Meridian in one.
Wherefore would
he wait, wronged
only of Night,
which he left
for us –
Without a spec-
ulation, our
little Ajax
spans the whole –
Pass to thy
Rendezvous of
Light,
Pangless except
for us,
Who slowly ford
the Mystery
Which thou hast
leaped across!
Emily –

October 1883

On October 5, 1883, Susan and Austin's seven-year-old son Gib dies from typhoid fever. Devastated by the death, Susan secludes herself for over a year and does not leave her home. Emily retreats as well. In an attempt to assuage the family's grief, Susan's other children, Martha and Ned, stop speaking their brother's name aloud.

235

Perhaps the
dear, grieved
Heart would
open to a
flower, which
blesses unre-
quested , and
serves without
a Sound.
Emily.

early October 1883

236

Dear Sue –
A Promise
is firmer than
a Hope, although
it does not hold
so much –
Hope never knew
Horizon –
Awe is the first
Hand that is
held to us –
Hopelessness in it's
first Film has not
leave to last –

That would
close the Spirit,
and no
intercession could
do that –
Intimacy with
Mystery, after great
Space, will usurp
it's place –
Moving on in
the Dark like
Loaded Boats
at Night, though
there is no
Course, there is
Boundlessness –
Expanse cannot
be lost –
Not Joy, but
a Decree
Is Deity –
His Scene,
Infinity –
Whose rumor's
Gate was shut
so tight
Before my Beam
was sown,
Not even a
Prognostic's push
Could make
a Dent thereon –

The World
that thou hast
opened
Shuts for thee,
But not alone,
We all have
followed thee –
Escape more
slowly
To thy Tracts
of Sheen –
The Tent is
listening,
But the Troops
are gone!
Emily –

early October 1883

237

Climbing to
reach the
costly Hearts
To which he
gave the worth,
He broke them,
fearing punishment
He ran away
from Earth –
Emily –

October 1883

238

The Heart
has many Doors –
I can but
knock –
For any sweet
"Come in"
Impelled to
hark –
Not saddened
by repulse,
Repast to me
That somewhere,
there exists,
Supremacy –
Emily –

late 1883

239

Thank Sister
with love, and
reserve an Apart –
ment for two
Cocks in the
Cocks
Thanksgiving plan –
ning –
Mattie is almost

with you –
The first section
of Darkness is
the densest, Dear,
After that, Light
trembles in –
You asked would
I remain?
Irrevocably, Susan –
I know no
other way –
Ether looks
dispersive, but
try it with
a Lever –

Emily –

late November 1883

240

Twice, when
I had Red
Flowers out,
Gilbert knocked,
raised his sweet
Hat, and asked
if he might
touch them –
Yes, and take
them too, I said,
but Chivalry

forbade him,
Besides, he
gathered Hearts,
not Flowers –
Some Arrows
slay but whom
they strike,
But this slew
all but him,
Who so
appareled his
Escape,
Too trackless
for a Tomb –

Emily —

late 1883 to early 1884

241

Dear Sue –
I was
surprised, but
Why? Is she
not of the
lineage of the
Spirit? I knew
she was beauti-
ful – I knew she

was royal, but
that she was
hallowed, how
could I surmise,
who had scarcely
seen her since
her deep Eyes
were brought in
your Arms to her
Grandfather's '
Thanksgiving?
She is a strange
trust – I hope
she may be saved –
Redemption Mental
precedes Redemp-
tion Spiritual.
The Madonna
and Child
descend from
the Picture '
while Creation
is kneeling
before the Frame –
I shall keep the
secret –
Emily –

about 1882
This letter-poem may refer to poems sent to Emily that were written by Susan's daughter Martha.

242

Dear Sue –
Your little
mental gallantries
are sweet as
Chivalry, which
is to me a
shining Word
though I dont
know its meaning –
I sometimes re-
member we are
to die, and
hasten toward
the Heart which
how could I woo

In margin on right side

in a rendezvous where there

In margin on left side

is no Face? Emily –

1880s

243

I felt it no
betrayal, Dear –
Go to my Mine

as to your own,
only more
unsparingly –
I can scarcely
believe that the
Wondrous Book
is at last to
be written, and
it seems like
a Memoir of
the Sun, when
the Noon is
gone –
You remember
his swift way
of wringing and
flinging away
a Theme, and
others picking it
up and gazing
bewildered after
him, and the
prance that
crossed his Eye
at such times
was unrepeatable –
Though the
Great Waters
sleep,
That they are
still the Deep,
We cannot doubt –
No Vacillating
God

Ignited this
Abode
To put it out –

I wish I could
find the
Warrington Words,
but during
my weeks of
faintness, my
Treasures were
misplaced, and
I cannot find
them – I think
Mr Robinson
had been left
alone, and
felt the opinion
while others were
gone –

Remember, Dear,
an unfaltering
Yes is my
only reply to
your utmost
question –

With constancy,
Emily '

about 1884
The "Wondrous Book," "Memoir of the Sun," refers to biographer George S. Merriam's *The Life and Times of Samuel Bowles* (1885). With "Go to my Mine / as to your own," Emily tells Susan that she does not mind that Merriam was given access to personal information about their friend Samuel Bowles, for

which Emily was a source. This letter-poem shows that Emily continues to mourn and celebrate Bowles' life. She meditates on the words of William S. Robinson (known as "Warrington" in the *Springfield Republican*): "This life is so good, that it seems impossible for it to be wholly interrupted by death."

244

Dear Sue –
One of
the sweetest
Messages I ever
received, was,
"Mrs Dickinson
sent you this
Cardinal Flower,
and told me
to tell you
she thought
of you."
Except for
usurping your
Copyright –
I should
regive the
Message, but
each Voice
is it's own –
Emily –

1880s

245

That any
Flower should
be so base
as to stab
my Susan,
I believe un-
willingly –
"Tasting the
Honey and
the Sting", should
have ceased
with Eden –
Choose Flowers
that have no
Fang, Dear –
Pang is the
Past of Peace –

Sister –

about 1884
It is possible that this letter-poem refers to Austin's ongoing affair with Mabel Loomis Todd, which began less than three months after Gib's death. Mabel had been Susan's friend.

246

Morning
might come
by Accident –
Sister –

Night comes
by Event –
To believe the
final line of
the Card would
foreclose Faith –
Faith is Doubt.

Sister –
Show me
Eternity , and
I will show
you Memory –
Both in one
package lain
And lifted
back again –

Be Sue, while
I am Emily –
Be next, what
you have ever
been, Infinity –

1880s

247

No Words
ripple like
Sister's –
Their Silver
genealogy is

very sweet
to trace –
Amalgams
are abundant,
but the lone
student of
the Mines
adores Alloyless
things –
Emily –

1880s

248

Tell the Susan
who never
forgets to be
subtle , every
Spark is
numbered –

The farthest
Thunder that
I heard
Was nearer
than the Sky,
And rumbles
still,
Though torrid
Noons
Have lain

their Missiles
by –
Emily –

1880s
This letter-poem reflects the nineteenth century belief in electricity and its frictions as a life force.

249

Who is it seeks
my Pillow Nights,
With plain in-
specting face.
"Did you" or
"Did you not,"
to ask'
'Tis "Conscience,"
Childhood's
Nurse –

With Martial
Hand she
strokes the
Hair
Upon my
Wincing Head –
"All" Rogues
"shall have
their part in"
what –
The Phosphorus
of God –

mid-1880s

Here Emily alludes to the New Testament scripture — "But the fearful, and unbelieving and the abominable, and murderers, and whoremongers, and sorcerers, and idolators, and all liars, shall have their part in the lake which burneth with fire and brimstone: which is the second death." (Revelation 21:8)

250

Dear Sue –
I could
send you no
Note so sweet
as the last
words of
your Boy –
"You will look
after Mother"?
Emily '

summer 1885
Emily probably writes this note just before Ned leaves to vacation at Lake Placid in the Adirondacks. By this time Emily's final illness, called Bright's disease, is in remission. She is very ill in the fall of 1884, recovers later that year, and is well through the summer of 1885.

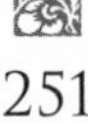

251

The World
hath not
known her, but
I have known
her, was the
sweet Boast

of Jesus –
The small Heart
cannot break –
The Ecstasy of
it's penalty
solaces the
large –
Emerging from
an Abyss, and
re-entering it '
that is Life,
is it not,
Dear?

The tie between
us is very
fine, but a
Hair never
dissolves.

Lovingly '

Emily '

late 1885
Emily falls ill again in November 1885. This letter-poem suggests that even death cannot disengage Emily from Susan nor Susan from Emily.

252

Dear Sue –
The Supper
was delicate
and strange –

I ate it with
compunction
as I would
eat a Vision –
The Blossoms
only were too
hearty – those
I saved for
the Birds –
How tenderly
I thank you –
I often hope
you are better –
Beneath the
Alps the
Danube runs –

late 1885
A section of this manuscript is torn away. Attached to this letter-poem is a note from Susan on blue-ruled paper, which says, "Signature Taken out to give a begging friend." The practice of giving signatures as gifts was common in the nineteenth century. This signature, from one of Emily's late letters, would have been a particularly precious offering from Susan.

253

I was
just writing
these very
words to you,
"Susan fronts
on the Gulf
Stream," when

Vinnie entered
with the Sea –
Dare I touch
the Coincidence?
Do you remem-
ber what whis-
pered to
"Horatio"?
Emily –

1886
Emily conveys her feelings to Susan through the innuendo of Shakespeare's *Hamlet*, when Horatio hears rumors of war and ill fortune.

254

How lovely
every Solace!
This long,
short, penance
"Even I regain
my freedom
with a Sigh"
Emily –

early 1886
According to Susan's daughter Martha, this letter-poem is "One of the latest." Emily quotes the final lines of Lord Byron's "The Prisoner of Chillon." Throughout Emily's final illness, Susan is her constant caretaker. Martha Dickinson Bianchi described the months before Emily's death: "The rest of the winter was spent in the country with books and music, still consciously making adjustment of being a family of four not five; and though Susan was giving us the happiest times in reach, we realized that she was not only far from strong herself, but under a shadow of apprehension about Aunt Emily. We carried the little notes back and forth as we always had."

CODA

EMILY DICKINSON lost consciousness on May 13th or 14th and died a little after 6:00 in the evening on May 15, 1886. The cause of death was diagnosed as Bright's disease resulting in kidney failure.

A neighbor and friend of the Dickinsons who was with Lavinia when Emily died gave her son the following account: "Just after dinner Vinnie sent over word — if I could come over I might see Miss Emily — and very glad was I of the privilege — She looked more like her brother than her sister, with a wealth of auburn hair and a very spirituelle face — She was robed in white — with a bunch of violets at her throat.... Sue & Emily were friends from girlhood and Vinnie was perfectly satisfied that Sue should arrange everything knowing it would be done lovingly as well as tastefully."

It is no surprise that it was Susan who swaddled Emily's body for burial, "arranged violets and a pink cypripedium at Emily's throat and covered her white casket with violets and ground pine," and "lined the grave with boughs."[1] Susan wrote the following commemorative paragraphs within hours of Emily's last breath. Printed in the *Springfield Republican*, Susan's obituary, "Miss Emily E. Dickinson of Amherst," publicly voiced her regard for her beloved friend. Susan's memoir portrays a strong, brilliant, and loving woman given to a life of thinking and writing, and fully involved with her family, her household, and the community in which she lived.

Miss Emily E. Dickinson of Amherst

The death of Miss Emily E. Dickinson, daughter of the late Edward Dickinson, at Amherst on Saturday, makes another sad inroad on the small circle so long occupying the old family mansion. It was for a long generation overlooked by death, and one passing in and out there thought of old-fashioned times, when parents and children grew up and passed maturity together, in lives of singular uneventfulness unmarked by sad or joyous crises. Very few in the village, except among older inhabitants, knew Miss Emily personally, although the facts of her seclusion and her intellectual brilliancy were familiar Amherst traditions. There are many houses among all classes, into which her treasures of fruit and flowers and ambrosial dishes for the sick and well were constantly sent, that will forever miss those evidences of her unselfish consideration, and mourn afresh that she screened herself from close acquaintance. As she passed on in life, her sensitive nature shrank from much personal contact with the world, and more and more turned to her own large wealth of individual resources for companionship, sitting thenceforth, as some one said of her, "in the light of her own fire." Not disappointed with the world, not an invalid until within the past two years, not from any lack of sympathy, not because she was insufficient for any mental work or social career — her endowments being so exceptional — but the "mesh of her soul," as Browning calls the body, was too rare, and the sacred quiet of her own home proved the fit atmosphere for her worth and work. All that must be inviolate. One can only speak of "duties beautifully done"; of her gentle tillage of the rare flowers filling her conservatory, into which, as into the heavenly Paradise, entered nothing that could defile, and which was ever abloom in frost or sunshine, so well she knew her subtle chemistries; of her tenderness to all in the home circle; her gentlewoman's grace and courtesy to all who served in house and grounds; her quick and rich response to all who rejoiced or suffered at home, or among her wide circle of friends the world over. This side of her nature was to her the real entity in which she rested, so simple and strong was her instinct that a woman's hearthstone is her shrine.

Her talk and her writings were like no one's else, and although she never published a line, now and then some enthusiastic literary friend would turn love to larceny, and cause a few verses surreptitiously obtained to be printed. Thus, and through other natural ways, many saw and admired her verses, and in consequence frequently notable persons paid her visits, hoping to overcome the protest of her own nature and gain a promise of occasional contributions, at least, to various magazines. She withstood even the fascination of Mrs. Helen Jackson, who earnestly sought her co-operation in a novel of the No Name series, although one little poem somehow strayed into the volume of verse which appeared in that series. Her pages would ill have fitted even so attractive a story as "Mercy Philbrick's Choice," unwilling though a large part of the literary public were to believe that she had no part in it. "Her wagon was hitched to a star" — and who could ride or write with such a voyager? A Damascus blade gleaming and glancing in the sun was her wit. Her swift poetic rapture was like the long glistening note of a bird one hears in the June woods at high noon, but can never see. Like a magician she caught the shadowy apparitions of her brain and tossed them in startling picturesqueness to her friends, who, charmed with their simplicity and homeliness as well as profundity, fretted that she had so easily made palpable the tantalizing fancies forever eluding their bungling, fettered grasp. So intimate and passionate was her love of Nature, she seemed herself a part of the high March sky, the summer day and bird-call. Keen and eclectic in her literary tastes, she sifted libraries to Shakespeare and Browning; quick as the electric spark in her intuitions and analyses, she seized the kernel instantly, almost impatient of the fewest words by which she must make her revelation. To her life was rich, and all aglow with God and immortality. With no creed, no formalized faith, hardly knowing the names of dogmas, she walked this life with the gentleness and reverence of old saints, with the firm step of martyrs who sing while they suffer. How better note the flight of this "soul of fire in a shell of pearl" than by her own words?—

Morns like these, we parted;
Noons like these, she rose;
Fluttering first, then firmer,
To her fair repose.

KEY TO MATERIALS

SYMBOLS USED TO IDENTIFY MANUSCRIPTS

A	Manuscripts at Amherst College will be indicated by this initial and the library catalog number.
"Annals"	Dickinson, Susan. "Annals of the Evergreens." Box 9. Dickinson Papers. Houghton Library, Harvard University, Cambridge, Massachusetts.
Brown	Manuscripts and other documents in the Martha Dickinson Bianchi Collection, John Hay Library, Brown University, Providence, Rhode Island.
H	Manuscripts at the Houghton Library, Harvard University, Cambridge, Massachusetts, will be indicated by this initial and the library catalog letter and/or number.
Morgan	Manuscripts at the Morgan Library, New York, New York.
Princeton	Manuscripts at the Princeton University Library, Princeton, New Jersey.
Smith	Manuscripts at the Neilson Library, Smith College, Northampton, Massachusetts.
Yale	Manuscripts at the Beinecke Library, Yale University, New Haven, Connecticut.

ABBREVIATIONS OF FREQUENTLY CITED SOURCES

AB	Bingham, Millicent Todd. *Ancestors' Brocades: The Literary Debut of Emily Dickinson.* New York: Harper & Brothers Publishers, 1945.
CP	Bianchi, Martha Dickinson and Alfred Leete Hampson, editors. *The Complete Poems of Emily Dickinson.* Boston: Little, Brown, 1924.
FF	Bianchi, Martha Dickinson. *Emily Dickinson Face to Face: Unpublished Letters With Notes and Reminiscences.* Boston: Houghton Mifflin Publishers, 1932.
L	Johnson, Thomas H. and Theodora Ward, editors. *The Letters of Emily Dickinson.* Cambridge: Belknap Press of Harvard University

Press, 1958. References to this edition will use this initial and give the number assigned by Johnson.

LL Bianchi Martha Dickinson. *The Life and Letters of Emily Dickinson.* Boston: Houghton Mifflin, 1924.

P Johnson, Thomas H., editor. *The Poems of Emily Dickinson.* Cambridge: Belknap Press of Harvard University Press, 1955. References to this edition will use this initial and give the number assigned by Johnson.

PF This refers to the Prose Fragments printed in Volume III, *Letters* (911-929). Citations will use these initials and give Johnson's number.

SH Bianchi, Martha Dickinson, editor. *The Single Hound: Poems of a Lifetime.* Boston: Little, Brown, and Company, 1914.

YH Leyda, Jay. *The Years and Hours of Emily Dickinson.* New Haven and London: Yale University Press, 1960.

NOTES

Citations for the following Houghton call numbers should be translated as follows:

H80b	MS Am 1118.3 (80b)
H L2	MS Am 1118.4 (L2)
HB1	MS Am 1118.5 (B1)
H SH	EDR 1.3.18
H ST	bMS Am 1118.95 Box 12
H Box 8	bMS Am 1118.95 Box 8
Photostats	MS Am 1118.99b

Watermarks and embossments are described using symbols from the Houghton Library's Manuscript Condition Survey. Our special thanks to Jana Dambrogio for compiling these facts about the manuscripts and their present state.

INTRODUCTION

1 H L20; L 93.

2 *Springfield Republican* May 18, 1886; *Writings by Susan Dickinson,* ed. Smith et al. Dickinson Electronic Archives.

3 iii.

4 Letter to Richard Watson Gilder, December 31, 1886.

5 Letter to Higginson, December 1890.

6 December 1890 letter.

7 H Lowell Autograph; 14 March 1891 to William Hayes Ward; *Writings by Susan Dickinson.*

8 *Poems* 1568n.

9 H Lowell Autograph, 8 February 1891; *Writings by Susan Dickinson.*

SECTION ONE NOTES

1 YH I, 183.
2 YH I, 212.
3 YH 1:267.
4 A 596, L 109.
5 A 597, L 110.
6 A 608, L 128, A 597, L 119.
7 YH 1:302-303.
8 YH 1:315.
9 YH 1:316.

1. Ink, gilt-edged, embossed "PARIS" (I). "Susie Gilbert" on verso, and "Read – No" penciled in Susan's handwriting, probably much later. That notation may indicate a decision not to read this letter to friends at a gathering in her home or not to include this letter in her book of Emily's writings. [H B131, L 38. *FF* 186-187.]
2. Ink, one sheet, four pages, end of letter may be missing. Coffee stains (rings of mug) are on manuscript, perhaps from Susan. Text of every paragraph has faint penciled lines, as if someone (presumably Susan) were reading and marking passages for editorial purposes. A calligraphic "g" in "hight" underlines the first part of the word in the "last" sentence (last of the surviving holograph). Ellipsis indicates end of letter may be missing. Thomas Johnson omits "left" from the line, "for there will be none left to interpret..." [H L5, L 56. *FF* 205-208.]
3. Ink, one sheet, four pages, multiple folds, faint lines across text. "G's" in "ugly things" dramatically underline letters preceding them. Johnson omits the article "a" before "a broken back." [H L10, L 73. *FF* 182-184, in part.]
4. Ink, one sheet, four pages, folded in half. "Susie" on verso, and "No" in Susan's handwriting. Johnson creates a final paragraph from the marginalia. [H L22, L 74.]
5. Ink, blue paper, embossed "J Prout / Stationer / Worcester" (JFJ), multiple folds. "Chuck" or "Church" penciled in Susan's handwriting across the last page. Here and on other letters "Chuck" may mean that Susan has not selected a letter or a section to read or to include in her book of Emily's writings. There is a blot of ink where Emily writes, "Dont see the blot." Exclamation mark after "him" after upside-down marginalia is inverted. A letter written to Austin Dickinson at the same time, beginning, "I will write while they've gone to meeting," erases or cuts away all references to Susan. Johnson omits "would" in the first sentence: "when the world and the cares of the world would try so hard ..." and he records "did'nt" rather than "didn't." He forms a paragraph from the

marginalia and places it after the signature. [H L9, L 77. *FF* 177-181, in part.]

6. Ink, embossed "Paris" (SFHBP), faint pencil marks across paragraphs, folded in half, then in thirds, very worn. In the first paragraph, last sentence, Johnson mistakenly transcribes "much" instead of "such," and at the end of the letter he regularizes Dickinson's one quotation mark for two quotations in: ". . . forever . " Herein. . . ." [H L13, L 85. *FF* 197-200, in part.]
7. Ink, embossed "Superfine" (SFHBP), folded in half, then in thirds, and worn. Faint pencil lines in Susan's handwriting cross the body of text; "Baltimore" at end of first sentence; and "Chuck" or "Church" across the text of the first two sentences. Johnson omits the article "a" from "where I have none – and a sister . . ." [H L18, L 88. *LL* 20, three sentences in part; *FF* 213-215, in part.]
8. Ink, small sheet, folded in thirds, bottom third torn away. Johnson omits "little" from the last sentence, "till this little heart. . . ." [H B173, L 92. *LL* 27, in small part, and altered.]
9. Ink, embossed "Paris" (SFHBP), one sheet, four pages, folded in half, then in thirds. "Dont" and "CFS" or "CPS" are scribbled across paragraph beginning "God is good, Susie." Emily's handwriting is noticeably different. Underlinings are very wavy, calling attention to themselves. Johnson mistranscribes Dickinson's "This union, my dear Susie, by which two lives are one" as "These unions"; he prints "if that great blessedness" instead of Emily's "of that great blessedness"; in the last paragraph before the signature Johnson prints "it had no parting," rather than "it has no parting more"; he transcribes "gather" as "gathers" and omits the word "me" from "if they promise me not to lose you." [H L20, L 93. *LL* 43, in part.]
10. Ink, no embossment, one sheet, four pages, lightly ruled, folded in thirds, pinholes, holes on each third similar to some of those made on the fascicles for binding. Addressed "Miss Susan H. Gilbert./40-Lexington St./Baltimore./Md-" "May want again," in Susan's or Martha Dickinson Bianchi's handwriting just above the address. A pencil line down the left side of text on the third leaf marks the passage from "Dear Susie, I have tried hard" to "never slumbers nor sleeps"; and a heavier line on the left side of the postscript marks "Why cant I be a Delegate." Johnson transcribes "fears" as "years" in the first paragraph. [H L2, L 94. *FF* 215-217, in part.]
11. Ink, no embossment, one sheet, four pages, folded into rectangles. Penciled lines across the final three paragraphs. Dashes dramatically point down. Johnson mistranscribes "I'd" for "I'll" in the sixth paragraph. [H L7, L 96, *FF* 217-219, in part.]

12. Ink, gilt-edged, no embossment, two sheets torn precisely down left side, making small leaves, multiple folds, pinholes, and rust marks from paper clips. [H B176, L 97. *LL* 55, in part, with changes.]
13. Ink, embossed XSTR, multiple folds, quite worn. Lines penciled across paragraphs from "It made me feel so lonely" to "At Dover"; "Manchester" (where Susan was visiting) penciled above the date. "T's" in this letter have an extraordinary flair, and most of the dashes are noticeably longer than in previous missives. "X" on verso in Susan's handwriting. [H L16, L 102. *FF* 220-223, in part, with changes.]
14. Ink, no embossment, one sheet, four pages, folded in rectangles. Lines penciled across second, fifth, sixth, and eighth paragraph. In the first paragraph, Emily uses "it" to refer to her emotional "heart" in a way that recalls her use of "it" in the "Master" letter Johnson calls the third and Franklin designates as the second. [H L8, L 103. *FF* 188-189, in part.]
15. Pencil, no embossment, a torn half sheet, folded in fourths, paste marks. Line between stanzas drawn by Emily, which parallels Susan's practice of putting lines between stanzas in her own poems. The dash after "Comrade" points up to the right, heightening the excited, exclamatory tone of the heading's command. Susan transcribed this poem twice. There is another version of this poem in the fascicles. [H B73, H ST 23e, H ST 24, P 4. *Poems* (1896) 200, titled "Eternity"; *LL* 78-79.]
16. Ink, embossed, one sheet, four pages, folded in half, then in thirds. Handwriting is markedly shaky. Lines penciled through all paragraphs. Johnson mistranscribes "shadow" in the sixth paragraph as "shadows." [H L4, L 107. *FF* 190-192, in part.]
17. Pencil, embossed with capitol building (CNGRSS), "Congress" printed, folded in thirds, very worn, paste marks. "Susie" on verso. [H B152, L 135. *FF* 220, in part.]
18. Ink, embossed (BTH), folded in thirds, penciled lines across last five paragraphs. Over paragraph beginning "To get you all once more," "Shyness" penciled in Susan's handwriting. Emily's handwriting is noticeably shaky, and an ink blot appears over the word "beat" in the seventh paragraph. Johnson omits the clause "I flew – " from the second sentence. [H L19, L 154. *LL* 31, in part, with changes.]
19. Ink, embossed (SLP), blue-ruled, one sheet, two leaves, folded in rectangles. Lines penciled across most paragraphs; "Chuck" or "Church" penciled across the fifth paragraph. Johnson transcribes "good" instead of "great" in the next to last paragraph. [H L6, L 176. *FF* 211-213, in part.]
20. Ink, embossed (SLP), one sheet, two leaves, blue-ruled, rust marks from paper clips. Illegible note in Susan's handwriting, perhaps "Last" (?), penciled in the upper margin of first page, and penciled lines cross

paragraphs. Johnson forms final paragraph with the marginalia following the signature. [H L1, L 177. *LL* 33-34, in small part; *FF* 200-202 in part.]

21. Ink, embossed (SLP), one sheet, two leaves, blue-ruled, folded in rectangles, lines penciled through paragraphs. "Washington" in Susan's handwriting on top of the first page and across lines in sixth paragraph beginning "Vinnie met the other evening." The envelope, addressed by Edward Dickinson "Miss Susan H. Gilbert. / Amherst. / Mass," has been torn open, sealing wax is still attached, and bears paste marks on the verso, indicating preservation in a scrapbook. [H L14, L 178. *FF* 202-205, in part.]

SECTION TWO NOTES

1 H Lowell Autograph, 14 March 1891 to William Hayes Ward, *Writings by Susan Dickinson*, ed. Smith et al.

—

22. Ink, gilt-edged, embossed coat of arms (SMLY), one sheet, four pages, multiple folds, poem on pages 3 and 4, with corners turned to be inserted into scrapbook. Handwriting appears shaky. "Young" is penciled in Susan's handwriting on fourth page, "X" on verso. [H L17, P 5, L 173. *FF* 181-182, poem but not the letter; *Letters* (1894) 162; (1931) 159, *LL* 188, prose variant of the second stanza serves as the concluding paragraph in a "Late Autumn, 1853" letter to Josiah and Elizabeth Holland (dated "early 1854" in *LH* 38).]
23. Pencil, gilt, embossed "Paris" (A), writing on first of four pages, folded in thirds. "Sue" erased from verso. Another version of the poem is in the fascicles. [A 663, P 204. *UP* 46.]
24. Pencil, no embossment, neatly torn (8 x 13.5 cm), folded in quarters, paste marks. "Susie" on verso. "Send this back to me" in pen in Susan's handwriting of the 1860s, suggesting that she and Emily passed this note back and forth. [H B75, L 134. *FF* 185.]
25. Pencil, gilt, lightly blue-ruled, embossed (FNP), writing on first of four pages, folded in thirds. Address erased from verso. Two other versions of this poem were written; one is included in the fascicles. [A 654, P 130 (handwriting like that of "A poor – torn Heart"). Printed as "October" in *Drum Beat* (11 March 1864); as "Indian Summer" in *Poems* (1890) 100-101.]
26. Pencil, gilt, embossed (FNP), blue-ruled, writing on first of four pages, folded in thirds. "Sue" erased from verso. Another version of this poem is in the fascicles. [A 655, P 131. First and third stanzas in Frederick H.

Hitchcock, *The Handbook of Amherst, Massachusetts* (1891); *Poems* (1891) 173 titled "November."]

27. Ink, embossed "Paris," gilt-edged, two leaves, folded in thirds. "Sue" on verso, which Johnson does not note. This poem is divided into stanzas in the fascicle copy. [A 634, P 138. *Poems* (1891) 124, as "My Rose."]
28. Ink, two leaves, blue-ruled, folded in thirds, "Susie" on the verso. "Letter from Emily Dickinson to Sue Dickson," written by an unknown hand, is in ink on verso. [A 70.]
29. Ink, embossed (V), one sheet, four pages, multiple folds. "Church" or "Chuck" written on top of first leaf. [H L3, L 194. *LL* 28-29, in part.]
30. Ink, on two blue-ruled leaves, pinholes. "X" in Susan's handwriting on verso. Earlier editions delete the heading and alter the signature to "Emily." [H SH 1, P 14. *SH* 1-2.]
31. Ink, writing on three pages of two-leaf sheet, multiple folds. Addressed "Susie" on verso. "E.D." penciled in unknown hand on first page. The "I" in "Immortality" is scripted with flourish at an angle so that the letter looks as if it is wearing a fancy hat. There are three other versions of this poem, two in the fascicles. [A 71, P 7. *SH* 90-91.]
32. Ink, blue-ruled, no embossment, half sheet torn at left, folded in thirds, pinholes. "F's" are crossed with flourish. "Earth" is raised above the line because Dickinson originally wrote "world," which she crossed out. Another version of this poem is in the fascicles. [H 255, P 6. *Poems* (1891) 157.]
33. Ink, blue-ruled paper, no embossment, half sheet torn at left, multiple folds, with many stains. "Sue" in pencil on verso. [H 349, P 8. *Poems* (1896) 83, titled "Forgotten."]
34. Ink, no embossment, on two-thirds of half sheet folded in quarters. Marked with "X" and "E" in Susan's handwriting. Another version of this poem is included in the fascicles. [H 359, P 9. *CP* (1924) 297-298.]
35. Ink, no embossment, on half sheet torn at left, folded in thirds, many stains. Another version of this poem is in the fascicles. [H 291, P 10. *SH* 19.]
36. Ink, gilt-edged, embossed "Crown," folded in rectangles. Two dots in "sail," and the ending dash is elongated. Another version of this poem is in the fascicles. [H 273, P 11. *SH* 48-49.]
37. Ink, blue-ruled, no embossment, half sheet, carefully torn at left, multiple folds. "X" in Susan's handwriting on verso. The "T's" are all crossed extravagantly. Another version of this poem is in the fascicles. [H 344, P 12. *Poems* (1890) 102, titled "Autumn."]
38. Ink, embossed wreath (FNP), half sheet, bottom third is partially torn away, folds very worn, pinholes. "Sue –" on verso. Dash after "Crimson" points down. Envelope from "The National Arts Club / 15

Gramercy Park / New York N.Y." has Bianchi's notes for the book of Emily's writings. Another version of this poem is in the fascicles. [H 387, P 15. *FF* 185.]

39. Manuscript to Susan is "lost"; text reproduced from *The Single Hound.* "Signor" penciled on the surviving manuscript (first poem in Fascicle 7), is in Emily's handwriting of much later date. In the fascicles, Susan marked a poem with a similar theme — "Musicians wrestling Everywhere!" [H 289, P 157, marked by Susan with a "P." P 59. *SH,* 110; *New England Quarterly*, XX (1947) 148.]
40. Pencil, gilt-edged, embossed "Paris" (A), one sheet, two leaves, folded in thirds, pinholes. "Sue" on verso. Another version of this poem is in the fascicles. [H 321, P 62. *SH* 105.]
41. Ink, no embossment, two leaves. "Sue" on verso, crossed-out "C" in Susan's handwriting, multiple folds and two incisions in vertical fold as if for an attachment. Punctuation has a sportive kick to it: "Period" on exclamation at end of first line appears to be a comma turned on its side. Another version of this poem is in the fascicles. [H 319, P 64. *Poems* (1890) 76-77, titled "Summer's Armies."]
42. Pencil, embossed (FNP), blue-ruled on half sheet torn at left, folded in thirds, pinholes, top corners folded over, as if for insertion in a scrapbook. Another version of this poem is in the fascicles and a copy was sent to Higginson in July 1862. [H B189, P 67. *Brooklyn Daily Union*, 27 April 1864; *A Masque of Poets*, ed. Helen Hunt Jackson (1878); *Poems* (1890) 13.]
43. Pencil, blue-ruled, no embossment, torn upper half of sheet, folded in half. "X" on verso in Susan's handwriting. "Y's" written with flourish. Corners folded as if for insertion in a scrapbook. Another version of this poem is in the fascicles. [H 233, P 68. *SH* 113.]
44. Pencil, gilt-edged, embossed (FNP), blue-ruled, half sheet torn at left, folded in thirds, pinholes on top. Dashes more exaggerated, scooped (as in that after "Like you – " in "Master" letter). The cross of the "T" in the last line almost underlines "my" in preceding line. Dickinson changed "Thy pe" to "Thy" to "Thine," and crossed out "pe." [H 286, P 69. *SH* 86.]
45. Pencil, gilt-edged, embossed (FNP), half sheet torn at left, folded in thirds. Marked with "P" by Susan. Another version of this poem is in the fascicles. [H 239, P 71. *Poems* (1891) 226.]
46. Ink, gilt-edged, embossed "Paris" (A), half sheet torn at left, folded in thirds, pinholes. "X" in pencil in Susan's handwriting on verso. Bold "Y" in "Emily" spans the entire word. Another version of this poem is in the fascicles. [H 377, P 73. *Poems* (1891) 29, titled "Triumphant."]

47. Pencil, faintly embossed "Holyoke Co." (X), half sheet torn at left, folded in thirds. The "Y" in "Away" is scrawled so boldly that it extends between "of" and "spotted" in the following line. Pencil "X" and triangle on verso in Susan's handwriting, including a list: "Remember Mister / Austins Hold / *[illegible]* Waltzes – Labitax / Bobolink Polka / Remember (?)." [H 310, P 75. *SH* 38; *CP* 269-270.]
48. Pencil, no embossment, half sheet torn at left. Addressed "Sue" on verso, with "X" in pencil in Susan's handwriting. Descending and differently shaped arcs, perhaps of "E" and "Y" in "Emily," make it appear that signature was torn away. Johnson does not note that this manuscript is addressed to "Sue." There is another version in the fascicles. [H 254, P 76. *Poems* (1890) 116, titled "Setting Sail."]
49. Pencil, gilt-edged, embossed (FNP), two leaves, multiple folds. "P" and "X" on verso in Susan's handwriting. Another version of this poem is in the fascicles. [H 305, P 80, late 1850s. *Poems* (1896) 55, titled "Alpine Glow."]
50. Pencil, gilt, embossed (FNP), blue-ruled, multiple folds, pinholes. There is another version in the fascicles. "Sue" erased from verso. [A 651, P 84 (handwriting like that of "A poor – torn Heart"). *Letters* (1894) 215; *Letters* (1931) 202-203; *LL* 253.]
51. Pencil, gilt, embossed, lightly blue-ruled, writing on first of four pages, folded in thirds, pinholes. "Sue" erased from verso. Another version of this poem is in the fascicles. [A 653, P 121. *BM* 216.]
52. Pencil, embossed oval (stationery and handwriting like that of earlier pencil manuscripts at AC), half sheet, folded in thirds, torn at left, signs of wear and use. The dash after "charged" in last stanza points down, and the tail on the "Y" in "Emily" arches toward the signature. "X" in Susan's handwriting on verso. Another version of this poem is in the fascicles. [Morgan Library, MA 1488, P 152. *BM* 23.]
53. Pencil, gilt-edged, embossed (FNP), two leaves, folded in thirds. "Y" in signature scoops and cradles "Emily." "Sue" on verso, as is "Printed" in Susan's handwriting. Another version of the poem in fascicles. [H 251, P 154. *Poems* (1890) 142.]
54. Ink, embossed queen's head (Q), two leaves, blue-ruled, folded in thirds, pinholes. "Sue" on verso, and "X" in Susan's handwriting. There is another version in the fascicles. [H B195, P 155. *Poems* (1890) 71.]
55. Another version of this poem is in the fascicles. [P 160. First published in the *Independent*, XLIII, using Susan's holograph (see *AB* 145-146). Also published in *Poems* (1891) 85-86, with same title.]
56. Pencil, embossed (FNP), gilt, two leaves, blue-ruled, folded in thirds, paste marks. "Sue" on verso, and "X" in Susan's handwriting. Paste

marks reveal that this letter was mounted in a scrapbook. [H B133, L 231.]

57. Ink, small sheet torn to size, bottom has been torn away, missing as of June 20, 1963. Photostat confirms that Susan's note at the bottom of the letter-poem reads: "1860 – written on Ned's birth-day -/ Toby was the cat –." Johnson mistranscribes "I" for "you" in the line "If you could shut him up." "1860" may refer to the decade, since Ned was born in 1861. [H B140, P 218. *L* 232, *L* 53.]

58. Ink, no embossment, folded in quarters, last line and reassurance to Emily on verso. [H B94. Johnson, *Emily Dickinson* 117; *Rowing in Eden* 181.]

59. Susan's copy, now "lost," was most likely sent to the newspaper for printing. Another version is in the fascicles. [*Springfield Republican* (March 1, 1862).]

60. Pencil, gilt-edged, embossed (FNP), blue-ruled, paste marks. Another version is in the fascicles, and yet another was sent in Emily's first letter to Higginson. [H B74c, L 238.]

61. Ink, embossed with queen's head (Q), paste marks. "Emily –" and "Pony Express" (lower left corner) on verso. [H B74b, L 238, P 216.]

62. Ink, gilt-edged, embossed (FNP). Folded in thirds, pinholes. Another version is in the fascicles. [H B74a; L 238, P 216n; Susan's transcription is in H Box 9.]

63. Pencil, on Queen's head stationery. "Private" angles up to the right and the dash beside "kiss" angles down to the right. A little square of paper is scissored away beneath the words "If you have suffered this past / summer I am sorry *[square excision]* I" and "a thorn, why not we [!]" Scissorings are partially angled across the document. Though a word appears to have been cut out from the first incision, none is excised by this second in which the pieces on either side of the cut fit together perfectly. The shape of the second is cut to excise the last sentence and mimics the mark we use for long division. The cuts are probably the result of a letter opener or some editing process to place writings in scrapbooks. [H Box 8.]

64. Ink, blue-ruled, embossed "G." and "T.," folded in thirds. Franklin has placed this in Fascicle 19. "Sue –" erased from verso. [A 80-7, P 336. *BM* 177.]

65. Pencil, gilt-edged, embossed (FNP), two leaves, paste marks. "Sue" on verso with calligraphic extravagance, inscribed in large handwriting, with wide spacing between words, and written in the middle third of the page. [H B125, L 239, P 220.]

66. Pencil, embossed "A Pirie & Sons 1862" (Y), half sheet torn at left, folded in thirds and then multiple folds, pinholes. "X" in Susan's handwriting on verso. [H 374, P 1146. *SH* 9.]
67. Ink, gilt-edged, embossed "Paris" (A), two leaf sheet, corner folded over and pinned. "SHD's copy" and "5" penciled in top right-hand corner. Another version of this poem is in the fascicles. [H 309, P 217. *London Mercury*, XIX (February 1929), 358; *FP* 188.]
68. Two other versions: one in the fascicles, one sent to Higginson.[H 127a, P 228, (copy to Susan "lost"). Titled "Sunset" in three printings during Dickinson's lifetime: *Springfield Daily Republican*, 30 March 1864; *Springfield Weekly Republican*, 2 April 1864; *Drum Beat*, 29 February 1864.]
69. Ink, on two-thirds of half sheet, torn on right and bottom, folded in half, stains, paste marks. Last six lines repeat last part of "'Tis Anguish grander than Delight," which is dated "about 1865" by Johnson, though this letter-poem appears to have been sent to Susan earlier. [H B191, P 984 (last ll.). *SH* 96.]
70. Ink, gilt-edged, embossed (Q), four page sheet and poem continues onto the fourth page, rectangular folds. "X" and "60-70" in Susan's handwriting on verso, probably indicating the decade of the poem's writing. "This book" in Bianchi's handwriting. There are two other versions, one in the fascicles and one sent to Thomas Higginson in July 1862. [H B44, L258, P 229. *FF* 228, with poem omitted.]
71. Ink, on faintly embossed paper, half sheet torn at left, folded in thirds. "X" penciled in Susan's handwriting on verso. Another version is in the fascicles. [H 274, P 301. *Poems* (1890) 134, *CP* 313.]
72. Ink, half sheet torn at left, rectangular folds. "P" on verso. Another version is in the fascicles. [H 256, P 310.]
73. Ink, no embossment, half sheet torn at left, folded in thirds, paste marks. "Sue" on verso, and "X" in pencil in Susan's handwriting, as is "with gay flowers" and "Sent with very rich flowers." Another version of this poem is in the fascicles. [H B154, P 308, *SH* 60.]
74. Ink, half sheet torn at left, folded in thirds, paste marks. Addressed "Sue" on verso, and "X" in pencil in Susan's handwriting. "L" in "Largest" is noticeably large. There is another version in the fascicles. [H B28, P 309, *FF* 263.]
75. Ink, two leaves, no embossment, folded in thirds, pinholes, signs of everyday use (impressions from scribbling). Word choice and lineation is dramatically different from the copy bound in the fascicle and the other two versions. [H 278, P 311. *Poems* (1891) 174-175, titled "The Snow."]
76. Ink, two half sheets. There are two other versions, one in the fascicles. [P 312, 1935 photostat. *SH* 94.]

77. Ink, embossed (Q), half sheet torn at left, folded in thirds. "Sue" on verso. [H 246, P 313 (last stanza only). *Poems* (1891), 46-47, entire poem titled "Too Much."]
78. Ink, gilt-edged, embossed "Paris" (I), two leaves, folded in thirds. Pencil "X" in Susan's handwriting on verso. Another version is in the fascicles. [H 292, P 314. *BM* 245.]
79. Pencil, embossed "Paris" (I), gilt, two leaves, folded in thirds. Writing on first page, centered on page. "X" in Susan's handwriting on verso. [Morgan Library, MA 1357, P 1155. *SH* 126.]
80. Ink, half sheet torn at left, folded in quarters, pinholes, paper clip impressions. "Sue" and text on verso. Another version of this poem is in the fascicles. [H 262, P 315. *Poems* (1896) 86.]
81. Susan's copy is "lost," but may be that located at Amherst College by Marget Sands. There is another version in the fascicles and a copy was sent to Higginson. [A 457, P 322. *Scribner's Magazine*, VIII (August 1890), 240; *Poems* (1890) 58-59; *CP* (1924) 152-153.]
82. Ink, gilt, embossed "Paris" (I), half sheet torn at left, multiple folds. "P" on verso. Another version is in the fascicles. [H 249, P 675, *Poems* (1891) 210]
83. Ink, gilt-edged, embossed "Paris" (A), multiple folds. "X" in Susan's hand on verso. Another version of this poems in the fascicles. [H 276, P 446. *SH* 132.]
84. Pencil, gilt-edged, embossed "Paris" (I), folded in thirds, two leaves. "Sue" on verso, and "X" in Susan's handwriting on verso. Another version of this poem is in the fascicles. [H 330, P 305. *SH* 26; *LL* 195-196.]
85. Ink, embossed (V), folded in thirds, paper clip impressions. The dash after "Hum" slants down. Emily wrote "Combined Girl" on the middle third of the verso, as if it were a title or an address. "X" penciled in Susan's handwriting on verso. Another version of this poem is in the fascicles. [H B178, P 302, *SH* 65.]
86. Ink, torn at the right and bottom, folded in half vertically, then horizontally in thirds. "Sue" erased from verso. One version of this poem was sent to Higginson, another is in the fascicles. [A 690, P 683. *Poems* (1891) 37.]
87. Ink, two leaves, embossed (V), folded in thirds. "Dash" after "seldom" curves, with dot above, appearing as a kind of bird's eye. "Sue" on verso. [H 350, P 306. *SH* 35, concluding part I.]
88. Ink, embossed oval shield (E), blue-ruled, half sheet torn at left, folded in thirds. "Sue " on verso. Another version of this poem is in the fascicles. [H 226, P 666. *SH* 37.]

89. Ink, gilt-edged, embossed "Paris" (I), half sheet torn at left, multiple folds. "X" in Susan's handwriting on verso. Another version of this poem is in the fascicles. [H 293, P 668. *SH* 36.]
90. Ink, gilt-edged, embossed "Paris" (I). Two leaves. "Sue" on verso, inked with inch-long descending arc. Another version of this poem is in the fascicles. [H 296, P 669. *SH* 14.]
91. Ink, gilt-edged, embossed "Paris" (I), four pages. "X" penciled in Susan's handwriting on verso. Another version of this poem is in the fascicles. [H 304, P 670. *Poems* (1891) 214-215, titled "Ghosts." Facsimiles of holographs of this poem, *Harvard Library Bulletin*, VII (1953) 260 -261.]
92. Ink, two leaves, manuscript has not been folded. "Du-" on top of sheet. Another version of this poem is in the fascicles. [A 635, P 673. *FP* 147.]
93. Embossed "Paris" (I). Gilt-edged, two leaves, folded in thirds. "Dollie" on verso. The other version of this poem is a transcript made by Susan. [Princeton, H ST 22d, P 1691. *SH* 97.]
94. Ink, embossed "Paris" (I), small square torn at left and on bottom (bottom third of manuscript removed, possibly excising last line, "The Amber Quantity – " and other writing), numerous pinholes. Another version is in the fascicles. [H B180, P 676, *BM* 70.]
95. Ink, gilt, embossed "Paris" (I), two leaves, folded in thirds, pinholes. Part of signature and/or postscript is torn off. "X" in Susan's handwriting on verso. Another version of this poem is in the fascicles. [H 362, P 677, *SH* 11.]
96. Pencil, gilt, embossed "Paris" (I), half sheet torn at left, folded in thirds. [H 297, P 679 (last two and a half stanzas of "Conscious am I in my Chamber").]
97. Pencil draft, partial sheet torn on top and left, folded in half and then again. [H 242, P 682 (last ll. of " 'Twould ease – a Butterfly").]
98. Pencil, gilt, embossed "Paris" (I), half sheet torn at right, multiple folds. [H 368, P 680 (last stanza of "Each Life converges to some Centre –."]
99. Gilt, embossed "Paris" (I), half sheet torn at left, tear in manuscript, multiple folds. "X" in Susan's handwriting. [H 316, P 681.]
100. Ink, small sheet (11.2 x 12.5 cm.) torn at left and on bottom, folded in half. Dash after "Superlative" emphatically directed down. Franklin dates this handwriting around 1863. The fascicle copy is broken into stanzas, but, typically, the copy to Susan is not. Johnson did not know of this manuscript. Here this poem is associated with Susan for the first time. [Morgan Library, MA 1641, variant of Fascicle 38, P 800, *BM* 199.]
101. Pencil, gilt-edged, embossed "Paris" (I), half sheet torn at left, folded and refolded, paste marks. "Sue" on verso, and "X" penciled in Susan's handwriting. [H B 139, P 818, L 287. *FF* 270.]

102. Pencil, gilt-edged, embossed "Paris" (I), four pages, multiple folds, paste marks. [H B56, L 288. *FF* 267.]
103. Pencil, embossed "Paris" (I), four pages, folded in rectangles. [H B179, L 294. *FF* 231 and 266-267, excerpts only.]
104. Ink, gilt-edged, embossed "Paris" (I). [H B163b, P 303. *Poems* (1890) 26, titled "Exclusion." Verso: Pencil, gilt-edged, embossed "Paris" (I).] Johnson does not note that these two poems are back-to-back on a half sheet torn at left. [H B163a, P 826. *SH* 122.]
105. Pencil, gilt-edged, embossed "Paris" (I), half sheet torn at left, folded in thirds. "Sue" penciled on verso. Another version of this poem is in the fascicles. [H 315, P 808. *SH* 138. Susan sent out two transcripts of this poem.]
106. Pencil, gilt-edged, embossed "Paris" (I), four pages, folded in thirds. "X" and an exaggerated "E" in Susan's handwriting on verso. Another version of this poem is in the fascicles. [H 264, P 810. *SH* 135.]
107. Pencil, embossed "Paris" (I), half sheet torn at left, folded in quarters. Stanza upside down on the sheet (thus "Paris" is at bottom left instead of at top left). "170 x 15" multiplied on verso, presumably by Susan. Another version of this poem is in the fascicles. [H 371, P 811. *BM* 51.]
108. Pencil, gilt-edged, embossed "Paris" (I), four pages, folded in thirds. "Sue" penciled on verso, and "X" in Susan's handwriting. Luxurious spacing between words and lines. There are three other versions of this poem, one of which was sent to Higginson. Another version is in the fascicles. [H 341, P 815. *SH* 119.]
109. Pencil, gilt-edged, embossed "Paris" (I), four pages, multiple folds. "X" in Susan's handwriting on verso. Another version of this poem is in the fascicles. [H 257, P 817. *Poems* (1896) 145.]
110. Pencil, no embossment, half sheet torn at left, folded in quarters, paste marks, paper clip impressions. "Sue – " on verso and "C" inked in Susan's handwriting on verso. [H B18, P 809, L 305. Published by Bianchi in *Atlantic Monthly*, CXV (1915) 40; *FF* 263.]
111. Pencil, gilt-edged, embossed "Paris" (I), four pages, multiple folds, paste marks. "Sue –" on verso. [H B78, L 312, P 825. *AM* CXV (1915) 37, in part; *LL* 49, in part; *FF* 236, in part.]
112. Pencil, gilt-edged, embossed "Paris" (I), writing on first and third pages of four, folded in thirds. Children's scribblings, probably Ned's, are prominent on the verso. There are three other versions, including one sent to Higginson. [A 699, P 829. *Poems* (1891) 207, as "A Country Burial."]
113. Pencil, gilt-edged, embossed "Paris" (I), half sheet torn at left, folded in quarters, paste marks, paper-clip marks. "Sue." penciled on verso. [H B162, L 306. *LL* 100, in part; *FF* 270.]

114. Pencil, gilt-edged, embossed "Paris" (I), folded in quarters, half sheet torn at left. Asterisk-like mark on top of page (recto), slightly to the right. "3" also on recto. "Sue" on verso, and "X" in Susan's handwriting. Another version of this poem is in the fascicles. [H 342, P 985. *SH* 23; *LL* 195.]
115. Pencil, gilt-edged, embossed "Paris" (I), on half sheet with bottom third torn off, paste marks. These lines, with a second stanza, are in the fascicles. [H B53, P 989. *FF* 227.]
116. Ink, gilt-edged, embossed "Paris" (I), leaf carefully torn from sheet down right side, folded in thirds. Variant of second stanza is in loose sheets Franklin calls "sets." [H 331, P 992.]
117. Ink, gilt-edged, embossed "Paris" (I), two leaves, folded in thirds, pencil marks on recto and verso, drawings of animals on verso. There are precise triangular cuts between the first two lines of the second stanza. There are two other versions: one sent to Higginson and one in the fascicles. [H 250, P 1067. In *Atlantic Monthly,* LXVIII (October 1891) 451, in article by Higginson about their correspondence; *Letters* (ed. 1894) 312; (ed. 1931) 282; also *LL* 268-269; *SH* 5; *New England Quarterly,* XX (1947) 16.]
118. Ink, gilt-edged, embossed "Paris" (I), four pages, folded in thirds. "Sue – " in ink on verso, and "X" penciled in Susan's handwriting. Another version is in the fascicles. [H B192, P 1071. *SH* 16.]
119. Ink, gilt-edged, embossed "Paris" (I), two leaves, folded in thirds. "X" penciled in Susan's handwriting on verso. Another version is in the fascicles. [H 328, P 988. *LL* 49; *New England Quarterly*, XX (1947) 46.]

SECTION THREE NOTES

1 YH 11, 186.

120. Ink, gilt-edged, embossed "Paris" (I), two leaves, folded in quarters. Illegible penciled words in Susan's handwriting: "Mr Sayed" or "W Soced" or "Saved"? Another version of this poem was probably sent to Samuel Bowles. [H 361, P 1072. *LL* 49-50; *CP* 176-177.]
121. Pencil, gilt-edged, embossed "Paris" (I), half sheet torn at left, folded in thirds. [H 277, P 812. *Poems* (1896) 103-104.]
122. Ink, gilt-edged, embossed "Paris" (I), writing on first, second, third pages, folded in thirds. "X" in Susan's handwriting beneath second of Susan's poems. Two other versions of this poem exist: one that is signed and included among Emily's ungathered poems, and another in the fascicles. [H 325, P 1104. *Poems* (1896) 130, titled "Evening."]

123. Pencil, blue-ruled, no embossment, two-thirds leaf torn at top and right, folded in half, paste marks. "X" and "Read with [illegible]" in Susan's handwriting on verso. [H B159, P 1106. *FF* 264.]
124. Pencil draft, half sheet torn at right, no embossment, multiple folds. First "A" is crossed out, "The" written in and crossed out, "A" written in again. [H 223, P 1108. *FF* 244.]
125. Pencil, embossed wreath (W?), sheet torn in half, blue-ruled, folded in quarters, pinholes. [H 271, P 1109. *SH* 88.]
126. Pencil, scrap paper torn at left and bottom, folded in quarters, pinholes, paste marks. "Sue." penciled on verso. [H B135, L 324. *AM* CXV (1915) 37, in part; *LL* 57, in part; *FF* 237, in part.]
127. Pencil, torn at bottom, folded in half, paste marks. Two lines are centered on the page. "X" penciled in Susan's handwriting on verso. [H B71, L 325. *FF* 247.]
128. Pencil on small sheet, no embossment, folded in quarters. "Sue" penciled in one quarter of verso. [H B80, L 327. *FF* 264.]
129. Pencil, gilt-edged, embossed "Paris" (A), four pages, folded in quarters, paste marks. Text is centered in the middle of the first page. [H B97, L 328.]
130. Pencil, gilt-edged, embossed "Paris" (A), four pages, folded in thirds. "X" in Susan's handwriting on verso. There is another version in the fascicles. [H 345, P 1115. First stanza only in Frederick H. Hitchcock, ed., *The Handbook of Amherst, Massachusetts* (Amherst, 1891) 21; first two quatrains in *Poems* (1896) 136, titled "Aftermath"; *CP*, without stanza divisions; all four stanzas in *New England Quarterly*, XX (1947) 26.]
131. This is a reproduction of Bianchi's version of the poem, which presumably follows the copy that Emily sent to Susan, now lost. There is another pencil draft of the poem. [P 1116. *SH* 20; *LL* 195.]
132. Pencil, gilt, embossed "Paris" (I), folded in thirds. Writing on first and third of four pages. Scribblings on verso, as is "X" in Susan's handwriting; bottom third also has mathematical calculations. [H 234, P 1117. *FF* 240.]
133. Pencil, single white sheet embossed "P & S" (JP), blue-ruled, folded in rectangles, as if for an envelope, pinholes through all four folds. "X" on verso, as is "Parts gone" in Susan's handwriting. [H 252a, P 1118. *SH* 13.]
134. Pencil, blue-ruled, third of sheet torn at left and bottom, multiple folds, paste marks. Text is centered on the page. "Sue" on verso. [H B20, L 334. *LL* 62.]
135. Pencil, gilt-edged, embossed "Paris" (A), one sheet, paste marks. "Sue '" penciled on verso. [H B70, L 335. *LL* 62.]

136. Pencil draft, no embossment, one leaf graph paper, torn at left, folded in thirds. "X" in Susan's handwriting on verso. [H 366, P 1135. *SH* 82.]
137. Pencil, half sheet, torn at left, folded in thirds. "X" in Susan's handwriting on verso. [L 336, P 1139, Smith College. *Daily Hampshire Gazette*, 18 December 1952.]
138. Pencil, gilt-edged stationery embossed "Paris" (I), four pages, multiple folds. "X" in Susan's handwriting on verso. There is also a transcript by Susan (H ST 15a). [H 335, P 1136. *BM*, 54.]
139. Pencil, folded in half, pasted onto the half-title page of a copy of *The Single Hound* once owned by Laura Scull of Langhorne, Pennsylvania. Bianchi has inscribed the copy: "To Laura – In memory of our Immortals – with Martha's love – 1914." This verse is the first stanza of a four-stanza poem among the ungathered writings. [P 1137, first stanza, privately owned, *SH* 54.]
140. Ink, watermark "A Pirie & Sons / 1866" (Y), two leaves, folded in thirds. "X" penciled in Susan's handwriting on verso. [H 364, P 1247. *SH* 147.]
141. Pencil, gilt-edged, embossed "Paris" (I), four pages, folded in thirds. "Sue." on verso, which also has a "P" in Susan's handwriting. [H 238, P 1138. *Poems* (1891) 147, titled "The Spider."]
142. Pencil, graph paper, multiple folds. Glued on a leaf with Susan's transcript on blue-ruled paper (embossed AMB), to which Susan has added Emily's signature. [H 333, P 1141. *SH* 144; *LL* 197.]
143. Ink, watermark "A Pirie & Sons 1866" (Y), paper-clip marks, bottom two-thirds of second leaf are cut away, folded in thirds. Dashes after "one" and "aggregate" point down. [H 308, P 1243. *SH* 143; *LL* 197.]
144. Ink, four pages, folded in rectangles, pinholes on central fold as if for binding. [H B185, L 333. *FF* 239-240, in part.]
145. Pencil, gilt-edged, embossed "Paris" (I), two leaves, folded in thirds. "X" in Susan's handwriting on verso. There is another version in the fascicles. [H 347, P 1142. *SH* 28.]
146. Pencil, gilt-edged, two-thirds of a leaf, folded in half. "X" in Susan's handwriting on verso. Dickinson's small "b" and "f" are often nearly indistinguishable, and that is the case here. Dash after "Balloon" points down. [H 268, P 1215. *SH* 32.]
147. Ink, embossed "A Pirie & Sons" (Y). Another version of the poem is in the fascicles. [H B193, P 986, L 378. *FF* 231-232.]
148. Ink with all changes in pencil, white paper embossed "A Pirie & Sons / 1870" (Y), ruled, folded in quarters. Dashes after "Child," "[behold," and "ineffable"] point down. "X" in Susan's handwriting on bottom right of verso. [H 378, P 1258. *SH* 116-117.]

149. Pencil, torn at right and bottom, folded in quarters, paste marks. On verso a shopping list in Susan's handwriting: "[S?L? wake or word ending in 'll'] Ink, Satin Ribbon, Young's Druggist." [H B23, P 1158 (first two lines), L 350. *FF* 145 and 242.]
150. Pencil, embossed "Paris" (A), half sheet torn at left, multiple folds, paste marks; stains on verso. "X" in Susan's handwriting on verso. Susan quotes this in "When Autumn Began," review letter "To the Editor of the Republican" by S.H.D. of "Autumn's Divine Beauty Begins" (August 2, 1906; Brown St. A 126). [H B49, L 347. *FF* 238.]
151. Pencil, small sheet torn to size at right and bottom, paste marks. Text is centered on the page. "X" in Susan's handwriting on verso. [H B57, L 348. *FF* 259.]
152. Pencil, embossed "Paris" (I), gilt, half sheet torn at left, folded in thirds, paste marks. "X" in Susan's handwriting on verso. [H B8, L 349. *FF* 241.]
153. Pencil, gilt-edged, embossed "Paris" (I), folded in thirds. "2" in red pencil on upper right of recto, full sheet plus half sheet torn at left. "Sue" on verso, as is "X" in Susan's handwriting; "in *[unintelligible]* Poems" on recto, which likely refers to the poem's printing in Loomis Todd and Higginson's second volume of Dickinson's verse and is Susan's editorial note as she worked on her book of Emily's writings. Versions of this poem were sent to Thomas Higginson, Elizabeth and Josiah Holland, and an unknown recipient. Other versions are in the ungathered poems. [H 356, P 824. *Poems* (1891) 158-159, titled "A Thunder-Storm."]
154. Pencil, gilt-edged, embossed "Paris" (A), half sheet torn at left, folded, as if for an envelope, paste marks. [H B33, P 1156, L 356. *FF* 225.]
155. Pencil, embossed profile (D), two leaves, paste marks. [H B107, L 365. *FF* 254.]
156. Pencil, gilt-edged, embossed "Paris" (I), two leaves, folded in thirds, paste marks. "Sue." on verso. "A" on "All" is emphatically large, and there is extended spacing between letters. [H B182, L 366. *LL* 62.]
157. Pencil, gilt-edged, embossed "Paris" (I), half sheet torn at left, folded in quarters, paste marks. Text is centered on the page and words are widely spaced. "Sue." on verso. [H B10, L 346. *LL* 65.]
158. Ink, full sheet plus half sheet torn at left, folded in quarters, paper clip marks. [H B184, P 1179, L 364. *FF* 233-234, in part. The poem made out of the lines "Of so divine / a Loss . . . Bliss has been" is in *SH* 145; *LL* 197-198.]
159. Pencil, embossed with "Crown" (J), four pages, folded in thirds. "X" in Susan's handwriting on verso. [H 235, P 1177. *SH* 71. Two other versions of this poem are in the groups of unbound poems found after Dickinson's death (Sets 7 & 11).]

160. Pencil, gilt-edged, embossed "Paris" (I), two leaves, multiple folds, pinholes as if flowers were attached. [H 290, P 1178. *FF* 229.]
161. Pencil, gilt-edged, embossed "Paris" (I), two pages, folded in thirds. "Sue -" on verso. Emily sent one version of this poem to Thomas Higginson in 1871; another version is in the fascicles. [H 375, P 1181. *Poems* (1891), 65.]
162. Ink, embossed "A Pirie & Sons" (Y), half sheet torn at left, folded in quarters. "X" in Susan's handwriting on verso. Emily includes these lines in a letter to Higginson written about the same time. [H 306, P 1208. Lines to Higginson in *Letters* (ed. 1894) 316; (ed. 1931) 290; *LL* 277.]
163. Ink, embossed "A Pirie & Sons" (Y, 1866), two leaves, folded in thirds. Exaggerated spacing between letters and words. Another version of this poem was sent to Higginson; additional version in the fascicles. [H 302, P 1209. *Letters* (ed. 1894) 316-317, *Poems* (ed. 1931) 301-302; (ed. 1931) 290; also in *LL* 277, 323-324, 304, printed as though it were part of a letter written in 1876; *SH* 30; *CP* 266; *FP* 197.]
164. Ink, embossed "A Pirie & Sons 1870" (Y), full sheet plus half sheet torn at left, folded in thirds, paper clip and paste marks, "125" penciled on recto of first leaf. [H B150, L 392. *LL* 63, ending only; *FF* 234-235, in part.]
165. Pencil, graph paper, no embossment, two leaves, multiple folds, paste marks. [H B95, L 393. *AM* CXV (1915) 37, in part; *FF* 235, in part.]
166. Pencil, no embossment, two-thirds of a leaf, torn at left and bottom, folded in quarters. [H 324, P 1246. *AM* CXV (1915) 38; *LL* 60.]
167. Ink, embossed "A Pirie & Sons 1871" (Y), two leaves plus half sheet torn at left, folded in thirds. Exaggerated crossing of "T's," as well as wide spacing. [H B123, L 397, P 1251. *FF* 232-233.]
168. Ink, embossed "A Pirie & Sons" (Y), half sheet torn at left, folded in quarters, paste marks. [H B153, L 383. *FF* 267.]
169. Ink, embossed "A Pirie & Sons / 1871" (Y), two leaves, folded in quarters. "X" penciled in Susan's handwriting on verso. Here spacing between letters is so exaggerated that the comma appears separated from the word it follows. [H 261, P 1253. *SH* 139.]
170. Ink, no embossment, two half sheets scissored and torn at left, folded in thirds, paper-clip marks. Page appears to have been cut off, possibly omitting last two lines included in other versions: "Restored in Arctic Confidence / To the Invisible – " Emily sent a version of this letter-poem to Higginson; two other versions are among the ungathered poems and drafts. [H B190, P 1259, L 407. *FF* 256-257; *Letters* (ed. 1931 only) 307.]

171. Ink, no embossment, two leaves, folded in thirds, paste marks. "X" penciled in Susan's handwriting on verso. Wide spacing between lines as well as words; at this point, all the "T's" are crossed with exaggeration, spanning words. [H B99, L 427. *FF* 247.]
172. Ink, no embossment, half sheet torn at left, folded in thirds, paste marks. [H B38, L 428. *LL* 87.]
173. Ink, embossed "A Pirie & Sons / 1862" (Y), two leaves, folded in quarters. Dashes after "Day," "lent," and "Staked" point down. "O.K." penciled in Susan's handwriting on verso. [H 367, B 3, P 1295. *SH* 34, *LL* 196-197.]
174. Pencil, no embossment, two-thirds of a large leaf, torn at top, blue-ruled, multiple folds. "Top" printer's margin of paper is at bottom of draft. "X" in Susan's handwriting on verso. [H 280, P 1302. *SH* 56.]
175. Pencil, same paper as 174 (H 280) (blue-ruled), no embossment, roughly torn on bottom, about two-thirds of a leaf, folded in half, corners are folded, most likely for inserting in a scrapbook. "X" in Susan's handwriting on verso. [H 299, P 1303. *SH* 89]
176. Pencil, no embossment, on rectangle of note paper (blue-ruled) torn at left and bottom, folded in quarters, pinholes. "X" in Susan's handwriting on verso. [H B6, L 429. *LL* 62.]
177. Pencil, embossed "A Pirie & Sons / 1870" (Y), multiple folds, pinholes, paste marks. "X" in Susan's handwriting on verso. [H B160, P 1248. *SH* 141.]

SECTION FOUR NOTES

1 *SH* vi.

178. Pencil, no embossment, small rectangle torn at right and bottom, folded in half, paste marks. [H B25, L 430. *FF* 237. Susan's card is in H Box 9.]
179. Pencil, no embossment, half sheet, torn at left, folded in quarters, pinholes, paste marks. [H B34, L 448. *FF* 245.]
180. Ink, no embossment, two leaves, folded in thirds, pinholes. [H B168, L 484. *FF* 255.]
181. Heavy pencil, no embossment, two leaves, multiple folds, paste marks. [H B42, L 443. *FF* 244.]
182. Pencil, torn at right and bottom, folded in half, paste marks. [H B76, L 447. *FF* 246.]

183. Pencil, no embossment, two leaves, folded in thirds. "X" in Susan's handwriting on verso. Another version was sent to Elizabeth Holland. [H 229, P 1333. *SH* 40; *LH* (1951) 106.]
184. Ink, half sheet, torn at left, folded in thirds, pinholes, paste marks. Marks on page and appears to have been used as ink blotter. Dashes are written with wavy flair. [H L25, L 456. *AM* CXV (1915) 40: *FF* 237, with facsimile.]
185. Heavy pencil, blue-ruled, no embossment, torn at left and bottom, folded in quarters. "X" in Susan's handwriting on verso. [H 300, P 1335. *Poems* (1896) 93 (first stanza only), titled "Dreams"; *SH* 101 (second stanza only, reproducing copy to Susan), apparently following Dickinson's scheme for lineation; *New England Quarterly*, XX (1947) 44, using the version in the fascicle.]
186. Ink, embossed "A Pirie & Sons / 1862" (Y), two leaves, folded in quarters. Marked with "P." Susan made a transcript of this poem, probably from this copy. A different version of this poem was sent to Higginson. [H 348, P 1356. *Poems* (1891) 156, titled "The Rat."]
187. Pencil. There are at least three other versions of this poem, including one which was sent to Higginson. Other versions are divided into two stanzas. [P 1357, privately owned.]
188. Heavy pencil, watermark "Weston's Linen / 1876" (T), two leaves, folded in quarters, paste marks. A version of this poem was included in a letter to Higginson, with a reference to "the Hope that opens and shuts, like the eye of the Wax Doll." [H B11, L 554. *LL* 62, in part.]
189. Pencil, watermark "Weston's Linen 1876" (T), text on first and third of four pages, folded in thirds. Red pencil marks "1–" on first page, upper right-hand corner. [H 337, P 1440. *SH* 146.]
190. Ink, on stationery, watermark "Weston's Linen 1876" (T), two leaves and folded into thirds. On second leaf, "were" is written sideways next to "With Love alone / had bent, / It's fervor the." "X" in Susan's handwriting on verso. [H 360, P 1597. *FF* 268.]
191. Ink, no embossment, half sheet torn at left, multiple folds. "Y" wraps "vilify" in the third line. A version of this poem was sent to Higginson. [H 355, P 1358. *Letters* (ed. 1931 only) 297 (version to Higginson). *SH* 127.]
192. Heavy pencil, graph paper, no embossment, two leaves, folded in thirds. "X" penciled in Susan's handwriting on verso. [H 340, P 1359. *SH* 58.]
193. Heavy pencil, print-like, embossed "Paris" (A), half sheet torn at left, folded in half, then in thirds, pinholes, paste marks. "X" with "Prose" beneath penciled in Susan's handwriting on verso. [H B96, L 467. *FF* 242.]

194. Ink, no embossment, half sheet torn at left, folded in quarters, paste marks. Letters and words widely spaced. Emily sent a two-stanza version of this letter-poem to Josiah Holland, and she sent a single-stanza version in a letter to Higginson. Another single-stanza version is among the ungathered poems. [H B54, L 480. *FF* 265.]

195. Ink, no embossment, two leaves, folded in thirds, paste marks. "1860-70" penciled in Susan's handwriting on verso. [H B4, P 1401, L 531. *FF* 243.]

196. Heavy pencil, half sheet torn at left, multiple folds, paste marks. There is an alternate draft version of the last stanza at AC. Loomis Todd transcribed a six-stanza poem. [H B62, P 1400, L 530. *FF* 260. Similar to last two stanzas of "What mystery pervades a well" in *Poems* (1896) 117-118, titled "A Well" (with second stanza omitted); lines are printed in *AB* 337; complete poem is printed in *New England Quarterly*, XX (1947) 23-24.]

197. Pencil, watermark "Weston's Linen" (T), half sheet torn at left, folded in thirds, pinholes, paste marks. Two other versions of this poem are included among the ungathered poems. [H B13, P 1403. *Atlantic Monthly*, CXV (1915) 39; *LL* 61.]

198. Ink, no embossment, two leaves, folded in thirds, paper-clip marks. "X" penciled in Susan's handwriting on verso. Two drafts exist. [H 287, P 1404. *SH* 53.]

199. Pencil, blue-ruled, no embossment, extensive revisions, half sheet torn at left, folded in thirds. [H 244, P 1416. *SH* 129.]

200. Pencil draft on thin brown paper (scrap paper), no embossment, torn at right, folded in half, very worn. "Miss L Dickinson" and "10c" in unknown handwriting on verso. Number in parentheses is on top of draft. [H 338, P 1425. *SH* 123.]

201. Ink, no embossment, two leaves, folded in thirds, paste marks. "X" and "Special" in Susan's handwriting on verso. [H B93, L 541. *LL* 62, in part; *FF* 241, in part.]

202. Heavy pencil, on blue-ruled paper, embossed capitol (O), half sheet torn at left, folded in thirds. Envelope addressed "Susan – ," elaborately lettered, with paste marks. [H B181, L 581. *LL* 57.]

203. Pencil, no embossment, two leaves, folded in thirds, pinholes, paste marks. Elaborate lettering. [H B37, L 583. *LL* 62, in part.]

204. Heavy pencil, watermark "Weston's / Linen / 1876" (T), two leaves, folded in thirds, bottom of second leaf torn away, paste marks. [H B55, L 586. *LL* 62; *FF* 255.]

205. Pencil, watermark "Weston's Linen 18??" (T), half sheet torn at left, folded in thirds. Susan made a transcript of these lines. [Yale, Za Dickinson 1, L 587. *AM* CXV (1915) 37; *LL* 57.]

206. Heavy pencil, watermark "Weston's / Linen / 1876" (T), half sheet torn at left with bottom third removed, folded in half, paste marks. [H B50, L 584 . *FF* 264, with facsimile reproduction.]
207. Pencil, watermark "Weston's / Linen / 1876" (T), two leaves, folded in quarters, pinholes, paste marks, dramatic calligraphy. "Susan –" on verso. Dash after "you" is elongated and pointed down. Another version of the poem is among the ungathered poems. Emily sent a version of this letter-poem to Sarah Tuckerman in December 1880, following the death of her friend Elihu Root, a professor at Amherst College. [H B32, P 1366, L 585. *LL* 79; *FF* 243.]
208. Pencil, no embossment, two leaves, folded in thirds, paper clip impressions, paste marks. "X" in Susan's handwriting on verso. The "L's" in "Lie" and in "Lothrop" are scored with particular flourishes, perhaps to call attention to the "Lying Culprit." Bianchi's note accompanies the letter-poem: "After the 'Lothrop Case' in which a local pious fraud was exposed." [H B157, P 1453. *LL* 91, with signature altered to "Pecksniff."]
209. Heavy pencil, half sheet, torn at left, folded in quarters, paste marks. [H B82, L 534. *FF* 254.]
210. Pencil, no embossment, two leaves, folded in thirds. "To read to friends" in Susan's handwriting on verso. "Y" in "Hyphen" is a straight line (/), crossing of "T" in "Easter" extends from one end of the word to the other. [H 358, P 1454. *FF* 267-268.]
211. Pencil, graph paper, no embossment, two leaves, folded in thirds. "X" in Susan's handwriting on verso. [H 314, P 1456. *SH* 21.]
212. Heavy pencil, watermark "Weston's / Linen / 1876" (T), half sheet torn at left, multiple folds, pinholes, paste marks. "Susan – " on verso. [H B26, P 1455, L 625. *LL* 62, prose part only; poem, *LL* 57.]
213. Pencil, watermark "Weston's / Linen / 1876" (T), a half sheet torn at left, folded in quarters, pinholes. [H B169, L 624. *FF* 240.]
214. Pencil, watermark "Weston's / Linen / 1876" (T), two leaves, multiple folds, paste marks. "Susan." on verso. [H B48, L 626. *FF* 243.]
215. Pencil, no embossment, two leaves, folded in thirds. "Susan" on verso. [H 230, P 1467. *LL* 80; *CP* 311.]
216. Pencil, "Weston's / Linen / 1876" (T), half sheet torn at left, folded in quarters, pinholes. [H 353, P 1470. *SH* 109.]
217. Pencil, watermark "Irish Linen / Fabric" (U), text on first and third of four pages, folded in quarters. "X" in Susan's handwriting on verso. Another version was prepared for an unknown recipient. [H 343, P 1528. *SH* 64.]
218. Pencil, brown graph paper, no embossment, two-thirds of leaf torn at top and left, text on recto and verso, folded in half. "Devil–" and "X"

penciled in Susan's handwriting on bottom half of verso. [H 329, P 1479. *SH* 99.]

219. Pencil, watermark "Weston's / Linen / 1876" (T), half sheet torn at left, folded in thirds, paste marks, bold script. [H B141, L 636. *FF* 247.]

220. Pencil, watermark "Weston's / Linen / 1876" (T), half sheet torn at left, folded in thirds, paste marks. [H B7, L 660. *FF* 241.]

221. Pencil, half sheet torn at left, folded in thirds, paste marks. "Susan ' " on verso. [H B43, L 661. *FF* 260.]

222. Pencil, no embossment, half sheet torn at left, folded in thirds, paste marks. [H B63, L 662. *LL* 65.]

223. Pencil, "Weston's / Linen / 1876" (T), two leaves, folded in thirds, paste marks. [H B72, L 664. *AM* CXV (1915) 37-38; *LL* 58.]

224. Pencil, embossed "Paris" (I), two leaves, folded in thirds, paste marks. [H B138, L 707. *FF* 237.]

225. Pencil, half sheet torn at left, watermark "Weston's / Linen / 1876," folded in thirds, pinholes, paste marks. Notes, scribbles, lists of phrases, as well as the address "40 Lafayette St." penciled in unknown hand(s) over most of the verso. [Yale, Za Dickinson 1, L 708. *LL* 62.]

226. Pencil, no embossment, two leaves, folded in thirds, paste marks. "Susan – " on fold. [H B89, L 722. *LL* 79, in part; *FF* 241, in part.]

227. Pencil, watermark "Weston's / Linen / 1876" (T), two leaves, folded in thirds, paste marks. "X" and tiny "x" and "1–" in Susan's handwriting on verso. [H B119, L 853, P 1537. *AM* CXV (1915) 39; *LL* 61 (with L 580).]

228. Pencil, no embossment, two leaves, folded in thirds, paste marks. [H B188, L 755. *FF* 265-266.]

229. Photograph indicates that the sheet has been torn across bottom of leaf, and folded into thirds. Photograph of verso shows paste marks. [Photostat H B2, L 757. Manuscript now missing. *LL* 64; *FF* 176.]

230. Pencil, watermark "Weston's / Linen / 1876" (T), on small (4 x 4 in.) leaf cut at right and bottom, folded in half, pinholes, paste marks. "X" in Susan's handwriting on verso. [H B12, L 768. *FF* 242.]

231. Pencil, watermark "Irish Linen / Fabric" (U), one full sheet plus one half sheet torn at left, folded in thirds. "Wanting" in Susan's handwriting on verso, perhaps Susan's suggested title or her note that this sheet had been separated from the rest. There are other versions of this poem among the ungathered poems, and one was sent to Higginson. [H 294, P 1561. *Atlantic Monthly*, LXVIII (October 1891) 454, titled "The Blue Jay," in Higginson's article about her letters and poems; *Poems* (1891) 176-177, also titled "The Blue Jay."]

232. Pencil, watermark "Weston's / Linen / 1876" (T), three-quarters of leaf torn at top and left, folded in thirds, paste marks. Addressed "Susan" on fold, with an elaborate "S." [H B24, L 854. *FF* 242-243, altered.]
233. Pencil, "The American Paper Company," half sheet torn at left, folded in thirds, paste marks. Calligraphy features large, bold letters. [H B51, L 855. *FF* 237.]
234. Pencil, watermark "Pure Irish Linen" (PIL), onion skin, two two-leaf sheets, multiple folds. Envelope torn at end, with paste marks. [H B79, L 868, P 1564. *LL* 85; *AM* CXV (1915) 42; *Letters* (ed. 1931) 319.]
235. Pencil, watermark "Weston's / Linen / 1881" (T), two leaves, folded in thirds, stains. [H L50, L 869.]
236. Pencil, watermark "Irish Linen / Fabric" (U), two sheets, writing on first and third pages of each sheet, multiple folds, paste marks. Lines in this letter, beginning "Whose rumor's / Gate" and ending "a Dent theron," appear in five other versions: letters sent to Maria Whitney, Charles Clark, and three drafts found among the ungathered poems. Johnson makes a poem from some of these lines, beginning "Expanse cannot be lost." [H B91, L 871, L 872, P 1576, P 1588. *LL* 87, prose only.]
237. Pencil, watermark "Linen Record" (LR), half sheet torn at right, folded in thirds. A version was sent to Higginson. [H 385, P 1566. *Letters* (ed. 1931 only) 321.]
238. Pencil, watermark "Weston's / Linen / 1876" (T), two leaves, folded in thirds. [H 386, P 1567.]
239. Pencil, no embossment, two leaves, folded in thirds, paste marks. [H B 67, L 874. *FF* 263.]
240. Pencil, two leaves, folded in thirds, paste marks. [H B145, P 1565, L 938, (compare with PF 49). *FF* 259.]
241. Pencil, watermark "The American Linen Paper" (TALP), two leaves, folded in quarters, pinholes, paper clip, and paste marks. "1882" in Susan's handwriting on verso. [H B102, L 886. *LL* 54, in part; *FF* 171, in part.]
242. Pencil, half sheet torn at left, folded in thirds, paste marks. [H B77, L 856. *LL* 79, in part.]
243. Pencil, watermark "The American Linen Paper" (TALP), two two-leaf sheets, folded in thirds, both sheets with paste marks. Four other versions of this poem exist: one was sent to Benjamin Kimball, a friend of Otis Lord, and three others are among the ungathered poems. [H B158, L 908, P 1599. *LL* 82, four lines; *LL* 296; *FF* 266, in part; similar message to a Mrs. Cooper in *Letters* (ed. 1894) 392; (ed. 1931) 381.]
244. Pencil, no embossment, two leaves, folded in thirds, paste marks. [H B144, L 909. *FF* 264.]

245. Pencil, watermark "Weston's / Linen / 1876" (T), two leaves, folded in thirds, paste marks. [H B106, L 911. *FF* 249, in part.]
246. Pencil, watermark "Linen Record" (?LNNRCD), two leaves, folded in thirds, paste marks. [H B90, L 912. *LL* 87.]
247. Pencil, watermark "Weston's / Linen / 1876" (T), folded in thirds, pinholes, paste marks. [H B134, L 913. *FF* 243.]
248. Pencil, two leaves, no embossment, folded in thirds, paste marks. There are two other versions of the poem. [H B108, L 914, P 1581. *FF* 265.]
249. Pencil, two leaves, multiple folds, pinholes. "Susan – " on verso, and "X" in Susan's handwriting. [H 376, P 1598. *SH* 106.]
250. Pencil, half sheet, torn at left, folded in thirds, paste marks. [H B41, L 999. *FF* 262.]
251. Pencil, two leaves, folded in thirds, paste marks. [H B148, L 1024. *LL* 63, in part; *FF* 270, in part.]
252. Pencil, watermark, "RCRD 1881," two leaves, folded in thirds, paste marks. [H B66, L 1025. *FF* 269.]
253. Pencil, watermark "RCRD, 1881," two leaves, folded in thirds, pinholes, paste marks. [H B65, L 1028. *FF* 242.]
254. Pencil, "Weston's / Linen / 1876," half sheet torn at left, folded in thirds, paste marks. With Bianchi's note, "One of the latest." [H B128, L 1029. *FF* 269.]

CODA

1 *FF* 61.

ACKNOWLEDGMENTS

In October 1986, we took a long walk beneath the sweet mountains of northern California and realized that we had been dreaming the same book separately for several years. Since that time, we have been dreaming and making the book together that you now hold in your hand, and our first thanks must go to our perspicacious and deft editor, Jan Freeman. Without her faith in the project and understanding of its depth and breadth, there would be no volume to open carefully.

We especially thank Leslie Morris, Curator of Manuscripts in the Harvard College Library; without her conscientious assistance and that of the Houghton Library staff, this book would not have been possible. And we thank John Lancaster, Special Collections Curator, and staff at the Amherst College Library, and Mark Brown, Curator, and staff of Special Collections, Brown University Library, as well as Barton St. Armand for access to papers in the The Barton Levi St. Armand Collection of Dickinson Family Papers. We are also grateful to the curators and staff at the archives and special collections at Yale University, Princeton University, Smith College, and the Morgan Library in New York. Ellen Louise Hart is grateful to the Houghton Library for a Stanley J. Kahrl Fellowship that enabled her to complete much of the research for this volume. For early support of research that led to *Rowing in Eden* and this volume, Martha Nell Smith gratefully acknowledges the American Council of Learned Societies and the National Endowment for the Humanities. And, for enabling that research to continue, the General Research Board of the University of

Maryland. And we are thankful to the Massachusetts Foundation for the Humanities for a generous grant which helped usher this volume into print.

The work of Ralph Franklin and Thomas H. Johnson, and the collegial advice of Ralph Franklin, deserve special mention. For her enthusiastic support and editorial insights, we thank Marta Werner. Numerous friends and colleagues have believed in this project's importance and possibility, and for their unstinting support we thank Vivian Pollak, Margaret Dickie, Polly Longsworth, Dan Lombardo, Sandra Gilbert, Susan Stanford Friedman, Katie King, Deb Price, Bart St. Armand, Jerome McGann, Ruth Stone, and Alicia Ostriker. Ellen Louise Hart is indebted to friends, family members, and colleagues for their interest in this project, and wishes to thank Priscilla W. Shaw and Theresa Louise McRae for their wisdom and long-term support. And for her enthusiasm, incisive critiques, endlessly generative discussions, as well as for her fulfillment of a promise to render a joke a day to realize Emily Dickinson's beatitude — blessed are those that play — Martha Nell Smith is ever and devotedly indebted to Marilee Lindemann.

SELECTED BIBLIOGRAPHY

Bennett, Paula. *Emily Dickinson: Woman Poet.* Iowa City: University of Iowa Press, 1990.

Bianchi, Martha Dickinson. *Emily Dickinson Face to Face: Unpublished Letters With Notes and Reminiscences.* Boston: Houghton Mifflin, 1932.

—. *The Life and Letters of Emily Dickinson.* Boston: Houghton Mifflin, 1924.

—. "Selections from the Unpublished Letters of Emily Dickinson to Her Brother's Family." *Atlantic Monthly* XV (1915): 35-42.

—, ed. *The Single Hound: Poems of a Lifetime.* Boston: Little, Brown, and Co., 1914.

—, and Alfred Leete Hampson, eds. *The Complete Poems of Emily Dickinson.* Boston: Little, Brown, and Co., 1924.

—, and Alfred Leete Hampson, eds. *Further Poems of Emily Dickinson.* Boston: Little, Brown, and Co., 1929.

—. "Life Before Last: Reminiscences of a Country Girl," eds. Barton St. Armand and Martha Nell Smith.

Bingham, Millicent Todd. *Ancestors' Brocades: The Literary Debut of Emily Dickinson.* New York: Harper & Brothers Publishers, 1945.

—. *Emily Dickinson: A Revelation.* New York: Harper & Brothers Publishers, 1954.

—. *Emily Dickinson's Home: Letters of Edward Dickinson and His Family.* New York: Harper & Brothers Publishers, 1955.

Cameron, Sharon. *Choosing Not Choosing: Dickinson's Fascicles.* Chicago & London: University of Chicago Press, 1992.

Crumbley, Paul. *Inflections of the Pen: Dash and Voice in Emily Dickinson.* Lexington: University Press of Kentucky, 1997.

Dandurand, Karen. "Another Dickinson Poem Published in Her Lifetime." *American Literature* 54 (1982): 434-437.

—. "New Dickinson Civil War Publications." *American Literature* 56.1 (1984): 17-27.

Dickie, Margaret. *Lyric Contingencies: Emily Dickinson and Wallace Stevens.* Philadelphia: University of Pennsylvania Press, 1991.

Dickinson, Emily Elizabeth. Dickinson Papers. Amherst College Library, Amherst, MA. Houghton Library, Harvard University, Cambridge, MA. Library of Congress, Washington, D.C. Morgan Library, New York, NY. Neilson Library, Smith College, Northampton, MA. Princeton University Library, Princeton, NJ. Beinecke Library, Yale University, New Haven, CT.

Dickinson, Susan. Dickinson Papers. Boxes 9, 10, 12. Houghton Library, Harvard University, Cambridge, MA. Martha Dickinson Bianchi Collection, John Hay Library, Brown University, Providence, RI.

Dobson, Joanne. *Dickinson and the Strategies of Reticence: The Woman Writer in Nineteenth-Century America.* Bloomington & Indianapolis: Indiana University Press, 1989.

Eberwein, Jane. *Dickinson: Strategies of Limitation.* Amherst: University of Massachusetts Press, 1985.

Erskine, John. "The Dickinson Feud," *The Memory of Certain Persons.* Philadelphia & New York: J.B. Lippincott Co., 1947.

Ezell, Margaret J.M. and Katherine O'Brien O'Keeffe, eds. *Cultural Artifacts and the Production of Meaning: The Page, the Image, and the Body.* Ann Arbor: University of Michigan Press, 1994.

Faderman, Lillian. "Emily Dickinson's Letters to Sue Gilbert." *The Massachusetts Review* 18.2 (1977): 197-225.

—. *Surpassing the Love of Men: Romantic Friendship and Love Between Women From the Renaissance to the Present.* New York: William Morrow and Co., Inc., 1981.

Farr, Judith. *I Never Came to You in White.* Boston & New York: Houghton Mifflin, 1996.

—. *The Passion of Emily Dickinson.* Cambridge, MA & London: Harvard University Press, 1992.

Franklin, R.W., *The Editing of Emily Dickinson: A Reconsideration.* Madison, Milwaukee, & London: University of Wisconsin Press, 1967.

—. "The Emily Dickinson Fascicles," *Studies in Bibliography* 36 (1983): 1-20.

—, ed. *The Manuscript Books of Emily Dickinson.* Cambridge: Belknap Press of Harvard University Press, 1980.

—, ed. *The Master Letters of Emily Dickinson.* Amherst: Amherst College Press, 1986.

Fuller, Jamie. *The Diary of Emily Dickinson.* San Francisco: Mercury House, 1993.

Gilbert, Sandra Caruso Mortola and Susan Dreyfuss David Gubar. "Ceremonies of the Alphabet: Female Grandmatologies and the Female Autograph," *The Female Autograph: Theory and Practice of Autobiography From the Tenth to the Twentieth Century,* ed. Domna C. Stanton. Chicago & London: University of Chicago Press, 1987.

Grabher, Gudrun, Roland Hagenbuchle, Cristanne Miller, eds. *The Emily Dickinson Handbook*. Amherst: University of Massachusetts Press, 1998.

Grahn, Judy. *The Highest Apple: Sappho and The Lesbian Poetic Tradition*. San Francisco: Spinsters Ink, 1985.

Halpin, K.D. and Kate Nugent. *EMILY unplugged*. Northampton, MA: Sleeveless Theatre, Inc., 1995-.

Hart, Ellen Louise. "New Approaches to Editing Emily Dickinson." Diss., University of California, Santa Cruz, 1996.

—. "New Light on Manuscripts Addressed to 'Sue.'" *The Emily Dickinson International Society Bulletin* 8.2 (1996): 14-15, 23.

—. "The Elizabeth Whitney Putnam Manuscripts and New Strategies for Editing Emily Dickinson's Letters." *Emily Dickinson Journal* 4.1 (1995): 44-74. *http://www.colorado.edu/EDIS/journal/articles/IV.1.Hart.html*

—. "The Encoding of Homoerotic Desire: Emily Dickinson's Letters and Poems to Susan Dickinson, 1850-1886." *Tulsa Studies in Women's Literature* 9.2 (1990): 251-272.

Holland, Jeanne. "Scraps, Stamps, and Cutouts: Emily Dickinson's Domestic Technologies of Publication," *Cultural Artifacts and the Production of Meaning*, eds. Margaret J.M. Ezell and Katherine O'Brien O'Keeffe. Ann Arbor: University of Michigan Press, 1994.

Horan, Elizabeth. "To Market: The Dickinson Copyright Wars." *The Emily Dickinson Journal* V.1 (1996): 88-120. *http://www.colorado.edu/EDIS/journal/articles/V.1.Horan.html*

Howe, Susan. *My Emily Dickinson*. Berkeley: North Atlantic Books, 1985.

—. *The Birth-mark: Unsettling the Wilderness in American Literary History*. Hanover & London: Wesleyan University Press, 1993.

—. "Women and Their Effect in the Distance." *Ironwood* 28 (1986): 58-91.

Johnson, Thomas H. and Theodora Ward, eds. *The Letters of Emily Dickinson*. Cambridge: Belknap Press of Harvard University Press, 1958.

—, ed. *The Poems of Emily Dickinson*. Cambridge: Belknap Press of Harvard University Press, 1955.

Kauffman, Linda. *Discourses of Desire: Gender, Genre, and Epistolary Fictions*. Ithaca & London: Cornell University Press, 1986.

Leyda, Jay. *The Years and Hours of Emily Dickinson*. 2 vols. New Haven & London: Yale University Press, 1960.

Longsworth, Polly. *Austin & Mabel: The Amherst Affair and Love Letters of Austin Dickinson and Mabel Loomis Todd*. New York: Holt, Rinehart, Winston, 1984.

—. *Emily Dickinson: A Letter*. Amherst: The Friends of the Amherst College Library, 1992.

Love, Harold. *Scribal Publication in Seventeenth-Century England*. Oxford: Clarendon Press, 1993.

Luce, William. *The Belle of Amherst*. Boston: Houghton Mifflin, 1976.

McGann, Jerome. *Black Riders: The Visible Language of Modernism*. Princeton: Princeton University Press, 1993.

—. "Composition as Explanation (of Modern and Postmodern Poetries)," *Cultural Artifacts and the Production of Meaning*, eds. Margaret J.M. Ezell and Katherine O'Brien O'Keeffe. Ann Arbor: University of Michigan Press, 1994.

—. "The Rationale of Hypertext." Institute for Advanced Technology in the Humanities (IATH), University of Virginia, 1993.

Miller, Cristanne. *Emily Dickinson: A Poet's Grammar*. Cambridge, MA & London: Harvard University Press, 1987.

Mudge, Jean McClure. "Emily Dickinson and 'Sister Sue.'" *Prairie Schooner* 52 (1978): 90-108.

Ostriker, Alicia. *Stealing the Language: The Emergence of Women's Poetry in America*. Boston: Beacon Press, 1986.

Patterson, Rebecca. "Elizabeth Browning and Emily Dickinson," *Educational Leader* 20.1 (1956): 21-48.

—. *Emily Dickinson's Imagery*, ed. Margaret H. Freeman. Amherst: University of Massachusetts Press, 1979.

—. *The Riddle of Emily Dickinson*. Boston: Houghton Mifflin, 1951.

Petrino, Elizabeth A. *Emily Dickinson and Her Contemporaries: Women's Verse in America 1820-1885*. Hanover & London: University Press of New England, 1998.

Pollak, Vivian. *Dickinson: The Anxiety of Gender*. Ithaca & London: Cornell University Press, 1984.

St. Armand, Barton Levi. *Emily Dickinson and Her Culture: The Soul's Society*. Cambridge: Cambridge University Press, 1984.

Sands, Marget. "Re-reading the Poems: Editing Opportunities in Variant Versions," *The Emily Dickinson Journal* V.2 (1996): 139-147.

Sewall, Richard. *The Life of Emily Dickinson,* 2 vols. New York: Farrar, Straus, Giroux, 1974. Reprint. Harvard University Press, 1994.

Smith, Martha Nell. "Editing Emily Dickinson's Manuscripts," *The Emily Dickinson Handbook*, eds. Gudrun Grabher, Roland Hagenbuchle, and Cristanne Miller. Amherst: University of Massachusetts Press, 1998.

—. "The Poet as Cartoonist," *Comic Power in Emily Dickinson*, eds. Suzanne Juhasz, Cristanne Miller, and Martha Nell Smith. Austin: University of Texas Press, 1993.

—. *Rowing in Eden: Rereading Emily Dickinson*. Austin: University of Texas Press, 1992.

—. "Suppressing the Books of Susan in Emily Dickinson," *Cultural Correspondences: Essays on Epistolary Writing*, eds. Amanda Gilroy and Wil Verhoeven. Charlottesville: University Press of Virginia, 1998.

—, with Ellen Louise Hart, Laura Lauth, Lara Vetter, and Marcy Tanter, eds. *Writings by Susan Dickinson*. Dickinson Electronic Archives. *http://jefferson.village.virginia.edu/dickinson/susan*

Swanson, Don R. "Undiscovered Public Knowledge." *Library Quarterly* 56 (1986): 103-118.

Walker, Cheryl. *The Nightingale's Burden: Women Poets and American Culture Before 1900*. Bloomington: Indiana University Press, 1982.

Werner, Marta. *Emily Dickinson's Open Folios: Scenes of Reading, Surfaces of Writing*. Ann Arbor: University of Michigan Press, 1995.

Wolff, Cynthia Griffin. *Emily Dickinson*. New York: Alfred A. Knopf, 1986.

Wylder, Edith. *The Last Face: Emily Dickinson's Manuscripts*. Albuquerque: University of New Mexico Press, 1971.

INDEX OF FIRST LINES

INDEX OF NAMES AND SUBJECTS

E

F

T

U

V

W

ABOUT THE EDITORS

Ellen Louise Hart

Ellen Louise Hart teaches for the Writing Program, the Educational Opportunity Program, and the Literature Department at the University of California, Santa Cruz. She is the author of articles on editing Dickinson that have appeared in *The Emily Dickinson International Society Bulletin, Emily Dickinson Journal, An Emily Dickinson Encyclopedia, Tulsa Studies in Women's Literature, The Women's Review of Books,* and *The Heath Anthology of American Literature.*

Martha Nell Smith

Martha Nell Smith is professor of English at the University of Maryland, College Park. She is the author of many articles on Emily Dickinson, as well as of *Rowing in Eden, Rereading Emily Dickinson* (University of Texas Press, 1992); she is co-author of the *Comic Power in Emily Dickinson* (University of Texas Press, 1993) and coordinator of the *Dickinson Electronic Archives* project (http://jefferson.village.Virginia.edu/dickinson).

The text of this book is composed in Bembo.
Text design by Ivan Holmes Design.
Cover design by Judythe Sieck.
Composition by Potter Publishing Studio.
Index by Patricia Hollander Gross.
Photograph on the cover: *Calla 2, about 1925* by Imogen Cunningham